YEAR OF THE RATTLESNAKE

YEAR OF THE RATTLESNAKE

TALES OF REVENANTS, REVOLVERS, AND A WEIRD WEST THAT NEVER WAS.

STEVE VAN SAMSON

WEIRD HOUSE

ISBN: 978-1-957121-60-4

Year of the Rattlesnake © 2023 by Steve Van Samson

Foreword © 2023 by Steve Van Samson

Cover artwork © 2023 by Wayne Miller

Cover design by Steve Van Samson
Interior design by Cyrus Wraith Walker

Editor and Publisher, Joe Morey

Weird House Press
Central Point, OR 97502
www.weirdhousepress.com

This book is dedicated to my personal Four Horsemen of the West-Pocalypse: Joe R. Lansdale, Larry Blamire, Ed Kurtz & Owl Goingback. Though they never knew it, these notorious bad men were doggin' my heels as I wrote. In addition, I'd like to tip my hat to the father of the Weird Western itself, Robert E. Howard.

FOREWORD

The interwoven concept of the stories in this book is directly inspired by (and would not exist without) two specific books. Both of which I strongly urge anyone to read and then read again and again.

The Dying Earth, written by Jack Vance, was first published in 1950. Upon my first reading of this unique blend of dystopian sci-fi and high fantasy, I was utterly unprepared for what was in store. When Turjan of Miir (the hero of story 1) showed up at the end of story 2 as the prisoner of an evil magician, it was like a lightbulb of possibilities had been switched on. As I continued reading, I enjoyed speculating on which characters might reappear in later stories. I read the book twice almost in a row and had an even bigger blast the second time. That was it: I knew I wanted to try the concept out myself, but I wasn't sure what the right vehicle might be.

Some time passed and I began writing and releasing novels and short stories in some of my favorite genres—though admittedly none strayed far from horror, which remains my first love. About this time, I should probably mention that I also have a serious thing for Westerns, especially ones that fall into the WEIRD category.

Back in 2008, I discovered a short story collection written by Larry Blamire called *Tales of the Callamo Mountains.* I already knew Blamire from his hilarious pastiche films such as *The Lost Skeleton of Cadavra,* but Callamo was about as far from Cadavra Cave as Tulsa is from

Jupiter. These stories were weird with a capital *W.* Sometimes terrifying, but more often just bizarre and thought-provoking in a *Twilight Zone* kind of way. But what struck me most was the fact that these stories seemed to dodge the typical stock characters we usually see in Western films. There was no emphasis on gunfighters, desperadoes or lawmen out for revenge … just regular folks. The sort that felt unexplored, unrepresented and, therefore, fresh.

Well, folks, I think by this point you can see where I'm headed here. Thing of it is, all creators are fans of something. And what is art, if not the physical expression of all those shreds and whatnots that slither around their creators' heads?

—Steve Van Samson
August 31, 2023

TABLE OF CONTENTS

ILLUSTRATIONS

WHERE DEAD MEN GROW

A traditional American folk song that never was

On the longest day in the hottest year
Billy rode out on a rail
He was full as a tick on red-eye juice
Ridin' the hoot-owl trail
Said Billy that day, he'd a hog-killin' time
As the devil knew quite well
He'd left twelve dead soldiers to recount the tale
And a bar dog with nothin' to sell

Like a lead plum Billy shot 'cross the waste
On the back of a piebald mare
Belly through the brush for at least a week
As he dodged the lawman's glare
The badlands stretched, seemin' without end
But the devil was at the reins
Billy got away by the skin of his teeth
And there was venom in his veins

Thirst came knockin' with the light of dawn
And Billy did air his lungs
He had burned the breeze for far too long
Now was speakin' all in tongues
When ole Diamond Jack told a pretty lie
Billy's elbow was want to bend
But he knew right then that a belly of hooch
Would quicken him to the end

Late that night 'neath a haunted moon
As an owl closed its eye
Billy felt the cold skin of a rattlesnake
Slither across one thigh
You can take my flesh for some beef and rye
And above the snakes you'll stay
It spoke of a place where dead men grow
Told him what he had to pay

On the hottest day in the longest year
Billy's thoughts hung on his deal
He was all heeled up and sweatin' hard
With five beans in the wheel
The river by the gulch was a long way off
But it wasn't hard to find
So he wiped his brow and took a deep breath
While the rattler licked his mind

The serpent's words moved Billy's tongue
As a blade drew 'cross his chest
Blood soon flowed from the symbols there
To sate the American West
The quake rose up and it split the earth
As the devil knew it would
The river drained away to reveal a hole
A door to no place good

Right into that gap, ole Billy dove
Sparin' one tear for the wind
Thoughts dwellin' on a checkered past
All the wages paid in sin
His soul was gone but it turned a lock
Let somethin' out of its cage
What then emerged was a monstrous sight
A beast of boundless rage

And so it was, in that far off place
Where a river once did flow
The ground was spoiled by a hellish curse
Which tended every row
Horns and claws from perdition's womb
The thing fed many a crow
It turned the Claim, once green and good
Into a place where dead men grow

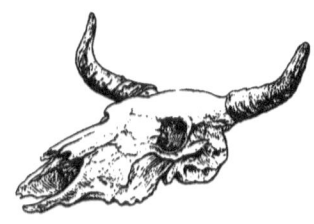

HELLFIRE IN A GLASS

Overhead, the clouds looked swollen. Not with rain, but something worse. Something infected. Seeing this, the rider's face sank into a grimace. The last thing he wanted right then was to be outside when those clouds finally let go of whatever they were holding.

The town had caught his eye about a mile back, but barely. Hell, if he hadn't been up on that ridge—if he hadn't stopped to adjust his hat—he might have ridden right on by. And that would have meant another night under the stars. Another ten hours of jumping at every sound, pointing iron at every snap and rustle. No doubt about it, after almost two weeks on the trail, Frank was ready to rejoin civilization.

Though few enough knew it, the man knew how to appreciate the finer things. Hell, he had even almost finished school, once upon a time. But that was long ago. Back in the life that was. Before circumstances had reshaped him into something unrecognizable. A creature better equipped to survive on the surface of the sun. It was almost funny. Now, after all he had done, Frank could hardly remember that other life. Or the boy who once peered into his school books with a secret dime novel inserted—dreaming of desperados and the kind of hellfire that comes out the end of a revolver ... or in a glass.

Goddamn, he needed a drink.

As open country became street, he looked for a sign marking where he was. Frank was pretty confident he was still in Texas, but to say his bearings were two days gone would be generous. Fact was, this town was the first he'd glimpsed since barreling out of the Devil's Claim in a storm of bullets.

Accompanied only by the sluggish plod of his horse, the man looked from one side of the street to the other, then he leaned to one side and spit. However bad the sky looked, it wasn't near late enough for the street to be so empty. Back on the ridge, the town represented an end to his long, lonely ride across mountain-riddled pain in the ass that was Young Territory. And right then, that had been enough. Now though, Frank's second-life instincts were starting to prickle. He didn't like not knowing things, especially where he was and who else might be there with him.

There were a handful of settlements along Young Territory's eastern fringe. This town might be Knox, Haskell or Taylor, but the only signs he could see were of no immediate help. *GENERAL DRY GOODS & MERCHANDISE* read one while another proclaimed *D.A. VIRGIL CIGARS*. These and more pointed to a thriving burg, but something felt off. Every building was just a little too dark, too run-down. The street didn't feel empty the way streets tend to when honest folks have all turned in or are just trying to stay out of the rain. What it felt was deserted.

As Frank mused on this, a sudden rustling turned his head. Next to what must have been the town livery was a corral holding a number of horses. The animals looked healthy and well tended-to, but they paid him no mind. It was a strange sensation, coming upon this sudden sign of life, but in that moment, Frank Hass was sure of one thing.

"This is no ghost town." He snickered. The words were the first he'd spoken in almost two days. As he said them, an insidious worm-tickle insinuated itself behind his tongue. Not wanting to announce himself just yet, the rider quietly cleared his throat. His mind shifted more and more to that drink he hoped was just around the corner.

It was a few minutes of slow riding and absorbing his surroundings before he heard it. The distinct tinkle of piano keys. Unless he had gone full loco, there was music up ahead. Urging his horse a bit faster, he stopped before a proper-looking establishment, erected right at the bend of the road.

Here at least, there was a sign. The letters were a bit hard to make out. Red paint over dark wood and more weather-beaten than his own face.

CASTIGATION SALOON.

For a second or two, Frank mused on whether or not the town and its only apparent saloon shared a name, but there were more important matters at hand. With mounting excitement, he dismounted—hurriedly latching the spotted Appaloosa to a post. As the animal lowered its head to a trough, his gaze lingered on the water. It looked like glass. Like the darkest shade of black he had ever seen. For an instant, he could see the reflection of those ugly, pregnant clouds, but then the water began to roil as the horse took its first good drink in days. On the brim of his hat, he could hear the first drops of rain, and that was just fine. He took a deep breath and smiled. Right then, it felt a little like God himself had finally chosen to bestow a break on old Frank Hass. With a slow creak, the door swung inward, banging against a small bell. The startling chime was like an explosion. It sounded like the only sound in the universe.

The newcomer's eyes scanned from left to right. To his pleasant surprise, the saloon was considerably less empty than the street. In fact, no small number of the Castigation's tables were occupied. These men were backwater types by the look, but that was fine. In general terms, these were the devils he knew. His second life had afforded countless opportunities to be surrounded by men of this ilk. Ugly, mean and usually without any notion of how excruciatingly dumb they were. Seeing them like that, hunched over their glasses, he couldn't help but feel a momentary swell of relief. It was good to be around folks again. Any folks at all.

But that one at the back. There was something about that one. Frank knew better than to turn and look in full, but there was recognition there. Not much, but enough to get his hackles up. Without breaking his stride, he kept moving until he reached the bar. Though there was no bartender, the shelves were fairly well stocked and there was a door. A back room through which he could see the faint flicker of candlelight.

"Hello?" he offered in a low voice, again feeling that same dry tickle in the back of his throat.

There came no answer. No response from the room or any of the customers. Feeling a tad unnerved, Frank slid his hand down the bar's surface. The wood was cool to the touch—polished and fine with brass accents that made it a fair bit fancier than any he'd seen in New Mexico. He thought about calling out again, but instead inclined his head just enough to see an old piano. Like the bar, the instrument sat unattended. Though he couldn't recall the moment the music stopped playing, it was so fresh in his mind he could've hummed a few bars if asked.

"You looking for work?"

The question sounded more like a statement of fact than a question. He turned to see an attractive woman emerge from the room behind the bar. Her hair hung just past her shoulders and was blond in the truest sense. Yellow like a prairie flower. Like a ray of morning sun. The sight stirred something. Reminding Frank Hass that a man needed more than a little red-eye to get him through.

"Well?" she playfully gibed.

As he looked into those pools of hazel-green, he suddenly discovered that he was no longer thirsty. Politely, he tipped his hat. "Ma'am?" he stammered like a boy of twelve, before straightening up. "I'm sorry?"

"Well," said the woman "You're eyeballing that piano like it owes you money. Thought maybe you knew how to play."

"Oh." Frank shook his head. "No, ma'am. Not me. Besides, from the sound of things you already got yourself a fine musician. Who was it I heard playing before?"

The woman crooked her head in confusion. "Before?"

"Not two minutes ago. C'mon, get him back out here. It's been too long since I heard real music. Truth is, I could use a bit more."

"Mister, I don't know what you're talking about. No one's touched that thing in months. Last player I had was Duncan Stiles, and he's been dead almost nine months." She pursed her lips, shook her head in apparent regret. "But if you're not looking for work, must be the other thing. So what'll it be?"

A glass was slammed down. The sound was so loud and sudden, it sent a jolt through the man's bones—one strong enough to make him feel as if his manhood had been questioned. "Whiskey." He nodded.

Moving with no great urgency, the woman procured a bottle and glass. And as she did, she flashed a quick glance at her newest customer, and unless

Frank had cracked, there was the start of a smile there. Seeing that combined with the alternating sway of hair and hip caused the aforementioned stirring to intensify in his guts. There and lower.

Wearing that same ghost of a smile, the blonde woman poured a stream of liquid gold from bottle to glass. The sight was perfection. All the sweetness and warmth of a lover's caress for five cents a whack. The sight and the smell alone were enough to make his knees buckle. Frank reached for the glass but the bartender pulled it back.

"You got money?"

Just like that—three little words was all it took to sour, the man's newly managed contentment. With a frown, he slapped a hand flat on the bar, than moved it away to reveal a nickel. "All right then," said the woman. "Can't be too sure around here."

Looking moderately annoyed, he eyeballed the woman before disappearing the glass's contents in one swallow. The whiskey was cheap stuff, but he reveled in it. Savored the heat travelling down his throat, past his ribs. And when it came to rest, deep in his belly ... Frank Hass was just a little closer to whole.

"Just where is *here*, anyway? Seems I misplaced my bearings at some point." He asked this in an even tone, placing down another nickel.

"Oh ... " She raised an eyebrow. "Just another bump on the road to tarnation. Most don't stay long enough to remember they were here at all." In that moment, the woman seemed to trail off, as if remembering she still had a kettle on. "What about you, mister? Where are you coming from? Nothing east of here but mountains and saddle sores."

As the fire died down in his belly, another one sparked elsewhere. He had asked a very straight and simple question. One which the woman would have no logical reason to dodge. He hated that. Didn't like when people assumed he was too dumb to smell bullshit.

"East?" Frank managed to keep his tone light. "Did I say anything about coming across the territory?"

The woman's smile faded.

"As it happens ... I'm coming from El Paso," Frank lied. Then, with a disdainful glare, he slid forward his empty glass. "Best to stick to what you know. Eh, darling?"

The bartender blinked real slow, the way only a woman can when they know something. For a second there, Frank thought that things had already started down the wrong path. He hated that too. How women were always treating him this way. Putting words in his mouth. Not answering simple questions. God above, this was the first person he'd seen in over a week and she couldn't be civil for five damn minutes?

"Suit yourself, mister." To Frank's surprise, the woman's tone verged on playful. Without another word, she raised the bottle and poured. This time, a drop splashed back out onto the dark wooden surface. Without missing a beat, the bartender took her finger and wiped up that drop. Then, inserting the tip into her mouth, she cleaned it with a crisp *pop*. Needless to say, the sight had quite the effect on her trail-weary customer. Never a fan of being transparent, the man cleared his throat and drank.

The first gulp was fire, but the second was something more. With shut eyes, Frank stopped worrying about labels and just allowed himself to drift—reveling in the whiskey's good work. "Sign out there says *Castigation Saloon*." He said this distantly and with a bit of sarcasm. "Is that what you call the town, or is Castigation just an old family name?"

"That sign has faded some over the years. Been meaning to have it repainted." She picked up a glass and began to clean it with a rag. "The family name is Costigan, but most call just me Ellie."

"Hmm." Frank prickled, feeling once again that he was being lied to. "Sure looked like Castigation to me."

"As I said," the woman went on, her words started to slow as she watched the man remove his hat and lay it on the bar. "The sign has faded some … over the years."

"You *did* say that." The words were dreamlike but they seemed to conceal a warning. The man's eyes were still closed and his head lolled back, relaxedly. He didn't noticed the woman's expression shift as she laid eyes upon the horizontal scar that ran across his forehead.

"You know …" said Elouise Costigan after a few quiet moments. "It's kinda nice to meet a man who can read. Have to say … most of my customers just recognize the two o's in *saloon* and call it a day. Not often I get a man of *culture* in here."

Again came the slow blink, but this time it held a different connotation.

Ellie shifted her weight to the other hip then leaned back. As she did this, her shirt collar moved to reveal the tanned skin of her collarbone. Frank was immediately frozen. Galvanized. He wanted to reach across the bar right then. But ... there was no need to rush. This was nice. A little talk. Plenty still to drink. The road had been long and he was still so damned thirsty. He reached out, but the bartender pulled back the bottle.

"Hey," he flared. "I ain't done with that."

Another smile flickered across the woman's lips. This one positively wicked. "Oh, I think maybe you are." Moving as slow as she pleased, Ellie Costigan put that bottle back on its shelf. Then she reached under the bar itself. Frank couldn't see what she was doing, but he heard the distinctive sliding sound of a metal latch being undone.

"Try this." Ellie appeared with a new bottle in hand. "A high-class customer like yourself deserves a higher class of drink."

The man looked perplexed. His eyes flitted from the woman's smile to the bottle. Inside was something that looked a little like liquid gold, but there was something else in there too. All coiled up in the bottom, the thing glared with hateful, slit eyes that seemed to be daring the man to make the first move. "That's a ..." Frank's voice trailed off.

"Rattlesnake."

The man's heart skipped. Of course this Costigan woman couldn't be calling him by name. He *knew* that. But hearing that moniker—the same one they put on all the posters ... caused the man's trigger finger to flex.

"Being as cultured as you are, I'm sure you've heard of the worm in tequila?" Ellie removed the topper, allowing a most alluring scent to prick at her customer's nostrils. "Well ... I find nothing gives that special *kick in the teeth* quite like a dash of rattler."

Trying to appear unshaken, Frank cleared his throat—wet his lips. "Is it ... *dead?*"

Ellie laughed. "Of course it's dead, silly. You know any snakes that can breathe whiskey?"

He stared back stupidly. Too perplexed to get mad, but just. In that moment, he wanted that golden liquid so bad, it hurt. But something was off here. Had she just insulted him? Called him, what was it..., *stupid?*

And for what? For asking a simple question. Hell, he had seen taxidermied snakes before, but this one was different. He knew the thing was dead…, but maybe it was too mean to give a shit.

"Well?" said Ellie with a playful lilt. "You want me to pour or what?"

Frank looked up, clearly stewing in his own vinegar. "This your good stuff?"

The bartender nodded.

"Then what have you been selling me so far? Horse piss?"

"Maybe." Utterly unflapped, Ellie winked and started to pour. "But I didn't realize I had a customer that could appreciate the finer things. My mistake. This first one's on the house."

The man's scar squirmed as hills and valleys appeared on his brow. And though his every fiber felt sure the woman was mocking him somehow, Frank could not stop staring at that snake. He kept expecting it to move. To shift or slide to the mouth of the bottle. In his head, he imagined what its teeth might sound like hitting up against the bottle glass—or if it might just pour right out with the drink. Maybe fall to the bar with a loud *splat*, and slither away. To his chagrin however, neither of these things happened. In fact, as Ellie poured, that old rattler didn't even budge. Wearing his frown like a badge, he was suddenly overcome with a powerful revelation. This woman had him so riled up, he had raised his voice. *Son of a bitch.* And after he had tried so hard to stay cool.

Taking care not to move too much, Frank looked from table to table. To his surprise, not a man present was looking his way. As they had when he walked in, the other patrons of Costigan's Saloon seemed content with the company they had. Each pondering their own glass as if it were the goddamned meaning of life. Subconsciously, he made a quick count. There were fewer men in here than he had thought. Maybe only four or five, and that was fine. Less was better.

Still looking with his peripheral vision, there was something that made him turn just a little more. Something about that big man in the back. And though he was standing in full view, Frank shot a glance at that table in the back. A second was all he dared. As such, a large black shape was all he could glean. But there was something about that shape—about that large man in the back.

Frowning, he picked up the glass. Then, like a flaming serpent, Miss Ellie's high-class stuff shot down into his belly like a bolt of lightning. The sensation was ecstasy. A river of either paradise or perdition—in that moment it was hard to know. "Hoe-Lee Shit!" The words were ejaculated as if by a man who just got bit by his own horse.

"Well," Ellie Costigan was smiling. "I guess I'll take that as a compliment." In that particular moment, she looked very pleased with herself.

Still marveling at the flavor, Frank smacked his lips. The stuff was definitely whiskey, but like none that had ever crossed his palate. He could detect notes of all kinds—caramel and barley, some kind of nut and just the right balance of smoke and honey. And there was something else. Something subtle, he couldn't place. Something beneath the symphony.

Slowly his eyes moved to the snake in the bottle.

"That there is an old family recipe," Ellie nodded proudly. "Since Daddy went to heaven, I've been making it myself. I am very pleased it is to your liking."

"*Liking* ... may not be a strong enough word." Again, the man moved the glass to his lips. Pausing to inhale before partaking of another sip. No use denying it, the drink had him, body and soul. In fact, the thrall was so strong, he almost forgot about how mad he had just been. Or about that big man in the back.

After the last fiery drops slid past his tongue, Frank opened his eyes. More relaxed than a moment before, he looked up at the bartender—appreciating for the first time the freckles on the bridge of her nose and the ample roundness of her hips. Noticing she was being noticed, Ellie Costigan placed a hand on her bar and leaned forward to enhance the view. By God, the woman was beautiful.

"How much?" All of a sudden, Frank was wearing a wolfish grin.

"*Excuse* me?" Ellie sounded offended, but only slightly.

"For the *bottle.*"

"Oh. Five dollars." Ellie backed off and turned to put the glass she had been cleaning away. "And worth every penny."

"Five dollars?" Frank's tone had picked up a discrete edge. "You trying to trick me, Freckles?"

13

The woman raised an eyebrow, but said nothing as four silver dollars were pushed across the bar.

"If the first glass was on the house, this should cover what's left."

The bartender didn't look at the money. Just kept staring at her only customer. After a few seconds, she set down the bottle, sliding it over.

"No." He held up a hand, not wanting to touch the bottle. "You can keep pouring." Without a word of response, the bartender did as requested and filled the glass once more. Frank's smile broadened. His head felt heavy, but otherwise, he felt like a king. Just like he had back in San Miguel, when things had still been good. Before he'd answered the call of an old friend and everything had gone to hell.

As he brooded on this, something seemed to be needling the nerves in his spine. It was an old itch. One he hadn't thought about in a very long time. Frank pressed the glass to his forehead. Then he closed his eyes and allowed the coolness to enter his skin. Beneath, that old scar across his forehead gave a single throb.

He didn't want to turn. Didn't want his night to be filled with any business that didn't involve this fine snake juice or the even finer woman who was pouring it. Problem was, *want* had nothing to do with it.

Slowly, carefully, Frank looked back over his shoulder. To the big man-shaped shadow in the back. That was when he felt every muscle in his body tense at once. The man back there was dark-skinned—a Mexican by the look. The biggest damn one he'd ever seen. And there was a strap of what looked like boot leather across one of his eyes.

"You all right, mister?" The voice pulled Frank from his thoughts.

"I'm fine," he lied again, his eyes moving to rest on the bottled snake. The head of that old rattler was completely free of the liquid now. He watched with dread as a single golden drop slid down one of the fangs. Whoever had done the taxidermy had posed the snake with its mouth open, its teeth bared. The damn thing looked ready to strike.

"Are you sure? You look a little pale."

"I said I'm *fine*," Frank hissed. "Might be better, though, if my glass wasn't empty."

As she poured, a sneer flashed across the bartender's face, but the expression went unnoticed. In fact, he did look pale. And as Frank reached for his drink, it was with a trembling hand. In his mind, he was miles away, years too.

There was no denying it. That was the scourge of Nevada County, Carlos Cortes his own self. They called him the Conquistador, but he sure as hell wasn't from Spain. That big, mean Mexican had killed between twenty and forty-six men, women and children—all in cold blood. The posters never seemed to agree on the number.

But why in Hell was he here? Just *sitting* back there? Had he not noticed or recognized Frank when he walked in? Or could it be possible that so many years had passed the bastard had forgotten old Rattlesnake Hass? No. Not possible. A man might forget many faces in his span. But the one responsible for his own missing eye?

And to think Frank had been stupid enough to raise his voice in a place he didn't know. Thereby inviting those who hadn't noticed him before to turn his way. Hell, the fact that he wasn't sporting a series of new bullet holes was a miracle. *Goddamn idiot!* he cursed in his mind. As furious at himself as anything. *Son of a clap-infested whore!*

Again the man drank deep of the snake liquor, though it completed him a little less now. Not trusting his peripheral senses, he looked back over his shoulder.

"Why do you keep doing that? Just you and me here." The statement was strange, but her lopsided grin eased his mounting nerves.

Frank leaned forward. "Damn it woman, keep your voice down! That bottled rattler isn't the only snake in this bar."

Hearing this, Ellie's face abandoned much of its warmth. "Is that right?" She sounded consummately unsurprised.

"You're goddamn right, it's right!" Frank's eyes were doing that bloodshot, bugging-out-of-his-skull thing. "Now I need you to listen to me very closely. All right?"

The woman gave a wide-eyed nod.

"Okay. Now you see that man in the far back. That big Mexican?"

Ellie looked with her eyes only. Real quick, just there and back. And though she gave no word, no nod of the head, Frank could tell she knew exactly who he meant.

"That there is Carlos Cortes." Catching the woman's gaze, he raised his eyebrows for emphasis. "One thousand dollars reward, though I haven't seen too many posters lately. Tell you the God's honest … I heard he was dead."

With an expression that was a bit difficult to read, Ellie pulled out a cloth and began to wipe imaginary spills. Without looking up, she spoke in a quiet voice. "So he's … real dangerous?"

"Dangerous?" Frank was shaking his head in disbelief. Sometimes women really were too stupid for their own damn good. "The son of a bitch is wanted in three states. He's killed at least three deputy marshals and maybe forty-fifty regular folk. Most importantly, though … he really doesn't like me."

"That a fact?" Ellie's voice was not nearly concerned enough. In fact, there was an undertone that gave the distinct impression that she thought this entire conversation was funny. "What's the matter? You cheat him in cards or something? Steal his favorite book?"

The expression of mild bemusement made no sense and it was going right up Frank's ass. He was already at that stage. The one he always reached sooner or later with members of the fairer sex. Right then, the bar woman was transmogrified. No longer an amalgamation of skin and curves, hair and lips. Now, she was a stupid mewling thing. A nail, begging to be hammered.

Problem was, Frank's typical knee-jerk reaction to this type of situation would draw too much attention. Though it tasted like bile in his throat, the man had to control himself. Right now, his best chance was to stay calm and casual. To hope that when the time was right, the Conquistador would be too deep in his cups to notice as he stood up and walked out the front door. In two swallows, Frank emptied the glass before pushing it forward again.

"What I did…," the words came in a low, slurred whisper. "Was shoot him in the face."

Ellie paused. Looking thrown for the first time.

"It all happened pretty fast. We had only been running together for a couple of days. Me, Hodge, Ted Campbell, some big ginger who kept talking about how he'd been struck by lightning … and *him*. Was Campbell who put the job together. Said it'd be easy. Clean."

Frank wiped his brow on one sleeve before continuing. "Little did I know that Cortes' definition of *clean* meant to leave no one alive in the bank. Teller … manager … customers. Turned out it was the wrong time and place for everyone." He lifted the newly refilled glass, again pressing it to his forehead though no relief came. When had it gotten so damn hot in here? He tried to remember, but his head was heavy. His thoughts, almost too thick to process.

"We got out of there pretty quick, but somehow there were two deputies on our trail. To this day, I don't know how they found us, but they did. One of them had a weird name like … Nothing or Nada—something like that." He shrugged. "Anyway, them bastards were good. Worked like they was possessed of a single mind. It wasn't long before they tracked us down to this little church, about five miles outside of town. There was a wedding going on, but Cortes didn't like that."

Ellie backed away, looking very close to horrified. Her voice was small and to Frank's ear … *womanish*. "And, that's when you did it? When you *shot* him?"

Frank raised an eyebrow, though both the man's eyes were more than halfway shut. "Those two deputies … they weren't far behind. If we were gonna have any chance at all, we needed Cortes. Unlike myself, that big Mexican is a hell of a shot."

Frank's eyes were wide and wet and trembled as they watched old events play again. "Once that first shot rang out, there wasn't a trigger without a finger. Our side started dropping fast. Ratchford was first, then the lightning guy. I remember stepping in mud at one point. Mud that wasn't mud. It was then that I saw them—really saw them. All them wedding folk. Guests were everywhere—laying in all manner of wrong-looking positions where they'd dropped. The bride and groom were still near the altar, one reaching for the other, both covered in blood."

Frank moved the glass to his lips, and nearly retched at the smell. It took a few moments before he recovered enough to continue.

"The worst was the little girl with the flowers."

A trembling hand was raised to prod beneath the hat. Lifting it just enough so an old scar was revealed. The skin there was raised in a long, ragged line and it throbbed. "Mr. Nothing? He did this. Just a graze, but enough to blind me with all that blood that came flowing out. He had flanked us—come round the other side while his partner held us off in the front. I aimed as best I could, but with all that blood in my eyes, I couldn't see for shit. Didn't realize that Cortes was between me and him. He turned just right and ... BANG."

Frank turned is fist into an explosion—splaying the fingers to drive his point home. As he did this, he pictured the long face of the deputy marshal who'd caused it all.

Mr. Nothing? Nada? No bueno?

Whatever the man's name was, something occurred that hadn't before. The pair of lawmen who'd led that small posse into the Devil's Claim a couple weeks back, had looked damn familiar. Then again, Frank had only seen 'em from a distance. Sensing what was about to occur, fearless ole Rattlesnake Hass had jumped on his horse. And while the rest of his gang reached for their irons, he was already galloping like a hurricane, making for the edge of Young Territory. Still, there was something about that pair in front.

"So that's it, then?" Ellie's voice was flat.

"Hmm?" Yanked from his thoughts, Frank was lost for a second.

"The big man over there. You're saying his eye was just an ... *honest mistake?*"

"Oh, uh, yeah. But try telling *him* that. Cortes was screaming and cussing in two languages. At first, I kept waiting for him to drop dead, but he just started shooting. And this time, it was in my general direction! In the commotion, I managed to hide. I don't know how, but Cortes ended up making his way to one of the horses and rode off."

"Huh," said the bartender, one hand on her hip. "So what happened to the deputies?"

"Cortes got one of 'em in the arm. It was bleeding really bad, but other than that, they got off scot-free. In fact, both got on their horses and rode after the real prize."

Ellie cocked her head to one side. "They just left you?!"

"Well, sure. Aside from being the biggest payday, for all they knew, Cortes was the only one left breathing. Hell, there were so many bodies around, all Hodge and I had to do was nothin'. Bet we laid there for twenty minutes before getting up and riding the opposite direction."

A look of distaste washed over the bar-woman's face. One which her customer didn't seem to appreciate. To him, it felt a lot like judgment.

"Don't fool yourself, Ellie darling" he spat. "Just because someone hides behind a tin star doesn't mean he gives a damn about right and wrong. People are just people. No matter what side of the law a man is on, dollars are all he really loves."

"You really believe that?"

"Hell yes, I do. My daddy used to say that every man's got a coin. And when he comes into the world, all covered in blood and takes his first breath … the devil flips that coin. You know—just to see where he'll end up. Thing is … whether it's heads or tails, the coin is *money*. And that's what we get a taste for. With enough of that, a man can have *anything*." Sweat cascading down his reddened face, Frank moved his hand to cover the woman's.

She could feel the wetness between his palm and hers. It was hot. Practically boiling. "Hold on there, Mister … I think you've got the wrong idea." Miss Ellie offered the statement calmly, helpfully. "This is not that kind of establishment. Besides … " She stepped away, wiping the back of her hand on her apron. "You look like pounded shit, Frank."

"What?" The man stood up so fast, it felt like his head hadn't joined the rest of his body. "I didn't give you my damn name." Part of him knew he was being too loud—making too much of a scene. But that part was difficult to hear. Overshadowed as it was by fever and a strange acrid taste down in his throat.

"Didn't need you to give it to me, *Frank*." She said the name as if it were an insult. Then with a foxy grin, and one eye on her customer, a piece of paper was produced from underneath the bar. This was flattened out and slid it over.

Blinking through the rage and searing sweat, Frank looked down and began to read.

REWARD 500.00 WANTED DEAD OR ALIVE! NOTORIOUS BAD MAN. RATTLESNAKE HASS. Real name - FRANCIS LEVI PLUNKET. Also known as - FRANK PLUNKET, WHISKEY BILL or FRANK THE SNAKE. For rape, murder and introducing liquor into the Indian Territory.

The picture was an old one, but it had depicted the man's unique scar quite prominently. Frank's eyes moved slowly over the type. His mind taking an extra second or two to process it all. Once it finally did, Ellie Costigan heard the distinct sound of a revolver sliding out of its holster.

In the man's mind, he was carrying out a fearsome display. Producing an iron and pointing it into that delightfully helpless face. The reality however, fell somewhat short. Frank's movements were sluggish, exaggerated—and when that pistol finally appeared, the bar-woman had no trouble swatting it out of his hand.

The man wheeled around, following the trajectory of his weapon as it soared. And the pistol was quickly forgotten. Repeatedly, Frank rubbed his eyes. First with his hands and then the backs of his sleeves.

What followed was a series of choked, partial vocalizations, as the man's eyes moved from table to table. All of them—even the one in the back, was empty. He stumbled back, his mind reeling—desperate to recall the state of things when he'd walked in. Though no eye contact was made, he'd been aware of a handful of men. Each with a table all to himself. Each pondering a single glass. Not drinking, just pondering.

For the briefest of seconds, his addled brain kicked over an explanation so simple, he almost laughed out loud. He looked to the door, and to the tiny bell that hung above. That was when his expression fell. The man shook his head, added more sweat to his sleeve. However badly he wanted the simple explanation to be the right one, all those other customers couldn't have just gotten up and left. Even if the sounds of scooting chairs and boots on wood had gone unnoticed … there was no way he would have missed that bell.

A shaky hand reached for his revolver before remembering it was no longer there. Frank spun back around to the bar, but before his vision stopped blurring there came an explosion of white pain. He was sent stumbling backwards and as he fell, he slipped away. Into another place. Another phase of matter.

The crack of skull on wood was too loud to be real. Though the man's eyes were open, it was a few seconds before he realized what the coppery taste in his mouth meant. In vain, he tried to speak, but with half a tongue, forming words was going to take some time getting used to. Likely more than he had.

And so he simply lay, listening to the mule-kick thrum of his heart—trying to understand what had happened. In that moment, the man looked astounded and mortified. Like someone had just caught him playing with his pecker.

"That look suits you, Frank." A woman's voice pierced through the veil of fog and consternation. "Or should I say ... *Rattlesnake*. That's what they call you, right?"

The man on the floor gurgled, coughed, sullying his shirt with brownish-red bile.

"Well, I think that's great." The woman's voice went on. "Almost poetic, considering what did you in at the end there. You do read poetry, right? I mean, I know you're a man of culture, being able to read my sign and all."

The footsteps were slow, plodding and they were moving from one end of the universe to the other. With what little control Frank had left, he tried to turn his head—causing a mouthful of hot blood to spill on the floor.

"Speaking of which ..." The bar-woman's face slid into a wooden sky. The expression was hard. It had transfixed the pretty thing into something else. Something better equipped to survive. "

"Wha? Wha?" sputtered the man on the floor. "Wha' y'gonn' do a-me?"

"Already done it, darling."

She got down on her haunches. Lord in Heaven, from his perspective, she seemed a hundred feet tall.

"You greedy sack of shit. This stuff isn't easy to make, you know. Hell, most of my previous customers only manage a single glass before getting to where you are now. Gotta say, you have a hell of a constitution, Frank."

Ellie sighed. Looked out over the tables with somber green eyes.

"I can see them too. Sometimes. Usually out of the corner of my eye. But when I look straight on ... they always disappear. Funny old world." She snickered. "That's why, every night I serve them what they came for. What they can only get here. Keeps 'em from roaming off. I reckon it'll work on you too, Frank."

She looked down, but the man was already dead.

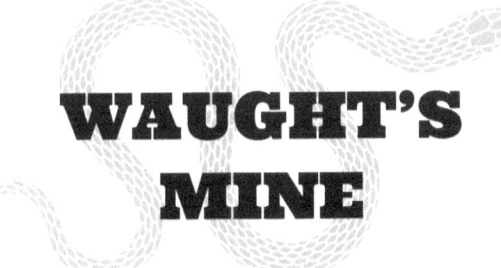

WAUGHT'S MINE

ONE

[August the 11th, 11:25 PM]

Edged in the subtle glow of an August moon, the mine loomed. In truth, the word *mine* felt too small, too singular. This was a complex. One with so many buildings, it was hard to know where it ended and the town of Broken Promise began.

Gable rooftops crested buildings of varying size. Some were high off the ground, supported by what looked like stilts. Others had been homes, once upon a time. Back when folks had come in droves. Salt-of-the-earth settler types looking for a better life for them and theirs—for their very own slice of the promise. The lucky ones left poorer than they had come.

The rest never left at all.

As the four men approached, they moved quietly, keeping to what shadows they could. Ahead, rising highest of all was a massive, brick building. The roof was lopsided—longer on one side to accommodate a row of chimneys. And on the very top, near high enough to touch the sky, there was a sign.

WAUGHT'S MINE EST. 1832

"That's the one." whispered Patch Briar, absently scratching the hidden line of his jaw. In the months spent working the Hurley ranch, his beard had grown long—thicker than it had ever been. "If the shaft is anywhere …" He looked to the man at his right. The one who shared his long, narrow face and uncanny knack for finding trouble.

"Yep." Russell gave a slow, thoughtful nod and said no more. The elder brother's clean shirt, well-groomed mustache and bowler hat made him look more like a banker than a man who had done three stints in the Virginia state prison system. Looks aside, if his present company could be likened to parts of a snake, Russell Briar was most certainly the head. "That's the one, gentlemen. We'll be checking there first."

From somewhere in the back came a deep grunt. Despite being near a head taller, the full-blood Choctaw moved with less sound than the three white men combined. One Horse Tom had long black hair, unreadable eyes, and features that looked as if they had been shaped with a hand ax. The man wasn't much for conversation, but he had been with the brothers since their daring escape of Fort Evans, back in '63.

The smallest of the group was also the most fidgety. Jimmy Laine hadn't known the others long and before tonight, had never felt welcome in their company. As the four men moved closer to the building with the sign, Jimmy seemed unable to take more than two steps without darting his head in one direction or another.

"Damn it, Jimmy," said Patch. "Will you stop doing that? You're making my teeth itch."

"S-sorry, Patch," stammered Jimmy. "I can't help it. N-never actually been this close to the mine before."

Patch wrinkled his nose, exchanging a knowing glance with the man at his right—the sort only siblings can. Aside from being a twitchy little weasel, Jimmy Laine smelled awful.

"I still don't know why you insisted he come along." Patch whispered, leaning closer to his brother's ear.

Russell frowned. "If we hadn't, who would have fit in that shithouse? Sure as hell not One Horse Tom."

Patch shrugged, conceding the point. "All right—but I'm telling you …" He turned to make sure Jimmy couldn't hear. "I'm not getting into an enclosed space with him reeking like that."

"You won't have to, little brother." Russell's eyes rested on something up ahead. "As it happened, it rained yesterday."

The four men stopped at an old coal tub which sat discarded, forgotten and filled to the brim with dark water.

"Jimmy." Russell waved the man over, than pointed at the tub. In the moonlight, the liquid looked like oil. It was only a couple of feet deep, but the bottom could not be seen. "Well?" He said.

"All right, all right …" said Jimmy, resigned like a man being shoved onto the gallows. "I get it."

After splashing a few handfuls over his back and face, Jimmy straightened up, looking far too proud of the effort. That was when the towering Choctaw grunted again and stepped forward. One Horse Tom had not been happy with the inclusion of Jimmy Laine. Their dynamic was a tenuous one. Tom was the wolf—the other, a festering thorn lodged in his paw. Quite unceremoniously, Jimmy found himself hoisted up and dropped into the tub with a large splash. And though it needed to be done, the big Indian seemed to take a bit more pleasure in the act than was probably required.

"What the hell?" sputtered Jimmy, flopping out of the tub and kicking like a trout in a rowboat. "You sons of bitches! *Sons of bitches!"* He clawed the water from his face, straining to see. "This old tub's been sitting here, twenty years! God knows what you just dropped me into."

"It's called water, Jimmy," Said Patch. "Now that the two of you are acquainted, maybe you'll get together on a more regular basis."

"Oh that's funny. Go on and laugh it up, Patch." Jimmy did not look pleased. "Just remember, the only reason I smelled like that was because you all forced me into that damn shit hole."

"We had to be sure." Russell stepped in. "Thorough. Had to exhaust every possible avenue before …"

With that, all four men turned to regard the mine and by God, the mine regarded them right back. After a few drawn-out seconds, Russell went on.

"Lippencott's cabin and wagon had to be checked first, but the outhouse, well ... like I said, we had to be sure. And you *are* the smallest, Jimmy."

"Yeah, yeah, I know." Jimmy wiped his face with the pit of one elbow. "But you listen to me." He stepped forward. "If we find this score tonight, you better not try anything funny. I've earned my part of this now ... and though it might surprise your refined ass, Russell Briar, I ain't afraid of you. *Neither* of you." He glared at Patch. "Y'hear me?"

With that, a shadow moved to swallow the small, dripping man.

"Don't need to be afraid of no Briars, Jimmy." The voice rumbled like distant thunder. "Just me."

One Horse Tom didn't talk much, but when he did, those around tended to listen. Right then, Jimmy Laine looked like a mouse on the train tracks. He skittered back, too frightened to say more.

"Tom." The voice of Russell Briar was calm but firm. Per usual, his hat was angled a bit forward. Just enough to help him think. "We're all partners here. Four working towards a single goal. As long as we all remember that ..."

"Everything is going to be just fine." Patch stepped in. It was the way the brothers talked sometimes. As if each could see the same conversation in their head and were trading off lines. He placed a hand on the Indian's broad back—spoke with a soothing lilt in his voice. "No one is getting the raw end of anything. You hear me, Jimmy? Size of this score ... there'll be plenty to go around. Tom—what'd Lippencott say again? About how big it's supposed to be?"

"Mmmm," grunted the Choctaw, "big as a baby's fist."

"*A baby's fist.*" Russell repeated the phrase slowly, savoring the words. "Make no mistake gentlemen, we can all walk away rich men tonight. Think of it Jimmy, you can start over wherever you want. *Be* whoever you want—for the rest of your life. Now, isn't that worth a couple hours of hell?"

"Well ..." said Jimmy Laine, scratching his head. "I *suppose.*"

"All right then." Russell smoothed the corners of his moustache. "To go over it once more—here's what we know. Last Tuesday in the Marigold ... Augustus Lippencott, renowned charlatan and general snake in the grass, got himself *deceased.* According to Tom here, who was the only one of us present at the time, Lippencott was spending cash like it was his last day on earth—which, as it happened, it was. He was up on a damn cloud. Celebrating something that had set him up for good—no more traveling salesman. No more snake oil. And, when he had swallowed enough whiskey, he started letting on to the reason for his mood."

"He said it was gold," said One Horse Tom in his low staccato. "Said he hid it somewhere ... *none of you stray dogs can look.*" The Choctaw's frown seemed to deepen then. "But Lippencott didn't know who he was talking to. Didn't see the man with the mark." With that, Tom drew a line down his face with two fingers. A line from the corner of one eye, down past his jaw.

"Weeping John Wraith," said Jimmy, shrinking away from the large Indian. "Not a good idea to name-call a man like that. Indirect-like or otherwise. Wraith's made himself quite a name ... runnin' with the Pete Decker gang. Probably wanted in three states by now."

"Four," said Russell "But we don't have to worry about him. Weeping John is gone. After the shooting, he left town just the way he had arrived earlier that day. In a cloud of hot dust and trouble we don't need." With that, the elder Briar removed his hat, inclining his eyes to the August moon.

As a warm breeze meandered past, he shut his eyes. "Stray dogs," He smiled. "As turns of phrase go, that one's pretty apt."

Patch nodded. "Remember, boys ... since Tuesday night, every cur in town has been sniffing around for that gold. Turning every stone, ripping up every floorboard—including, I've little doubt, the ones in this here mine. But, now that the dust has settled, it's our turn. And we can check the one place none of them would dare."

"Where none of you stray dogs can look," said Russell—repeating the phrase almost automatically. "Far as I'm concerned, the wrong word jumped out at Weeping John. Whether he meant to or not, Lippencott worked a real clue into that remark. He said ... *could.* Where none of us *could* look ... and that's the real reason we're here."

"What are you saying?" exclaimed Jimmy Laine in frustration. "That he tossed that treasure of his *down the damn mine shaft?!*"

"No, Jimmy." Russell put the bowler back on—adjusting the angle until it was just right. "Isn't it obvious? The reason why none of the dogs in this town have struck it rich is because Augustus Lippencott didn't hide the gold. He swallowed it." With that, Jimmy looked at the old mill once more, his eyes pausing briefly at the entrance before moving back up to the faded sign.

"Swallowed it?" Jimmy almost choked. "Something that big?"

"Or shoved it up his ass." Russell winked. "Point is, we find that dead salesman, we find our score."

Jimmy Laine stood frozen, unable to speak—looking as if he were faced with the ghost of his own mama. And though his brain tended to produce more smoke than heat ... even he understood.

"Damn this town," cursed Jimmy, kicking a rock. "Why can't folk here bury their dead six foot down, like everyone else?"

TWO

The door didn't put up much of a fight. One swift kick was all it took for the little chain to pop. Following this came a loud bang which ripped the fat man at the desk from his liquor-induced slumber. The shock caused one arm to flail wildly, knocking over a bottle he had been working on earlier that night. Expensive liquid began to pour over the desk in a series of slow glugs, but Roy Hurley took no notice.

He looked perplexed, dazed. Bloodshot eyes scanned the office, while trying not to blink. Around him, dust swarmed in the flickering candlelight. The room was small, only slightly wider than the desk he had passed out on. The wall opposite him had two primary features, a large window through which nothing could be seen but the pitch-black adjacent room … and an open door that gaped just as dark.

Through that door, the barrel of a very big gun slid into the light. A Colt Paterson, revolver by the look. Same weapon John Coffee Hays so famously used to fend off those Comanches back in '41. 'Course there was no Texas Marshal at the end of this iron. Behind the weapon emerged a hand, an arm and finally the rest of a man whom Hurley had not expected to see again. As he watched the gunman step into the light, the fat man's eyes flitted to his brand-new 1866 Winchester.

"Oh, I wouldn't worry about that," said Patch Briar, in a labored drawl. Without looking, he reached for the rifle himself, lifted it from the wall, then made it disappear in the shadows just outside of the door. "I'd say you got plenty of gun to worry about right here." He tipped the barrel of the Paterson. "Now why don't you pick up that bottle. I hate seeing something so fine go to waste."

The eyes of the man at the desk were wide and yellow. He did as instructed though, slamming the bottle down on its ass a little harder than he meant to. Before him stood one half of the infamous Briar brothers. To the eye of Roy Hurley, the man looked freshly returned from the brink.

"Patch?" Adrenaline coursed through every inch of the fat man—fear-sobered as he was. "What are you doing? Hell, son, you look like you just blew in from the ninth circle of hell."

"Well ..." said the man with the revolver. "Thereabouts."

Hurley heard the distinct clicks of a hammer being pulled back. It was a small enough sound, but in the confined space it seemed like a series of cannon blasts.

"Go on." Patch nodded, lowering his arm whilst keeping the barrel pointed right where it was. "Pour."

The fat man looked confused, but scooped up two glasses from the far side of the desk and filled them. His nerves were immediately audible in the rattlesnake clinking of glass. He was about to slide one forward, but the eyes of Patch Briar gave him pause.

"Oh no—both of those are for you, Roy. You'll be needing whatever's left in that bottle, more than me."

Wasting no time, Roy Hurley picked up one of the glasses and emptied it in two swallows. Then he pressed it to his forehead, praying for the respite of a few degrees. Then he looked—really *looked* at his assailant. Patch looked drained. The kind of fatigue that runs deeper than body or mind. And those streaks of white in his beard ... those were new. "Listen ... Patch," Hurley sputtered nervously "Whatever's happened ... whatever this is ... we can work it out. All right? Now, why don't you go and get Russell and we can all discuss things like civilized—"

BANGG!!

The gun went off in an explosion so sudden Hurley didn't know whether to grip the pain in his head, or the one in his chest. The bullet found its target dead center—shattering the bottle in a spray of what looked like hail.

"Careful now," said Patch—a tentacle of smoke drifting from the barrel of his revolver. "That other glass is all you got now. The very last bit of comfort in all the world. You can take my word on that."

Again came the repeated clicks of the Paterson's hammer. They were slower than before, more methodical. Every one dealing an impact to the fat man's bones.

"Also ..." Patch growled. "if I hear my brother's name exit your mouth again, the next bullet goes in your stomach. We clear?"

Hurley nodded, indicating that matters were in fact, transparent as crystal. "Damn it, Patch. Just talk to me." His voice was unsteady. "Where the hell have you been? Where's—" He was going to say Russell's name again, but wisely stopped himself. "... that big Indian you boys are always with?"

The question made Patch's eye twitch. "You mean ... *Tom?* Come on, Roy, he's worked for you the same four months we have, and just as hard." Patch took a deep breath—let it out slow. "But don't you worry about him. It's just you and me, boss. Though by my watch, I'd say it's a bit late to be playing games. You know full goddamned well where I've been. Where we've all been. You're the one who sent us there."

"What?!" Hurley's eyebrows leapt up. *"Sent you?* Patch—I got no damn idea where you went after quitting time today, and that was six hours ago! Far as I knew, you all were at the Marigold! Digesting some of Dill Blanchard's stew and working on a good Friday drunk!"

Patch took a deep breath. Let it out slow. In that moment he looked almost wistful. Unfortunately, the expression soured fast, like milk in the sun. Within seconds, the younger Briar looked positively haunted— as if darkness had suddenly gathered in the hollows of his eyes. Looking this way, Patch leaned forward. "The thing of it is ..." His voice was barely above a whisper. "I come here straight from the *mine.*"

The words echoed off old wood and already ringing eardrums— piercing the fat man's heart like a dagger.

"The *mine...?*" Hurley repeated the term with something like reverence. "Dear Lord—what in the hell were you doing out there, boy? Waught's Mine has been shut down for almost thirty years now! Ever since '36, when the miners hit that pocket of bad air and choked to death." His words were picking up speed. Coming now in furious bursts. "Why would I want to send you there? Better yet, how could I have? I've been here all night, romancing my fine Kentucky lady after a long, hot, pain-in-the-ass week. Listen, son ... I don't know what you think happened, or who lied to you, but ..."

BANGG!!

31

Another cannon blast sounded in the small room as a vase exploded. Hurley doubled over. To him, it felt a little like the business end of a shovel had just bounced off his head.

"First—," sneered Patch "I ain't your damn son, Roy. Second—it wasn't me who was lied to tonight."

The younger Briar dragged the back of a dirty hand across his face. His eyes looked right through the trembling fat man. Through the wall behind him too. He drew a long breath—the sort that helps old memories come back into focus.

"You know ... back when we was kids ..." Patch's voice had softened a bit "Mamma used to say that brother of mine could swindle the front teeth right off a rattler." He smiled, wagging the finger of a stern parental gesture. "But she warned him. When you deal with snakes, you're liable to get some poison in for the bargain." For a few long moments, Patch looked as if he were watching a play. One only he could see. Ghosts of various emotions flitted across his face, though none seemed to take root.

"Tell me something, Roy." Patch looked up, catching the fat man's gaze. "Earlier tonight, when Russell was picking up our wages ... what'd the two of you get to talking about?"

Hurley stiffened. Hand shaking, he took another sip of bourbon. The face of Patch Briar had gone stern again, but now there was something new in it. Something that seemed to be searching. In that moment, Roy Hurley got the distinct impression that the amount of breaths he had left was in direct correlation to the quality of his next few words.

The Briars might be wanted men in Virginia, but not for killing. And this one, Patch ... in the four months of employment, he had always shown himself to be the milder of the two. Maybe ... if Roy could keep him talking. Just maybe he'd get out of this yet.

"Not much talking, tell you the truth." Hurley's voice was as steady as he could make it. "It's been a bad week, as you plainly know. What with John goddamned Wraith blowing into town—all that mess with Lippencott. Damn fool." Hurley set the glass on the table. "No matter how many rounds you buy the room ... you disrespect a man like

Wraith and you don't get to buy another." He sighed, shaking his head. After a few quiet moments, a new series of those demon clicks filled the room, as the Paterson was made ready to yell.

"Last night." Patch nodded. "You and Russell."

"All right—okay." Hurley raised a supplicant hand. "But there's nothing to tell! We shared a few glasses before I handed over your wages and that's all!" Hurley's heart was in a gallop, but he pulled hard at the reins. He had to stay in control. If he lost it now ... the third bullet might indeed find purchase in his rather prodigious gut. "But, yeah okay—we may have discussed current events. Weather too."

"Lippencott," whispered Patch.

"The subject came up." Hurley frowned. "Augustus was no friend of mine, but ... we were kin. Cousins, twice removed. Though *twice* ain't nearly removed enough, far as I'm concerned." Roy scoffed, shook his head. "Truth be told, that man got under my skin like no one else ever has."

Patch grinned, but the expression didn't touch his eyes. "Family has a way of doing that."

The room fell silent for a few seconds. Just long enough for Patrick Briar to remember why he was *where* he was.

"Before Lippencott went and got himself shot to death, word is he paid you a visit, Roy. *Directly* before. You and Russell get around to talking about that by chance? Maybe after y'all were done jawing about the *goddamned weather?"*

Hurley's expression fell. Right then, the fat man felt as if he'd just stepped in fresh shit. Tentatively, Roy cleared his throat. "I believe we did, yes." The fat man licked his lips, then winced at the taste of his own salt and fear. "Just small talk. Augustus just going horizontal and all ... I suppose it was on my mind."

Patch raised an eyebrow. "Go on."

"Well ... the thing is, this isn't the first time that no-account cousin of mine got what was coming to him."

"That a fact?"

"Damn right it is." Roy Hurley frowned. "Augustus has been pushing potions and snake oils across half of Missouri for years—taking advantage of people who couldn't rightly afford it. And sometimes even decent folk can only be pushed so far before they decide to take a little back. That's how he got that limp." The fat man shook his head in obvious disgust. "The bullet was lodged deep in the thigh bone. By the time Augustus reached civilization, it was too late to save the leg."

"Damn." Now Patch was shaking his head. "Always wondered how he got that fancy wooden leg."

"That *fancy* wooden leg cost Augustus everything he had at the time. Every red cent he'd swindled. The sumbitch got most of what he deserved. And last Tuesday he got the rest."

Roy Hurley glanced up to the gunman's face, just long enough to notice something in his eyes. They were distant and cold—covered in a layer of fogged-up glass.

"As for what I may have said to your brother on the subject … well, I'm happy to tell you what I told him." Hurley picked up his glass. The next sip was bigger than the ones before and burned on the way down. The man winced, sucking air in through his teeth.

"Last time I saw Augustus Lippencott alive was last Sunday. Late. Just past midnight when I heard the knock. The man was drunk but not on liquor—flaunting some incredible good fortune he'd happened across on the trail. At first I thought he only came to rub my face in it but lo and behold, my dear cousin had himself a *business proposal.* Said he was looking to walk the straight and narrow for a while. That he wanted to buy up a not-so-modest share of my ranch. Even had the nerve to say how family was the only sort you could trust these days— bastard."

As he listened, the eyes of Patch Briar seemed to burn like lanterns in the utter dark of a cave—*or perhaps an old defunct coal mine.* "Go on," he said again.

Hurley suddenly looked as if there were an unsavory taste lingering on his tongue.

THREE

"It's the one thing I never understood about this place. Why do they do it?" Jimmy said this while approaching the shaft of Waught's Mine. "I've been in Broken Promise close to five years now and it still makes no damn sense."

"Ain't it got something to do with the ground? Same reason nothing grows 'round here?" Russell said this distantly, continuing to drink in the interior of the old mine tower. "The dirt's too full of rocks or some such."

"So they say. One thing for sure … a man dies in this town, he ain't getting no Christian burial." With that, Jimmy crossed his chest. Then he peered into the gaping mine shaft.

The sight transfixed the man. It was like seeing darkness—true darkness, for the first time. As he gazed down into that perfect void, Jimmy Laine began leaning forward. By degrees he pitched closer and closer to oblivion until a large hand grabbed onto his shoulder and pulled him back.

"The hell's the matter with you, Jimmy?" Patch Briar looked more annoyed than concerned. "You think there's a prize for the first one down?"

Jimmy backed away from the hole, panting, clutching his chest. His mouth kept opening and closing—once more bringing to mind some brainless river fish.

"Tom," came the voice of Russell Briar. *"You ready? Give it a try."*

"Mmmm," grunted the big Indian.

Having already asserted that no Choctaw was dumb enough to go poking around so deep in the earth, he was the obvious choice to stay topside. This was fine by Russell. After all, he didn't know much about thirty-year-old mines. There could be duplicate controls at the bottom of the shaft, but he sure as hell wasn't about to risk it. Better someone stay behind.

Currently up on a platform some ten feet away, One Horse Tom loomed before a large wheel. Like the connected winch drum and various pulleys it was chained to, the operator's wheel was covered in a thick layer of rust. Overall, the thing looked like it hadn't been turned in a hundred years.

The Choctaw glared down at the thing like it had done him wrong. Curling large fingers around the old metal, he gave an exploratory tug but the wheel didn't seem to notice. In that moment, the Indian's omnipresent frown turned ugly. Without a word, he slammed his other hand down and pulled with force enough to drag a pair of mustangs across the Ozark plateau. At first the only sounds were man-made ... but after a second or two there came a high-pitched shriek. The horrible whine increased before abruptly stopping as the old wheel relented to the considerable might of the large man.

The action produced a shudder which traveled through chains and pulleys, down to a small metal box suspended just above the shaft. It was the only way in or out of where they were going—a device the mining industry called a *cage*. As the wheel was turned, more and more chain was unspooled from the winch, causing that cage to plunge lower and deeper into the perfect dark of the inner earth.

"All right." Russell waved. "That'll do, Tom. Bring it back up."

The three men stared dumbly as the cage reappeared. It hadn't gone down but a yard or so but to their eyes, the thing might as well have passed right out of existence.

"Russ." Patch whispered so only his brother could hear. "Are you sure about this? I mean, are you absolutely positive that gold might not be somewhere—*anywhere*—else?"

Without taking his eye off the emerging cage, Russell gave a slow nod. "Only fools and salesmen are positive. I'll say this, though...." His voice suddenly increased in volume so everyone was sure to get an earful. *"If I needed to hide a gold nugget that big from a town full of wanted poster rejects, I'd probably have swallowed it too."*

Patch smirked "I don't know, Russ ... can a man even swallow something that size? Big as a baby's fist."

Russell looked back for Jimmy, who had thankfully wandered off.

Then he put an arm around his brother. "All right, all right … *listen*. Maybe I know a little more than I'm letting on. Okay? Maybe … I got a tip. Something only one other living man knows. Trust me. Our gold is most definitely with Lippencott's corpse." He winked. "You'll see. We're finding it tonight, and when we do, we can finally start over. Someplace where no one is looking for us. Someplace with beaches. Think about *that*, little brother."

"Beaches, huh?"

"With sand the color of milk," nodded Russell. "You know, I hear there are islands just off Mexico with nothing but sun, crystal-blue waves and dark-haired women, more beautiful than you can imagine."

Patch raised an eyebrow. Then he took a deep breath and did what he always did in this sort of situation. He shook his head and relented. "You can keep the first two … but the rest sound all right."

"Just *all right?*" gibed Russell with a grin.

"Come on." Patch rolled his eyes. "Let's find some lights. Might be some lanterns around somewhere."

"No need!" came a high, weasley voice. "Found something better." Jimmy Laine was carrying an old crate and sounded downright pleased with himself. When the Briars peered inside, what they saw were six small objects that looked like stunted tea kettles with hinged toppers. On one side, each featured a long spout and a rather wicked-looking hook on the other.

"What are they?" asked Patch.

"Oil lamps," Jimmy said, smiling. "Miners hook 'em on their hats so they can see down there. The oil should still be okay, I suppose. Of course if there's any gas down there … we are all going to explode and die."

Russell looked a bit conflicted then. He reached into the crate, pulling out a lamp and a box of matches. The first few proved useless but eventually he was able to strike a flame. The small object flickered to life, turning the eyes of the leering men to gold.

"Just hold on a minute, Tom." Russell called over to the big man at the wheel. "I want to try something."

With that, the elder Briar tossed the lit lamp into the shaft, which was actually several feet wider than the cage. Now it was all three men who leaned over the pitch-black opening. From the series of metallic clinks that followed, they were able to discern a few things. First— the lamp had hit the side several times on the way down. Second— the shaft was longer than any of them had imagined. Third, and most importantly of all—they were not likely to explode.

"Well," said Russell "That was informative."

"Yeah …" Patch looked troubled. "But something isn't lining up. The way we've heard it, this town has been dumping dead folk down there for over thirty years. Right?"

"That's right," said Jimmy Laine. "What about it?"

"Dead folk reek, Jimmy. Not as bad as you, but plenty."

Jimmy conceded the point. Then Patch looked to his brother. "I smell something weird down there, but it ain't the rot of men. I almost wanna say fish. Is it just me?"

The room fell silent for almost a full minute after that. "Naw, I smell it too." Russell admitted at last, sounding unworried. "Not *fish* fish, but … I don't know—day-old crawdads or something."

"Yeah," said Patch, "*Something.*"

Jimmy's eyes were darting from one Briar to the next. "So what are you boys saying? Are we going down there or what?"

Russell adjusted his hat, then his collar. After that he pulled out another lamp, which lit straight away. Holding the small device by its hook, Russell's usually comely face was lent an aspect of the demoniac.

"Of course we're still going down there." Under his well kept moustache, Russell Briar was smiling like a man possessed. Seeing this, Jimmy couldn't help but take a step back.

"Where you going, Jimmy?" Russell's voice had developed an edge.

"I—I was just thinking," stammered the little man, taking another step back. "That cage doesn't look big enough for all three of us anyway. M-maybe you two should just go. I'll probably just get in the way anyhow, and—"

"Sorry, Jimmy," said Russell without a drop of empathy. "Like you said … you've *earned* your part of this little expedition. You're in it right up to your elbows now. Besides … three search faster than two, and down there, time will be no friend of ours. Now, get in the goddamn cage."

Patch shot his brother a look—part surprise but with a hint of distaste. But Russell was already stepping into the suspended metal box and didn't notice.

"Well?" The sides of Russell's moustache twitched. "You boys gonna stand there all night? Or do you still wanna lay hands on the biggest gold nugget this side of forty-nine?"

Patch gave a resigned sigh. "All right, I'll take one of those." Jimmy set the old crate down, seemingly too stunned to do much else. A few seconds later, two more lamps had been lit.

"Here," said Patch, handing one over. Jimmy didn't seem to notice the thing at first, but upon hearing his name once more, snapped back to reality.

"Oh," he said, taking the lamp.

After that, no one spoke for some while—not that there was much to say. Once all three men were hunkered down in the cage, One Horse Tom gave another of his grunts. Then, with a fresh pig-squeal of rusty metal, the Briar brothers and Jimmy Laine began their descent into the pitch-dark bowels of Waught's Mine.

FOUR

Roy Hurley regarded his glass. Watched as a bead of condensation meandered down one side, and came to rest on one of the sausages he used for fingers. More than anything else, he wanted another kiss from his fine Kentucky lady, but the glass was nearly empty. Despite efforts to the contrary, the fat man's eyes darted to a bookcase on the far wall. His thoughts turning to the concealed wall safe, as well as the loaded Derringer inside.

"Whoever heard of Broken Promise, Missouri, anyhow?" The voice of Patch Briar yanked Hurley back into the moment. "We never should have come to this ass-end of the universe. This place is spoiled. Rotten from *beneath*." Patch continued, his Colt Paterson still pointed right where it needed to be. "Weeping John didn't blow through here by chance. He was just the latest devil called home to hell."

Hearing this, Hurley slouched a little more in his chair, releasing a long resigned sigh. "This town ..." Roy sounded dejected. Defeated. "It wasn't always a den of devils. Back when my daddy came here in '29, it was a place of hope. Back when the name was just *Promise* ... there was nothing broken about it. Like so many others, we had heard of Ulysses J. Waught and the paradise he was building around his affluent new mine." Hurley paused then, a nostalgic glint in one eye. "I was pretty young when we moved here from Kansas—ten or eleven. I remember Daddy built this horse ranch just beyond the outskirts because at the time, Promise was growing so fast, he thought the town would reach us soon enough."

Suddenly, the eyes of the fat man changed. Darkened as they considered old memories for the first time in years. "'Course that was before the accident. When all those miners died."

Hurley lifted an elbow, wiping what sweat he could from his brow. He had performed the act automatically—wholly without thinking. And to his surprise, the sudden movement elicited neither reaction, nor further threat from the clearly unstable Patch Briar. *Maybe ...* he thought *... maybe there was still a chance.*

Just keep him listening.

"That was when the screw turned. When Promise broke. After that, the only people who found their way here were … well …"

"It's okay, Roy. I get it. As citizens go, I ain't exactly upstanding." Patch smiled. Then, for a minute or more, the man with the Colt Paterson stared in thoughtful silence. He had slumped back against the door jamb, but his eyes remained vigilant. They slid to a bookcase—about four foot high and six foot long.

"Before you go on … I'm gonna need you to move that." Patch indicated the bookcase with the barrel of his gun.

"W-what?" stammered Hurley, trying to sound as clueless as possible.

"That bookcase, you've been eyeballing it for ten minutes. Now I may be a bit … *overextended* at the moment, but I ain't blind. So go on. Get to it."

After a few seconds, the fat man shuffled across the room, putting hands on the heavy bookcase. He needed to pull, but couldn't bring himself to do it. Instead, he turned to glare past the revolver, into the eyes of the man who had him on his knees. But a wave of that gun set him to work. Only after what felt to Hurley like a full turn of the earth, did Patch Briar speak again.

"That's a fine story, about you and your daddy." Incredibly, Patch sounded sincere. "Tell me, Roy … you like stories?"

Hurley ignored the question.

"Well," Patch went on—remembering. "Being on the trail with a full-blood Choctaw for so long, you tend to hear a few whoppers. Oh sure, there are some winters where he won't say more than ten words, but once in a while that man gets to talking. You know any good Indian stories, Roy?"

Again, Hurley did not reply.

"See … Tom's tribe believes that sometimes, just like people … *places* go bad." Patch began kneading the flesh of his temple with one thumb. "The way the Choctaw see it, this planet of ours is home to many things. Things older than the Ozarks … older even than God and all his pretty angels. Shadow spirits … or what the Bible might call *demons*. It's all stuff and nonsense, of course, but to One Horse Tom and his people, these things are as real as your sweaty gut, Roy. A few of the really bad ones even have names."

41

Suddenly, there was a loud slam as the bookshelf slid from its resting spot. The wall behind was a paler shade of off-white than the rest of the office. And in the center, recessed into that wall, was a safe, just as plain as you please. The sight put a smile on the gunman's face. He leaned in close again as Roy Hurley panted and glared his unblinking hate.

"Well, shit. Would you look at that." Patch gestured with the barrel of his revolver. "Break's over, Roy. Let's see what you got."

Lifting an arm, the fat man wiped his face. Then he hunkered in closer to the safe which contained the only means of surviving his current predicament. He knew that not only pulling the Derringer out in time, but squeezing the trigger was a long shot. Still, there was a part of him that felt a sudden surge of hope at the idea. He could picture the tiny pistol—knew it was lying flat atop numerous stacks of cash, just as he knew the thing was loaded. Hurley had made a show of moving the bookcase, but he also knew that Patch was liable to get wise to his stalling, should it go on too long.

"At the moment, only one comes to mind…," said Patch Briar—his free hand scratching at the hidden line of his jaw.

"One *what?*" Hurley was past trying to hide his disdain.

"One of the old things," Patch sounded annoyed. "The shadow things. Jesus, Roy … ain't you paying attention?"

Hurley fired a venomous look, then went back to addressing the small dial.

"*Impa Shilup.*" After saying the name, Patch looked as if he were about to spit out something foul. "He was one of the worst. One Horse called him the *soul drinker.* He (or *it*) was said to be part of some greater darkness that was here long before there was light to fill it. One Horse said that this Impa Shilup had a way of drawing people of ill-intent towards it, so it could creep inside them. Drink the rotted stuff of their soul."

"Why are you telling me this?" The voice of the fat man had gone eerily flat.

"Why?" Patch Briar sounded outraged. "Why?" His eyes were haggard, rimmed with red.

"Because tonight, Roy, because of you … I met the son of a bitch."

FIVE

"Smells like a fisherman's asshole down here." Jimmy Laine spoke in a nervous rasp, pushing his lamp light into corner after corner of the ample dark. "Russell ..." His nerves had given way to real fear. "... *where are all the bodies?*"

The question bounced off the walls, unanswered—echoing down and away.

"Y-you hear me Russell? This town's been dumping their dead down here for thirty years, so you tell me ... *where are all the goddamned bodies?!*"

"Jimmy's got a point, Russ." Patch was the last to step out of the cage "There should be a stack half a mile high by now. Hell, I expected us to hit the top of *that*, not the bottom of this damn shaft."

The group's de facto leader opened his mouth, than closed it again. Russell Briar pushed forward the small lamp an arm's length ahead, but in such prodigious darkness, the light was about as useful as rubber lips on a woodpecker.

"The bodies? The bodies?" Jimmy's mutterings were just above a whisper, though both men could hear them clear enough. Darkness, it seemed, wasn't the only thing which had been honed in this world below. Here it seemed, silence also reigned. A pure, perfect quiet unmatched by the sort they'd found on the trail, surrounded by open plains or hills. Down in the mine, the concept of silence had been refined. And every sound they produced—every breath and footfall— seemed a cacophonous thing.

"Hey, Russ." Patch's voice had become soft.

"Yeah?"

"It feels like ..." The younger Briar could feel tiny hairs on the back of his neck as they stood to attention. "I don't think we're alone down here."

"'Course we aren't alone." In the flickering lamp light, Russell Briar strained to see. "There's gotta be hundreds down here with us. One with a solid gold baby fist in his stomach."

"Yeah?" Patch swung his lamp around to reveal nothing but more rock and an endless supply of darkness. "So where are they?"

Right then, Russell looked at his brother. The man who had been the boy that'd followed him for as long as he had been able to walk. Patch was his caboose—that's what their mother had always said. Unable to stop himself from following the loud, smoke-belching engine with *RUSSELL BRIAR* written down the side. In twenty-six years—no matter how many friends had been shot and killed, or how many months had been spent in a jail cell—Patch had never given Russell cause to regret his decisions. Not once.

"Look—" Russell put a hand on his brother's shoulder. "Just calm down, all right? Think about it. It's entirely possible that whatever unlucky bastard has to put the bodies down here, takes that same cage we just did and hauls them off farther down that tunnel. Maybe he puts them in a special chamber, all nice and respectful. Fact is, we have no idea since, whenever the subject is brought up, no one in that damn town seems willing to talk details. But *think* about it for a second! Do you really think they *literally* toss bodies down that shaft?"

"I don't know...." Suddenly, Patch was nine years old again. "I guess I did but ... now that you mention it that does seem a bit ... I don't know—*shitty*."

"Sure does." Russell gave the man's shoulder a hard pat. "We just got to get the layout of these tunnels. Stands to reason—providing my special chamber theory is correct ... that the freshest body would be the closest. Gotta be, *right?*"

"Right." Patch nodded. "Makes sense."

And that's all it took. All it had ever taken. A few little words to reassure one brother that the other still knew what he was doing. That despite all evidence being to the contrary, everything was going to be all right.

"Okay, then," said Russell, flashing one of his hundred-dollar smiles in the low flickering light. "Now let's—"

Russell's words were cut by a metallic clang. The heads of the Briar brothers snapped toward the sound, both presuming that Jimmy Laine had dropped his lamp. But the light was still there. Still floating at eye-level some fifteen feet away.

"Hey, Jimmy...," Russell asserted. "Reel it in. You get lost, we might not have time to find your skinny ass."

The lack of response which followed was unnerving. Hearing that felt a little like sinking in quicksand.

"Jimmy?"

Patch's eyes feasted on the glow of Jimmy's lamp, but the longer he stared, the less lamp-like the thing became. Was it bigger than before? Steadier? More of a solid thing that the flicker cast from some old miner's light. Before Patch could decide on any of this, the light began to sway back and forth. It was as if it were attached to something. A luminous drop of dew tipping a blade of breeze-bent grass.

"What the hell are you doing, Jimmy?" Russell sounded annoyed. "Stop playing around."

In response, the light froze immediately in place. Then, quite inexplicably, it was joined by another of equal size and brightness.

The sight felt like a needle of ice sliding into Patch Briar's throat. It was impossible. Flew in the face of every sane, rational thought he had ever had—but here they were. A pair of what looked like eyes, glowing and staring out of the perfect black. For many seconds Patch found that he lacked the ability to move, or even breathe. And for what felt like hours—weeks, maybe ... he endeavored to do neither.

Then, the eyes did something which eyes simply do not do. *Can never do.* The younger Briar watched in abject horror as the impossible eyes began to separate. First only an inch or two, then more. He had no desire to imagine the face that held them, but the thought of a skull that could stretch and shift to accommodate the display before him was too much for any sane mind to bear. Grabbing his stomach, Patch doubled over—splashing bile and half-digested stew on the ground. When able, he looked again, but where those eyes had been was only darkness.

Perfect, unblemished void.

"They just ... *went out.*" The voice of Russell Briar was low—devoid of all emotion. *"Listen!"*

The sound was faint—non-directional. Like something heavy being dragged deeper into the tunnel ahead. Patch stood there for a second—unsure if his feet would take him where he needed to go. He held the lamp up to his brother's face but Russell didn't react. Didn't seem to even notice. Just kept staring at the spot where those unnatural lights had been.

"Jesus Christ, Patch ... what in God's name was that?"

"Don't know." Patch swallowed hard, tasting vomit. "Don't wanna know." He glanced in the direction of the cage, finding he could see it better than before. That his eyes were acclimating to the low light. "Damn it, Russ. What fresh hell did you lead us into this time?"

"I ... I just ..." Russell struggled to find a coherent thought. "The gold! He said it was big as a baby's—"

"*Screw the damn gold!* We gotta find Jimmy!"

With that, the elder Briar turned with confusion flickering on his face. It was like a part of the man had been burned away. "Jimmy?" Russell repeated the name in a confused drawl, as if it were some Chocktaw word he hadn't heard."

"The hell's wrong with you?!" It was all Patch could do to keep his voice down. "He may be a dumb, weasely little shit, but Jimmy Laine sure as hell doesn't deserve to die down here. Especially not after he sifted through other people's shit tonight, checking for your damn gold! *Now snap out of it and help me find the little bastard!*"

As the brothers stormed down the tunnel ahead, they did so in an order which had never before come to pass. Patch pushed ahead with long, dauntless strides as big brother Russell followed without a sound. When they reached the approximate spot where the eyes had been, there came the sudden crunch of metal.

"Stepped on something," Said Patch, reaching down. Lowering the light to reveal a mangled oil lamp—identical to the one in his hand. "Still hot." He spoke the name with regret. "That clanging sound was from Jimmy dropping it. Must have gone out when it hit." In that moment, Patch Briar looked like he was dangling at the end of a very short rope. "Come on."

To anyone who saw them coming, the brothers must have looked like a pair of eyes themselves. The light from their lamps, the only in all the world. Ahead, the tunnel came to a fork. Here Russell, whose mind had slowly been rekindling itself, stopped to shine a light on the ground. He checked the passage on the right, and then the left. Patch watched, unsure what his brother was up to.

"That way," Russell pointed to the tunnel on the left.

"What? How the hell do you know?"

"Can't you smell that?" Russell turned with a fiery glint in one eye. "Crawdads."

Unable to argue the point, Patch relinquished the lead. The tunnel went on for another fifty feet before emptying into a massive chamber. The echoes of every footfall seemed to go on forever, but behind them was another sound. A wet sound. A perverse slurping, like a horse at the trough. Locating the source of it was hard. One second it came from in front, then behind, or perhaps from some adjacent tunnel or back the way they had come.

Concentrating on the darkness, Patch's foot connected with something hard. Something he could feel snap like an old dried-out branch as he fell. In the calamity, his arm went wild—inadvertently hurling the small oil lamp. After a series of bone jarring bounces, it began to roll before finally coming to a stop beside what could only be a great and terrible heap of the dead.

The desiccated bodies of a hundred men, women and children lay contorted there. All of them had been gathered up and discarded in a massive pile. The vision hit hard, washing over Patch like a tide. Also, the slurping—he couldn't hear it anymore.

Suddenly, a brilliant light appeared and with it an extended hand.

"Come on!" It was Russell's voice. "Take my hand, you idiot!"

"Russ!" Patch exclaimed, doing as instructed. "I tripped! Feels like there's a table leg down here. Maybe an old support beam or some—" But Patch's word died on his tongue. Following his brother's eyes, he focused on the distant glow of his lamp. It had scooted and rolled across the ground—coming to rest beside one of the charnel mounds. For a few seconds, Patch hoped the lamp would not go out.

Then he wished to God it had.

The bodies went up like well-dried kindling. Flames moved fast over the surface of the mound in a wave—revealing many more such piles nearby. All around. Veritable hills of dead Promisinians. All dried out and twisted.

As Patch stared in disbelief, an old memory was triggered. A thought as preposterously out of place as it was fleeting.

Years earlier, out on the proverbial trail, One Horse Tom had managed to track and kill a pronghorn—a small one, but a welcome feast just the same. One of the group's members at the time, the one from Kentucky, had insisted on cooking up some of the less savory bits along with the meat—swearing he had grown up eating nothing sweeter. Now—Patch Briar had never prepared chitlins before but he was pretty sure that something like *intestines* needed to be cleaned before being thrown in the pan. In all the years since, he had staunchly maintained that the reek of those things cooking had been the foulest he had ever smelled. The olfactory equivalent of being mule-kicked in the balls. But ... as he stood in that cavern, watching the dead go up in flames, he experienced a powerful but woefully unhelpful revelation.

The goddamned chitlins have been dethroned at last.

As the blaze spread, more and more of their gruesome surroundings came to light. This was no simple cavern. Here was a charnel house. Bodies that looked a thousand years old were catching like bales of sunbaked hay. Arms and faces could be seen—all black and crisp and desiccated.

"Sweet baby Jesus!" Over the growing roar, came the voice of Russell Briar. "Patch! You found him!"

"What?!" Looking down, Patch watched his brother kneel before the thing that had tripped him. It was another dried-out mummy. As unfamiliar as any of the rest. He registered this in a dreamy sort of way—almost as if none of what he was seeing mattered. It was strange, but Russell was doing something with the dead fellow's leg.

"It's Lippencott!" Russell shouted his face awash with the coming inferno. "Look at the leg! Remember his wooden leg? It's hollow! None of them knew it! That was the tip—what Roy let spill into his cups earlier tonight. I'm sorry I didn't tell you before, little brother. I didn't want Jimmy and Tom to know everything and there wasn't time to pull you aside."

"The *gold!*" said Patch, understanding at last. "You're saying Lippencott hid it in his damn leg?"

"Must have!" Russell began to claw at the wooden limb, searching for a hidden catch. "The whole town has checked everywhere else, but none of them *stray dogs* knew about the leg. *Nobody did!*"

"Nobody ... but *Roy Hurley?*" Patch said this pointedly, turning to the wall of flames heading their way. Could feel the oppressive heat upon his face as more and more bodies joined the blaze. "I don't know, Russ. That doesn't make any sense."

"He knew because they were *cousins.* Twice removed or some shit." Russell coughed up a laugh as his hand continued sliding over the wooden surface of Lippencott's false leg. "That fat sumbitch said Lippencott came looking to buy up his ranch with a nugget of gold the size of a ...'"

"A *baby's fist*—I get it."

"That's right!" Russell's eyes glowed with orange light. "And Hurley saw the thing! Said Lippencott pulled it out of a compartment in his fancy wooden leg!"

"Okay ... and then what?"

"Then ... Roy said he turned down the offer. That he'd been bitten one too many times by that snake and didn't want any part of his ill gotten gains. He kicked Lippencott out."

"*Kicked him out?*" Patch did not sound convinced. "Let him just ... *walk* off with the gold?"

Russell stopped what he was doing. His upper lip was pulled back to expose a row of dark gums—transforming that hundred dollar smile into a slice of madness. "You got something to say ... *Patrick?*"

"*Russ,*" Patch's face was full of fear and of fire. "You'd have to be a saint to turn down a fortune like that. Roy Hurley is just a man. A man with a failing ranch that happens to be planted on the ass-end of perdition where nothing grows! Oh God, come on. You gotta know this ain't right! *None of this.*"

Russell Briar stared blankly. His hands, no longer searching, only trembled.

The flames were high enough to reveal the entire cavern. The ceiling was high, the walls were far ... and as more dead folk joined the blaze, the resulting heat and smoke were transitioning into threats.

"Listen to me now, okay?" Patch coughed—put a hand on his brother's shoulder. "We don't get back to that cage right now, the two of us will be dead as the rest of these poor bastards!"

"What?! *Leave?!*" Russell barked "But we're so close! The gold ... can't you smell it, Patch?"

"Be perfectly honest ..." Covering his mouth, Patch backed away. "Gold isn't what I'm smelling, Russ." In that moment, all Patch could do was watch in silent agony. Knowing he could no more alter his older brother's course now than when they were nine and fourteen—or five and ten.

"Mamma was right." Patch muttered this with a deep pang of regret. *"Nothing but his shadow ... just a goddamned caboose."*

Patch turned back to the flames, calculating the seconds that separated the Briar brothers from a thoroughly excruciating end. It was then that he thought of something he hadn't before. The path of any train is determined by the iron it rolls along. Fortunately ... you can always just derail the damned thing.

"Russell."

The sound of his name caused the man on the ground to look up—directly into the barrel of a very familiar revolver.

"Move!" shouted Patch.

Russell Briar skittered back as the Colt Paterson's hammer produced a series of clicks. A second later the weapon roared to life—tearing through the bony stub of Lippencott's left thigh. Bending down Patch lifted the false appendage. As he did, something shifted within. There was vindication in his eyes—as much for Russell as for himself. Patch shoved the leg against the chest of his dumbstruck brother and barked an undeniable command.

"Run!"

In unison, both men took off like bats out of the ninth circle of hell. They ran without thought—barely able to keep from colliding with the coming walls of the tunnel by the blaze at their heels. After the longest ten seconds of either man's life, they reached the fork. Turning back, Patch Briar saw the orange glow was too far behind them to be of any harm.

"Russ!" he shouted through panting gasps "The fire! It—"

CRACK!

Patch's head bounced off something hard. For an unknown span, he saw no more.

SIX

"How's that safe coming, Roy?" Patch Briar did not sound pleased. "For your sake, I sincerely hope you're not playing games."

"N-no. 'Course not!" stammered Hurley, wiping a profuse amount of sweat onto one sleeve. "It's my hands. They keep slipping. Every time I make a mistake, I have to start over. I'm s-sorry, Patch—you got me worked up something fierce, here. Listen—I still don't understand why we can't talk like civilized men. Please son, just put away the gun and I promise we can fix this."

"Can't fix gone, Roy." Patch Briar shook his head—smiled a joyless smile. "Can't fix dead. What you *can* do is open that goddamned safe before I blow your head off."

SEVEN

[August the 12th, 12:10 PM]

"Patch."

The voice called in through the fog.

"W-wake up, little br-other."

The voice, of course, was Russell's. He sounded close, but darkness had the man. The only light came from the feeble lamp at Patch's feet.

"Ther-re's no tim-me." The words were low, bland—chilling in their lack of urgency. Behind the words was a familiar, sucking sound. Just like in the chamber, it seemed to come from all around and nowhere.

"You h-have t-to ... get up-p."

Something in Patch's brain snapped into place. But as he rose, so too did the sound—surging with speed and volume before settling back into its previous rhythm.

"Agh!" came the voice of Russell Briar, suddenly in what seemed like agony. "Patrick ... *Please.*"

Patch wheeled around. The sound of his given name was usually made to sound like an insult but not here. Not now.

His eyes strained to see, to locate the source of the horrific, damnably unforgettable slurping. He reached for the lamp—finally beholding what it wanted to show him. The false leg had seen better days. It was broken, split down one side. Inside, Patch could see that the thing really was hollow. Moreover, it contained two very different objects, which Augustus Lippencott had taken to the grave.

The money clip was heavy, but looked to only be holding a few dollars. Beside that was a folded piece of paper and nothing else. No gold. No ticket to a new life in Mexico. Only a few bucks and a note with a single word scrawled on the outside.

And in that moment, Patrick Briar understood. Maybe not everything ... but enough.

"Russ?" Patch's voice trembled as bad as his hand when it reached for the lamp. "Where are you?"

The lamp was raised, thrust forward into the perfect dark. In response, a second light ignited some twenty feet away, and then a third. All three emitted an unnatural greenish hue that once again seemed to prevent Patch's body from doing anything but staying right where it was. The lights he had initially taken for eyes, moved closer—hovering just above Patch's head and tracing his general form. He could feel it. Feel *them*. The lights were inspecting him. He knew this as well as his own name, but remained powerless to do a damn thing about it.

Fear gripped him. Fear like he had only read about now shackled his every impulse. And behind it all was the sound. That sickening, gut churning sound.

Like a horse at the trough.

Suddenly, the smell of burning flesh pricked at his nostrils. The lamp—he had been holding it in his palm like a ball, instead of by the hook. White-hot pain kicked in with the force of a mule and suddenly Patch was on his feet! With a defiant scream, he reared back and hurled the old lamp at the ghost lights!

What happened next would later be reduced to a sequence of still images—flashes, seared into the man's brain for the rest of his days.

The lamp hit a domed surface which brought to mind the face of a gigantic horseshoe crab. Upon impact, oil splashed out and flared as unearthly screams filled the tunnel. Patch pressed hands to his ears, but the act did little good. The scream was legion. A thousand tea kettles boiling at once.

Teeth clenched and eyes squinted, as Patch forced open his eyes. The face of the creature was decorated with clusters of uncountable spider eyes—black like pools of crude oil. Patch looked to where the mouth should have been. His own eyes were expecting mandibles or fangs dripping hot venom. What he saw instead was a single curved appendage. Something massive and jointed like a long bony finger. It started at the center of the face, than curved back toward the body. Currently, the tip was inserted into the chest of a man Patch knew all too well.

"Russell!"

Lamp oil burning its face, the creature bucked and screamed—

crashing into the sides of the tunnel. God, it was huge. The size of an elephant at least. Finally the strange, finger-like proboscis was pulled from its victim. In the air it looked something like a segmented scythe—the crab-leg equivalent of Death's own blade. At that moment, Patch had visions of him and Russ catching wheel bugs and understood this was the thing's mouth. Whatever this monstrosity was, it had been feeding on his big brother. *Drinking* him, just as it had every other offering the citizens of Broken Promise had willingly laid at its door.

The body of Russell Briar slumped to the ground. His face looked up weakly, pitiably. It was deadly thin and covered in lines that hadn't been there before. It was as if the man had aged fifty years in a matter of seconds.

As the tea-kettle-shrieks rose, more and more lights winked into existence, revealing at last, their mechanism. Each of the ghost lights was set into the bulbous end of a long, squirming tentacle. The shrieking monster had a mane of them—each extending from behind its horseshoe crab head. They writhed and flailed about like a dozen faceless snakes—bathing the tunnel in flashing chaos.

Amid this, two brothers locked eyes for the very last time. What passed between them did so in a language all their own. That strange and wonderful dialect which none but siblings can hope to master. In that moment, nothing was spoken and yet, more than most say in a lifetime.

The elder of the two had lost the ability to move—his muscles already having atrophied into useless strips of jerky. Using the very last of his strength, his lips formed their final, soundless word.

"Go."

Tears streaming down his face, Patch turned and did just that. Running straight for the mine's only exit.

Unaccustomed to suppers that moved, the monster turned to cough up a confused bark. Now every oil-black eye was set and focused upon the scurrying thing that had dared fight back. With the segmented proboscis carefully folded along its belly, two massive arms shot forth. On massive knuckles, they began to drag the monster's bulk forward as the glow-tipped tentacles fought to keep its enemy in sight.

Glancing behind, Patch saw that the cage was there, not fifty paces away. He took a deep breath. In the greenish glow, all movement was reduced to blurs. Flashes. The proboscis shot out, piercing the ground by Patch's feet. It sounded thin. Metallic. The harsh strikes of a pickaxe. Again and again the monster lashed out like this. The attacks of its hideous scythe-mouth, lashing, stabbing, searching—all while strong arms dragged whatever unknowable bulk lay behind.

The remaining Briar backed away, but there was a weight on his skull. As if the shadows around him had started to bleed—to seep in and mingle with his already fractured mind.

That's when Patch Briar finally screamed.

He lifted the only weapon he had carried for three years. The revolver was a Colt Paterson by the look—the same weapon John Coffee Hays had so famously used to fend off those Comanches back in '41.

As the shrieking nightmare dragged itself closer, the man called Patch thumbed back the hammer. Then, with his dead brother's name on his lips, he aimed directly in the center of that cluster of oil-black eyes and pulled the goddamned trigger.

All at once, the ghost lights went out. A thousand candles snuffed by a single, undeniable breath.

EIGHT

The fat man's jaw worked like a gate with a busted latch. Open. Closed. Open again. Despite this, the rest of Roy Hurley remained perfectly still.

He had felt the tumbler inside the locking mechanism fall into place—heard the telltale click that to him, seemed louder than a rifle blast. At that moment, Roy Hurley prepared himself. He had one chance to get this right. Just one. The loaded Derringer—he could feel it just inches away. It was humming. Aching for his touch. Hurley could see a change had come over the last Briar brother. Something about his eyes—they seemed empty, though *devoid* might be a better word. Devoid of emotion, of color, even of wrath. The eyes of a wandering phantom having just realized that the grave up ahead was his own.

"You know ... it's kinda funny." Patch spoke in a low voice. "For months, my brother actually thought he was playing *you*, Roy. Offering to stay late. To pick up the wages or just share a drink. Russell liked to play the long game and like any good caboose, I went along. See, we were hoping that eventually, you'd get comfortable enough to spill something of value in one of them bourbon glasses."

Patch looked extraordinarily tired. As his free hand pinched the bridge of his nose while the one holding the revolver went slack. Hurley watched the Colt Paterson swing down to point at the floor. He knew his moment had come, just as he knew he wasn't gonna get another. Gently, he put a hand on the door of the cold and thoroughly unlocked safe.

"I asked you before ... what you told him. I gave you a chance." Patch said this as blandly as his brother's last words had been. "It turned out that our Mr. Lippencott's false leg was hollow—the perfect place to hide something *of value*. None of them stray dogs in town knew. But somehow my big brother *did*." Patch looked up. "You wanna know how?"

Hurley licked his lips, nervously tasting the salty twang of sweat.

"He knew because you told him, Roy. About the leg and what was *maybe* inside of it. Just enough to get the gears turning. My brother was no fool and you knew it. To get us into that godforsaken mine, you needed to make Russell believe the idea was *his*. That in fact, you had turned down Augustus Lippencott's *generous proposal*." At this, Patch laughed a little. "All so we'd chase that treasure of his down a damn mine shaft."

"You're crazy." Hurley growled, sliding a finger into the safe.

"Maybe." Patch grinned. "But you wanna know what's *really crazy?* Whatever that goddamned thing was ... Indian spirit monster or not— you were feeding us to it. Just like this town has been doing for twenty years—ever since Ulysses J. Waught closed down his fucking mine. Oh I've no doubt those miners released something beneath Promise, Missouri, but it sure as hell wasn't *bad air*. I don't know if you all worship that thing or are just scared shitless of it. What I *do* know is why you wanted us down there."

Roy said nothing.

"We were sacrifices." Patch's words came in a hiss, but he did not look up. "Thing is, that ugly *whatever-the-hell* was slow. Too accustomed to snacking on folk who can't skitter away. And the bitch of it is, Roy ... your God killed my brother."

When Patch met the fat man's eye, he found himself staring down the barrel of a very small pistol. For the first time all night, Roy Hurley was smiling. It was a crazed, maniacal smile. The sort that all masked men possess just beneath.

"You and your brother were good hands. Good men, or close as we get round these parts. You should know ... none of this was personal. It's just our burden. Sins of the father and all that." Hurley looked a bit regretful then, but the expression quickly turned hard. "You got a tiger in a cage, you best feed the thing. Last thing you want is for the thing to get restless."

Patch heard a high-pitched series of clicks and then—

POOOMB!!!

In the confined space, the blast was ear-splitting. Flesh parted and was flung through the air—splatter-painting the office walls. The fat man looked surprised. No … He looked downright flabbergasted. The large window beside the door was broken. In the center of the glass was a hole about the size of a cannon ball. The existence of the thing was inexplicable. As he fell, Hurley did his best to make sense of it, but such things are difficult to ponder when part of your brain is sliding down a wall. So, Roy Hurley stopped trying and just died—one hand still clutching an unfired Derringer.

Ears ringing, Patch Briar dusted glass off his shoulder. Then he pressed a palm into his right ear. One eye in a squint, he turned to see an incredibly large man walk through the office door. In his hands, a brand-new 1866 Winchester rifle. The same one Patch had taken off the wall and handed over to the large man just outside.

"Jesus, Tom. My ears are never gonna stop ringing." Patch worked his jaw open and closed a few times. "Nice timing, though."

"Mmm," grunted One Horse Tom. "What's in the safe?"

Almost too tired to move, Patch craned his head to the safe. Slowly, he took two paces, kneeled in a smear of blood, then peered inside.

"The only thing that can be." He pulled out a hunk of solid gold approximately the size of a baby's fist. "The one place no one could look. Hell, I knew Roy was full of shit. No one's dumb enough to let this kinda fortune walk out of his own damn office." Patch took a deep breath, then shook his head. Without his brother, the revelation was bland—tasteless.

The large Chocktaw proceeded to empty the contents of the safe into a cloth sack—same sort banks used. Along with the gold, there were numerous stacks of cash money. Absently, Patch reached into his pocket and pulled out Lippencott's money clip and threw it in as well.

For a second, One Horse Tom stopped to ask a silent question with his eyes.

"Courtesy of Augustus Lippencott," Patch said blandly. "Twenty-three whole dollars."

"Did … he swallow it?"

Patch snickered, than realized how genuine the question was. "Naw … it was in his leg. The wooden one. Along with this." He produced the folded piece of paper, held it up to the light and read the one word on the outside.

"Says *CONTRACT*." He unfolded the paper and glanced over what was inside. Of course, he had read it all before. By the light of the August moon. After he and One Horse Tom had put a sufficient number of steps between themselves and Waught's Mine. "My guess is ... this here is what Lippencott was really celebrating last Tuesday night. Seems, despite what Roy asserted, he did not refuse Lippencott's offer. This looks to be a letter saying they were going to split the Hurley property right down the middle. Roy even signed it."

"Hmm...," said a disinterested One Horse Tom.

"Kinda makes you wonder though, doesn't it?" Patch scratched absently at his jaw. "Lippencott trusted his estranged cousin enough to leave this gold in his safe ... but was Roy really gonna hold to what it says in this note? The more I think on it ... it does seem awfully convenient that Weeping John did what he did, just in time to make sure that Roy not only got to keep the gold all for himself ... but that any proof of this gentleman's agreement would be lost down the mine shaft."

The last Briar brother was more than exhausted, more than drained. He felt as if he were the last strand of an already frayed length of rope. As such, his words came out in a slower than usual drawl.

"I dunno ... maybe I think too much. You were the one who was there, Tom. Lippencott called the whole town a bunch of what—*stray dogs*? And Wraith just decides to go and take it personal? I know the man has a reputation and all but ... don't that strike you as strange?"

The Chocktaw stood up slowly and finished tying off the end of the sack. Then he frowned. "Everything white men do strikes me as strange."

"Welp. Fair enough." Patch drew in a sharp breath through his nose. "Hey, how about we saddle up a couple of Roy's best horses on the way out. I always liked that buckskin gelding."

"Already picked that one," grunted One Horse Tom.

"Of course you did." Patch smiled a little, yawned, then he closed his eyes.

They were waiting for him, of course. Right there in his own personal darkness just as he knew they would be. No matter how far he'd ever get from that mine … the ghost lights were *his*. Now and always. He would walk with them until the end of his days, and he would do so alone.

"Russell." One Horse Tom, grunted this, though his eyes remained fixed on the floor. "Would be proud. For this," he held up the money sack. "And for *him*."

For a few seconds, Patch didn't know what to say. His mind swirled—from trauma and exhaustion, yes … but also at the sound of his brother's name.

"Thanks," was all he said.

And without another word on the subject, the two men shuffled towards the door of the small, blood-stained office. But before they left, the big one turned back to regard what was left of his former employer.

"Oh … someone will find him eventually," said Patch Briar, with a shrug. "I reckon they'll get old Roy where he needs to go."

A FEAST
OF FLIES

When He broke the third seal, I heard the third living creature saying, "Come." I looked, and behold, a black horse; and he who sat on it had a pair of scales in his hand.

John Wraith had never much liked surprises. In fact, that was the primary reason his loaded Remington 1858 was pointed where it was. Why his thumb had already forced back the hammer, and why his trigger finger was currently fighting off an itch.

The fact of it was, the stranger had appeared out of nowhere. Without a sound of warning or apparently a single lick of sense, he had ridden right out of the ample dark. Like one of the night's many shadows breaking off from the herd. And now, whoever he was, the idiot was about to get his head blown off.

"I'm unarmed," said the stranger, holding up both hands. *"Saw the fire is all, and, well ... I've been riding for a long time."* It was a voice that fell uncomfortably upon the ears. One which seemed to vibrate the air—buzzing, like the drone of a thousand flies.

Using only his peripheral senses, John Wraith saw his men were on their feet now—all pointing iron at the same target. Unfortunately, the Wraith gang had only six members left, and that was counting one half-blind cook and the Chavez twins, who were still out with their snares. A sad state, but things would be better when they got to Dallas. They had to be.

Wraith smirked. "The saddles got a price, friend." He offered in a coarse tone. "A toll. Longer you sit in one, the more it takes from ya. Seems yours's been glutting itself on your good sense."

The stranger made no immediate response to this. Most of his face was obscured—hidden behind long, scraggly hair the color of moldy hay. Though he could make out little else in the flickering light, John could make out a sharp line of cheekbone that bordered on the skeletal.

"What's the matter, stranger?" barked a third man. "You deaf or something?" Jim-Jack Hodge was big, bearded and generally about as subtle as a stampede.

"Shut up, Hodge," said Wraith without turning from the stranger. "Tell me, friend … are you riding alone on this fine evening?"

"Alone. Yes." The stranger said this solemnly, than nodded. *"Things are better that way."*

"Is that right?" Wraith said this with a lilt to his voice. "Better for *who*, I wonder?"

The stranger started to put his hands down, but this only caused every arm holding a weapon to renew their aim.

"Please," said the stranger. *"I'm not looking for any sort of trouble. I don't need water, or supplies and if I'm speaking plain, I never had much in the way of an appetite."* His hands were still up—still empty but for a loop of reins around one thumb. *"All I'm after is a seat by the fire on a long, cold night. That and nothing more."*

Wraith could feel the words entering his skull, working their way inside like something alive.

"But … if that's asking too much …" The stranger bowed his head. *"Then I'll be on my way."*

"You'll be deader than a whore with compunction—that's what you'll be." Hodge grinned maniacally, allowing firelight to dance across the glistening, tobacco-stained surfaces of the few teeth he had left. Then he raised his Winchester repeater—leveled it to one eye.

"Damn it Hodge, I said *shut up*." Wraith worked something loose from between his teeth. Spitting into the flames resulted in a hiss that might have been inaudible if not for the fact that no one present was willing to exhale.

"Come on then." Wraith made a come hither sweep with the barrel of his pistol. "Off the horse, friend."

The stranger nodded, then slid from his saddle, kicking up a small cloud of dust upon hitting the earth. As for the horse, it didn't seem to notice one way or the other. The animal was rather gaunt with a solid black coat. It was also still to the point where a fourth man, in old cavalry greys, wondered if the stranger hadn't ridden in on a statue of a horse, rather than the real thing. This was Waylon 'Wrongway' McRabe—the closest thing to a navigator John Wraith had left.

After a few steps, the Wraith gang could better see their uninvited guest. The stranger wore a long greatcoat that clung like a second skin. The garment betrayed a most emaciated form—one that, to John Wraith, didn't look formidable enough to saddle his own ride, let alone be a physical threat to four seasoned desperados such as they.

"Wrongway," Wraith's tone was calm but inflexible as ever. "Check him."

McRabe shot back a glance to the man whose orders he knew better than to decline. Over the last eighteen months, he had seen John Wraith do terrible things. Though most of the really unjustified stuff had been fueled by whiskey, there were one or two incidents that tended to keep him up at night. And so, though he'd rather be doing just about anything else, McRabe trudged forward, holding his pistol out at arm's length.

After a few steps he shot back a nervous glance. To his relief, John only had eyes for the stranger—or rather, eye. Really, the right was the only one that mattered. The skin on that side was hideous. Stained bruise-purple and covered in warty bumps of varying size. The birthmark was unmistakable. A feature every wanted poster artist made sure to embellish. It surrounded the inner corner of the man's right eye, then trailed down past his chin. It was as if the face were displaying the only tear it had ever cried. Weeping John, some called him, just never to his face.

McRabe stopped, mere feet from the mysterious stranger. With one shaky hand, he reached out—perfunctorily patting a narrow pair of hips. These transgressions elicited no reaction from the stranger, but the man doing the frisking didn't feel right. His head was off. His stomach too. Doing this was like padding down a corpse. There was too much bone and not enough of everything else.

"There a problem?" The voice of John Wraith pulled the man back into his boots. McRabe hadn't realized it, but after the hips he had just sort of frozen there for a minute.

"No. No problem, John." McRabe swallowed, wet his lips. Then, eager to avoid the stranger's eyes, he ran a quick hand down each leg before checking the boots.

"Like I said ... I'm unarmed." The stranger smiled from behind his long hair. *"Never much liked guns."*

Ignoring this, McRabe stood up, squeezing both wrists and biceps before he slid a hand into the left side of the stranger's coat. As those finger moved around the man's side they learned the contour of every rib along the way—but, there was nothing to find. No weapons, no hidden pockets. Hell, the coat was even missing anything that resembled a lining. Suddenly, emboldened and well past ready to get the task over with, McRabe plunged that hand into the other side. That was when something moved. Something that wasn't the stranger, but rather, on him.

The hand of the man doing the frisking shot back faster than a bolt of fresh lightning as a chorus of fresh clicks sounded from behind. If every firearm hadn't been ready to fire before, they sure as hell were now.

McRabe backed up one step and then more—watching slack-jawed and horrified as the thing, whatever it was, wriggled beneath the coat. Right where shoulder met chest.

"My apologies, Wrongway. Seems I forgot to mention the Judge." The stranger gave a narrow smile.

To this, McRabe didn't know what to say. His mind was spinning. The Stranger not only had some kind of creature riding under his coat, he had just used a moniker only known and used by the other members of the John Wraith gang. Had someone else called him *Wrongway* in the last couple of minutes? McRabe tried like hell to recall. He took another step back as one hand moved to cradle his belly. It was an unconscious gesture. The body reaching for some threadbare measure of relief.

As for the stranger, he seemed to be whispering into his shoulder. Coaxing and calming whatever was hiding there. Slowly, an open hand was extended. The bulge moved again. Then it skittered nearer and nearer down to the end of the sleeve.

The face that emerged was that of a small lizard. After pausing for only a second or two, it proceeded to crawl out, filling the open palm and then some. It was a reptile unlike any the men had ever seen. The color of charcoal with a fiery orange back and a massive armored tail covered in thick scales and small, thorny spikes. The creature looked up—glaring with its beady black eyes, making the man called Wrongway feel as if he were suddenly on trial.

"He's harmless." The stranger's voice had adopted an amused quality. *"I picked up the Judge here some time back and well, we've been inseparable ever since. Sorry about the start, friend."*

"Harmless. Sure." McRabe sneered. He wanted to blurt out that he wasn't the man's goddamned friend. Instead he kept his mouth shut and scrambled back across the remaining ground to his outfit's leader. "He's clean, John." Adding; "Except for the lizard." Then he leaned in and spoke more softly. "But I don't like him. Not one bit. A man rides through Choctaw territory with no weapon, no supplies, no hat?! And I know it's dark but I'm telling you, there ain't no bags hanging from that saddle—not even a damn rope. Then there's that *thing*. You ever see a lizard like that? I sure as hell haven't. I'm telling you, John … something about this feller ain't right. Wouldn't we be better off sending him on his way? Or maybe …" McRabe's eyes flitted to the Remington pistol and back like a hummingbird betwixt the blooms of a honeysuckle.

For a few seconds, all was silent as John Wraith stood considering what he had learned. His eyes, locked with those of the stranger.

"It really is mighty cold out here." The stranger's voice buzzed hotly in the brain. The more John heard it, the more it felt like the call of slumber.

The other men watched intently. Focused on their leader. A man they had seen shoot to kill over the slightest insult, now stand uncharacteristically idle in the presence of a wandering vagabond who, more and more, was putting the *strange* in stranger.

"Really could use some of that fire."

Wraith had a severe look to him. Like he was circling a major decision in his head. Finally, he spat into the fire and slid his Remington 1858 back between belt and hip.

"Put 'em away, boys," he said at last. "I reckon this fire here is big enough for one more."

"What?" blurted out Jim-Jack Hodge, sounding down right flabbergasted.

"You deaf, Hodge?" bellowed Wraith—orange light flickering in his bad eye. "The rest of you too … I said put 'em down." The pistol had found its way into his hand again and by God, it looked angry. Despite a wash of confused expressions, the men did as they were told. Every one of them eyeballed the tall stranger as he stepped slowly into the camp proper.

"Well, then." The stranger said this with an appreciative nod. *"Much obliged, gentlemen. Much obliged."*

The words were like a cold shiver down the spine of every man unfortunate to hear them. Every man that is, except for John Wraith who looked about ready to fall asleep in his boots. The rest watched as their leader proceeded to plop his carcass down and kick up his boots as if none of the past ten minutes had happened. Unable to make sense of it all, they began exchanging glances. Things like consternation and all manner of objection passed between them but not a one had a mind to speak. Instead, all eyes moved to the stranger. Already he had set himself down about a foot from the fire. Just beside a three-legged spit, which supported a pot containing about a fifth of the gang's remaining beans.

As for Waylon McRabe, he trudged back over to his bedroll.

"Never had much of an appetite." He grumbled this under his breath—too low for anyone to hear. "I'll just bet."

Setting down he picked up a small leather-bound book. It was laying right where he had dropped it just fifteen minutes prior—right when the night had gotten interesting. After dusting off the cover, he flipped past a number of pages until he found the right one. Then, eyes in a squint, he read over the last couple of lines.

'*Hot again today.*' The words had been scrawled in slate pencil. '*Was hoping for rain but none came.*'

McRabe glared at the words, wishing to God he had something better to record. Something a mite less bleak … but bleak was all there was anymore. Touching pencil to page, he added…,

'*Food is almost gone.*'

As if on cue, his belly let lose a growl like a pissed-off bear. Something was wrong in there. His insides were in knots. His gut, empty and bloated at the same time. Though it wasn't easy, with a shaky hand, he managed five words more....

'*Never been so damn hungry.*'

The tip of the pencil snapped.

"Shit." He said to no one in particular. For a fleeting second, the only literate member of the Wraith gang considered reaching for his knife and whittling a fresh point. Problem was, his mind wasn't on the work. Looking over, McRabe found that the stranger was staring directly at him. His yellow eyes shining and stabbing like a pair of knives.

"Hey there, Wrongway." The voice was a mule kick to the side of the head.

McRabe looked up. Frowned. Standing there, just a bit too close for comfort, was one Jameson Jackson Hodge. Per usual, the man smelled like the corner of a pig pen farthest from the trough. The one where all the shit goes.

"How's them pretty poems going?" Hodge said this with a nasty grin, then offered a wink.

"Fine." McRabe clapped the book shut. Tucked it away in his bedroll. "But you know I ain't writing no damn poems, dumb-shit."

"Fine, huh?" Hodge stroked pensively his great bush of a beard, twisting when he came to the end. "Don't look fine to me, Wrongway. In fact, it looks more like something with quills crawled up your ass and turned sideways."

In that moment, Waylon McRabe wanted to reach up and slap the beard from the man's face. *Wrongway*. God, how he hated that damn nickname. A man makes one mistake that costs barely half a day's ride and his compatriots brand him a fuck-up for life—just one more entry for that oh-so-legendary code of the West. *Shit*, McRabe thought. Maybe his mama was right. Maybe he should have been a banker like his old man.

"Hot spit and holy shit!"

The exclamation shattered the momentary still that had settled. All eyes shot to a half-blind cook called Jerral Crooms. The scrawny, old black man was waving a wooden spoon in the air and cussing in a long glorious stream, as if he was being paid by the syllable. John Wraith was first to his feet.

"Jerral," Wraith barked. "What are you—"

"The beans! It's the dodgasted, mother-grabbin' beans!" Crooms dropped the pot onto the ground using a long metal hook. Then waving the steam away. "Look, damn you! Look!"

In absolutely no mood for more excitement, Wraith stomped around the fire and peered through the steam at what had become of their supper. Then, his stomach did something it had never done before ... it turned.

In the pot which had been making an absolute racket only minutes before, was a revolting, almost unrecognizable mass. The beans had turned an ashen grey and were joined together with what looked like a fibrous sludge that was most definitely not gravy. Crooms thrust in the spoon and scooped out a heaping portion which he proceeded to squint at.

"Jesus Christ in a rodeo!" Jim-Jack Hodge exclaimed. "You trying to poison us, you blind old fart?"

The cook screwed up his face. "Jameson Hodge … I ain't never been in less of a mood for your shit than I am right in this moment." He pulled out a finger. Poked the big burly son of a bitch in the chest. "Them beans were fine when they went in that pot. Just fine, like every other damn night! All a'you can look for your own selves!"

Jerral Crooms stamped over to a meager pile of cooking sundries which included a bent-handled fry pan and a burlap sack. This he threw open and held out proudly for all to see.

"There may not be much left, but my beans are—"

An audible gasp could be heard above the pops and the roar of the fire. Hideous black mold had taken the inside of the sack. Taken it so utterly that veins of the stuff were creeping up the sides. Accompanying the sight was a hideous smell which struck the onlookers full in the face.

"Shit!" Hodge spat this with rare sincerity as he bent over coughing, gasping for clean air. "Just … holy fuckin' shit!"

The men started to argue then. Each one shouting with outstretched fingers and clenched fists until Wraith stepped in and fired a single shot into the air. The report hit like a clap of lightning … the thunder of which rolled out slow over the plains of the Choctaw Nation.

There was no more shouting after that. In fact, for almost a full minute, no one said a damn thing.

"What are we gonna do, John?" The voice belonged to Waylon McRabe. One shaking hand was cupped over his stomach. "There's nothing left. Nothing."

"Step off, Wrongway." Wraith's voice was low. "And calm the hell down. All of you. I don't know what happened to those beans, but we're all gonna be fine—you hear? By this time tomorrow, we'll be in Texas. And once we hit Dallas, we'll be able to sit tight for a few weeks, all comfortable-like."

"Sure. 'Cause the Silver-Fish is got a big score for us—that right?" Jim-Jack Hodge said this with a bit too much venom. In response, one of the boss man's eyebrows adopted an arc. Then he walked over real slow until the sour reek of Hodge's exhales were in his nose.

"Good to know you been paying attention … *Jim-Jack*." Wraith pinched the brim of his hat, making a minute adjustment. "Some friendly advice, though. Unless you want to die knowing the taste and texture of one or both of your intestines … I'd lose that Silver-Fish shit. Pete Decker takes even less kindly to nicknames than I do."

A wide-eyed Hodge backed up a step. Looked around like he didn't know where he was. "Got it, John. Sorry. I don't know what came over me."

"You don't, huh? Well I do." Jerral Crooms kicked the pot, painting the ground with its steaming black corruption. "Dallas ain't gonna do shit for us if we all starve to death before we get there. Wrongway's right. There ain't nothing left for us to eat, John. Nothing."

The old man's comments birthed another wave of bellyaching, which was cut short by the dramatic arrival of two men on horseback. The Chavez twins were both brandishing their rifles and wide-eyed.

"John!" said Dwayne Chavez. "We heard the shot! Is it the Choctaw? The Chickasaw?" The two horses came to a stop as both men shot glances off into the distance. The first one, Dwayne, was a large dark-skinned freedman wearing a dirty green shirt, brown vest and a full handlebar mustache. The unlikely pairing of a crucifix and the skull of some small animal dangled from a rawhide cord around his neck. The other one was called Stu. He was a smaller, coffee-skinned, clean shaven Mexican with long black hair and twin bandoliers that hung across his chest. As it happened, the so-called Chavez 'twins' weren't related by blood, but rather the happenstances of a common surname, as well as a knack for the art of trapping.

"No Indians, boys," said John Wraith. "Just tell me you didn't come back empty-handed."

Both men dismounted. "That I can do," said Dwayne. "Stu? How about you show 'em the bounty our Lord has seen fit to provide."

Stu Chavez held up three good-sized jackrabbits, which dangled triumphantly from a length of rope—looking to the rest about the most beautiful thing in the whole of creation. The wave of relief which washed through the camp was palpable. As for Wrongway McRabe, his gut gave a kick so strong, he felt a slight tug in his spine. In the moment, it was about all he could do to stop himself from taking a bite out of one of the carcasses right then and there.

One by one, the rabbits were handed off. Then Crooms and each Chavez began working at the heels of their respective animal. Pink legs appeared amidst a series of dull rips as the hides were removed. Stu Chavez was the first to finish—his technique of flicking the animal with one quick wrench being the most effective. His small knife moved fast, severing the back legs, then the front before sliding into the animal's belly.

While this was going on, McRabe's eyes began to drift. The stranger didn't seem bothered by the comotion. He was still sitting on his haunches, with both hands out as if he were letting them dry.

"*¿Que demonios?*"

McRabe heard the exclamation distantly. It took him a second or two before he turned.

"Son of a bitch …" Dwayne Chavez made a cross. "This just ain't possible! The little shits were alive less than an hour ago!"

As he heard the words, something was rising in McRabe's throat. Something foreboding that tasted of panic and bile.

"No way! There just ain't no fuckin' way!" Now Hodge was the one raving. McRabe pushed the walking pigsty aside—peered down where the men were gawping.

"The thing's full of goddamn maggots!" cried Hodge. "Chavez, you liar! You two didn't bag these rabbits, you fuckin' found 'em. By the look, they probably been dead near a week!"

The Mexican Chavez jumped up and jabbed his knife within an inch of the bearded man's face. From his mouth gushed a furious tirade, though none but his so-called twin could understand the words. McRabe's eyes went wide with horror. That first rabbit's stomach hung open like a satchel filled with a black tar as well as a concentration of plump white maggots so thick, so dense, not a one of the animal's internal organs were left.

In that moment, the knees of the gang's navigator buckled. When McRabe's ass hit the dirt, a mouthful of vomit was expelled to splash on the ground between his legs.

"It's all of 'em," shouted the half-blind cook. "All three rabbits is rotten. And I just figured out why." He got up, shaking from finger to toe. "It's this place. This ain't Oklahoma—no sir. This ... this be the devil's country." Crooms was smiling as he spoke. "Somehow, we wandered right into Perdition ... but we ain't wandering out."

"Shut up! Just shut the hell up!" The voice belonged to Jim-Jack Hodge. His Winchester repeater was leveled at the old man. "You're fuckin' crazy Crooms. This is all your fault! You let our beans get wet in the last rain, you're just too damn blind to notice. That's the only explanation! You're the reason we come to this!"

The gunshot was sudden and louder than the voice of God. Loud enough to crack the sky. Jerral Crooms clutched at his chest—not from any newly made holes, but for the pain his heart was currently putting out.

The Chavez twins looked in awe at the man in the white hat. Once again the right hand of John Wraith was gripping his trusty Remington 1858. The pistol's barrel was still smoking—still pointing in the direction of Jim-Jack Hodge. Everyone watched the burly son of a bitch stumble one step to the right, then fall in a bearded heap of dead meat.

After the last of the gunshot echoed away, the primary sound was a steady roar, accented by the occasional pop and snap. But there was another sound too. A wet, greedy sound.

Heads turned. Jaws fell slack to gape in silent horror.

There was a man on the ground. A man in old cavalry greys was hunched over with his back turned to the rest, and he was eating. The Chavez twins exchanged a look, but neither said a single, damn word.

"Wrongway?" came the voice of John Wraith, sounding good and rattled for perhaps the first time in his life. "What you got there?"

No response. Just more chewing. More smacking. Like feet tramping through mud.

"Hell ... you find something good? Something we can all share?" Wraith's voice had adopted a placating tone. Silently he motioned to the twins—to circle round and flank the man, just in case.

"Ain't sharing shit." Came a voice that sounded only vaguely like a man they had known. "This one's mine. All mine." McRabe stopped for a second but didn't turn. Then he tucked back into whatever had his attention. "Hodge was wrong, you know. This is all *your* fault, John. Yours and nobody else's." More chewing, ripping, gulping. "Back in Missouri—that mining town had supplies. Had food. If we'd bought some as was the plan, we'd all be fine right now. But no. Oh no. You had to get all drunk, as usual. Had to kill that idiot snake-oil man with the limp. AND FOR WHAT?!"

McRabe's whipped round. He looked like a predator. There were strings of rabbit meat dangling from his mouth. His lips were flecked with what looked like grains of rice. Rice that crawled.

"For nothing, that's what!"

As the man they called Wrongway rose to his feet, the others could see just how off he was. His skin, yellow. The lines of his skull, far too prominent. His eyes contained undeniable madness but also stark, raving truth.

"Make no mistake." McRabe drew the back of one arm across his mouth. "We *are* in hell ... but Crooms got it backwards. Don't you get it, John? We didn't wander in ... you led Perdition straight to *us*! Invited it to share our fucking fire!"

With that, Waylon McRabe shot forward—hands out and grasping like claws. The first bullet slammed into his chest and spun him round, but it was the second one that tore off the top of his head. The man's body, already in motion, danced all the way to the fire, which accepted the gift without protest.

The old cook, still clutching the skin above his heart, gave a jerking sort of sound then dropped. And like Jim-Jack Hodge, Jerral Crooms did not get up again. John Wraith blinked, speechlessly. He had acquired the look of a deposed emperor after watching his kingdom burn. He turned for the twins but they were already on their horses. Already riding in full gallop for anywhere else. Apparently, taking out the crazed man in the cavalry greys had been their last official act as members of the Wraith gang.

John dropped—fell hard upon his knees. Bloodshot eyes scanned the ruins of his campsite, absorbing how it had been decorated with the cadavers of his own hand-picked soldiers. Just then, he had a sudden and powerful need to retch, but he fought the urge ... because

he was still him, damn it. Still *Weeping* John Wraith. The white hat
with the black heart. Killer of eleven men, six women and two dogs.

"Well … I suppose that's that," said a man he'd forgotten was there.
"I do appreciate the fire, John … and the show."

The stranger stepped past, either ignorant or ambivalent to the slew
of freshly dead. In his hand was that damn ugly lizard. It looked down
its snout at the man in the white hat, blinking real slow. Seeing this,
Wraith's insides gave a pulse. He lurched forward, clapping both hands
over his mouth. His cheeks all puffed out, just like a trumpet player's.

The stranger gave a whistle, summoning the black horse he had
ridden in on. As it clopped nearer to the fire's light, John could see the
beast through hot streaming tears. This was no regular horse. There
were no muscles, no meat …. only a charcoal pelt stretched tight over
bones. The worst part though, were its eyes which shimmered like
pools of sickly yellow light. With one swift motion, the stranger slid
up into the saddle, but before turning to ride off, he looked down—
just once more.

"The Judge thinks it'll be easier if you just let it happen." A shrug. *"I'd
listen to him, I was you. Better out than in, John."*

With that, the man's will simply gave out. In a great series of
convulsions, a mass composed not of bile but fat, buzzing flies was
vomited forth. Big and black, they were. Thousands of them. Millions.
All pouring from the man's throat and into the air, a veritable legion.
The droning of their wings was loud. Maddening. Sufficient by far to
drown out the screams of a man called Weeping John Wraith.

TRAVELING MENAGERIE

ONE

I t had been over a week since the last show. Eight long days of traveling and shrinking portions at supper.

Being something of a crossroads, Henderson had plenty of people, though most were just passing through or too busy for idle distractions. The place wasn't the worst payday they'd ever had, but the next destination had to be better. Supplies were running low and in the menagerie, there were a lot of mouths to feed.

Ben sighed, adjusted his position on the floor for the hundredth time. His back had been positively on fire all day. It was that bastard kind of pain that shot up the neck and made it hard to breathe. Not that the endless bumps and jostling of the wagon were helping any.

With a groan, he grabbed onto one of the vertical bars and hauled himself up. Ben's short, wrong-bent legs almost buckled at the prospect of supporting his weight, but that was nothing new. Still holding the bar, the man arched his back, then twisted sharply to one side. Two cracks for the right and another for the left, but the resulting relief was nothing to write home about.

Opening his eyes through the pain, Ben glanced over at his bed. The picture of modesty, the simple cot had been nailed to the floor. Now it glared back, offering no solace. When his back got like this, the floor was always better. Or maybe, all he deserved. Then again … it was good enough for Rosie Jones Thomas, and she never complained.

HUMMPH …

The breathy sound huffed from beyond the steel bars.

"All right, all right—keep your shirt on. I'm havin' a look. Just give me a minute, all right? Need to collect me bearings." Ben turned to the darkness of the cage then. "Bearings! That's a joke, luv."

RRRRRMMMPH. The large animal did not sound amused.

Ben hobbled along the line of bars, using them for support. Then he reached out an arm—pulled back the flap of canvas with short, gnarled fingers. At first, the daylight hurt his eyes, but the pain was insignificant when stacked up to his existing cornucopia of aches and ailments. Squinting, forcing his eyes to work correctly, as so many of his other parts refused. He could see it. The town was in the distance now.

Without warning, the man driving the lead wagon called out.

"Nacogdoches, dead ahead!" boomed the thunderous voice of Finneas Faraday. "I know it's been a long drive, but I need everyone up and ready as soon as they're able. Come on, folks, let's bring some want and whimsy to the fine people of east Texas!"

Ben rolled his eyes, and let go of the flap. Then he waddled over to the wall where he'd been sitting. The animal in the cage shifted causing a wall of shaggy black fur to press against the bars. With a crooked smile, Ben reached out and began to stroke his enormous friend's shoulder.

"Want and whimsy? How long's he been savin' that one?" He snickered. "Well, what d'you say, luv? Ready to show 'em a right monster? Aye?"

HUMMFFF! The loud snort was followed by the appearance of a broad pink tongue that slapped Ben in the face.

"That's the spirit." With a chuckle, he dug his fingers in and really scratched the spot he'd been patting. Rosie always loved that. "Just go easy on me this time, all right? Don't know why but the pain has been wretched all day. Even my aches have bloody aches."

The four wagons rolled into town at just after two in the afternoon. They were all connected like a miniature train—pulled in the front by a pair of Clydesdales (one white, one black), and trailed by the most peculiar cow anyone had ever seen. It had an impressive set of upward pointing horns and was covered in shaggy red-brown fur that hid the animal's eyes.

The sides of all four wagons had been painted with fancy gold letters that all read the same thing—*Faraday's Fantastic Traveling Menagerie.*

After turning their heads, some folk began footing it in the opposite direction, or to the closest indoors. Others, especially those with young 'uns, began to gather. They stood in rapturous silence, watching as the wagons pulled up and formed a half circle in the center of the town square. The bearded man sitting in the driver's seat was waving—his smile so broad it looked big enough to split his head wide open. His aspect was that of a circus ringmaster, complete with red jacket, white gloves and a top hat. That said, the first thing most noticed about Finneas Faraday was his size.

"Hello! Hello!" boomed the large man. "Greetings, good people of Nacogdoches! Mr. Faraday is the name, and this is my show! I bring to you fantastic creatures and culture from my travels around this vast world. Sights well beyond the mundane that are sure to excite and to thrill! Come! Don't be shy! Gather round, for the show is about to begin!"

Suddenly, a man emerged from behind the third wagon. He was significantly more slight and scrawny than the driver but nearly as tall. He had long gray hair and a prodigious curled mustache that looked like it weighed more than the rest of him. With a wink and a wave, he hopped down and began to unfasten and untie unseen things on the wagon's side. Faraday was there soon enough and wasted no time helping in the effort. A few seconds later, the whole side of that third wagon creaked open and was gently lowered as legs were attached and a set of stairs was unfolded. Since the hand-painted canvas with the fancy gold letters remained attached to the roof, it provided a fitting backdrop to what was clearly fixing to be a stage.

From behind the backdrop, a Chinese girl of no more than sixteen or seventeen rushed out of wagon number two, carrying something flat, red and almost bigger than she was. After setting this on the ground, the girl gave the thing a swift kick, causing it to change shape and settle into a rather sturdy looking stand-up shelf.

As the set up continued, more and more residents of Nacogdoches gathered round. There were men, women and children of all ages. Even the busy ones had a hard time curbing their curiosity—especially after *she* stepped out on that stage.

The woman looked like the young girl, only older—more developed. She was a vision of exotic beauty and grace with flowers in her long black hair. Her dress was as rose-red as the cheeks of the wide-eyed men who couldn't turn away.

"Ladies and gentlemen," boomed Mr. Faraday, offering his bear-paw hand to help the woman down the set of steps. "While we continue to set up, allow me to present a bit of pre-show entertainment."

Stepping down on porcelain-white legs, the woman moved with an almost supernatural grace. With a tight-lipped smile, she gave the growing audience a shallow bow, then lifted her hands in the air to a round of boisterous hoots and whistle-calls.

Up on the stage, the scrawny older man and the young girl appeared from behind the canvas holding an enormous snake. Six feet long with a striking yellow and white pattern. With some effort, the two handed the animal over to Mr. Faraday.

"Please put your hands together for the delicate but deadly, the emerald rose of the Orient … Miss Li-Mei, the *Serpent Lady of Shanghai!*"

Right on cue, the woman curled her hands around the snake's thick body as it was lowered onto her shoulders. Then, wearing it like some sort of living garment, she moved toward the crowd—gliding on those mesmerizingly long legs as if the enormous animal weighed nothing at all. The gasps from the crowd told her she had them … but the way they backed up when she advanced was a thing to cherish. There were no hoots, no hollers, only a growing mass of folks too nervous to exhale.

Miss Li-Mei loved making the first impression like this and Finneas Faraday knew it. The big man turned from what he was doing just long enough to see the look of satisfaction on her face. Seeing that always made him happy. It had been seven years since he'd first laid eyes on that face—not in Shanghai but San Francisco. And yet, each time he looked her way brought him back to the moment they'd met. On that day, she had tears on her cheeks, but now?

He watched her strut around the square—pointedly offering the head of the albino python to anyone who hadn't stepped too far away. Warming up the crowd meant showing them what tough guys they weren't. It worked in every state, every town and it was working in Nacogdoches.

Before going back to setting up, Faraday smiled. God, he loved that woman.

Off to the side, a small man emerged from around the back of the final wagon. He couldn't have been more than four and a half feet high and was wearing a red vest and striped bandanna. In his stubby hands was a rope that'd been connected to a strange shaggy cow which followed behind. After leading the animal to a visible spot, not too far from center, the man waved his free hand in a flourish. Forgetting the snake woman for a second, the audience began to laugh and point.

"What in the heck is that?" Someone yelled.

"Ah … not what but who!" Mr. Faraday turned, swinging his show cane in a glint of solid gold. "Allow me to introduce … all the way from jolly old Londontown … our resident master of beasts … say hello to Big Ben!"

The introduction made the crowd explode in laughter. It always did.

Holding his smile through clenched teeth, Ben hammered a wooden stake into the ground, tied off the cow, and bent into an exaggerated bow.

"Never should have agreed to that name." He grumbled into the dirt. "*Bloody* Americans."

As he stood up, he patted the cow's face while Mr. Faraday went on with the sales pitch.

"Consider all that you see as but a taste of what's to come." He swung both arms wide, as the others continued to set up stands for cages of varying size. "Our show is separated into three acts and will culminate in a grand finale that is one hundred percent guaranteed to leave you changed forever. There are some things in heaven and earth that mortals are not meant to meddle with ... and yet meddle I have, ladies and gentlemen. And for the cost of one ticket per customer—I will personally reveal the contents of our fourth and final wagon."

All eyes moved then to the last car in the train. The one with the painting of a hulking black monster on the side. The crowd stole a collective gasp.

Snickering to himself, Ben scratched the cow's face before heading back around the last wagon, to his private backstage area. When he got there, the unexpected presence of a strange man made him freeze. The stranger was pale, and had bulgy light blue eyes. Overall, he had the look of a lost hound.

"Oye! What the hell are you doing?" asked Ben. "Put that down."

The man blinked sleepily, but did not respond. In his hands was a large horned skull he'd picked off the ground. Neither bull nor ox but that of a gigantic buffalo. The skull had been cleaned and hollowed out—transformed into something that could be worn, just not by any man. Li-Mei's dress was definitely something, but the one bit of costume no one ever forgot belonged to Rosie Jones Thomas.

"I said, *drop the skull!* You deaf?" Ben's words gathered ire and gravitas like a rolling snowball. His eye went to a little hand ax. It was propped up against the stairs some six feet away. Suddenly, he wished he hadn't left it there. "This area is off-limits. If you're here for the show, it's around the corner."

Still no response.

"Oye! Are we going to have a problem? *Mate?*"

"What? Oh, I'm ... no—no problem here." The man shrugged,

then set the skull back on the ground. His voice had the pitch of youth, but sounded detached somehow. There was definitely something off about the man. Maybe a few somethings.

"Didn't mean any harm." The stranger went on. "I's just curious, is all. Never seen a real live circus 'afore."

"You still haven't." Ben shook his head. "We're a beast show, mate. A *Traveling Menagerie*. Can't you read the signs? We've got enough of 'em."

The pale man looked up at the back of the wagon—at the worn letters that'd been painted there. Then he shook his head.

"Can't read nothing. Never was much for book learning." He scratched the side of his neck. "You're Big Ben." He wasn't asking. "I heard the big man say it afore. That's funny. Seeing how you're not very big."

Ben forced a thin smile. "More ironic than funny, but yeah. That's the joke."

"Well my name's Esau." said the stranger with a wide-eyed look.

"Great." Ben rolled his eyes. He could feel a headache coming on. "Look, it's been lovely making your acquaintance and all, but I've got work to do. So, if you'll kindly exit the backstage area, I'd—"

"Oh sure, sure. Of course I'll get out of your way. Didn't mean to be a bother." Esau shrugged. He started turning to leave, then stopped. "Oh, silly me. I almost forgot, there's something I wanted to tell you."

"And what might that be?" At this point, Ben had to try to sound conversational.

"Oh, just that something bad is gonna happen here. Tonight. Something real nasty. Seemed the neighborly thing to say something. You know … since we's friends now and all that."

Utterly unprepared for what he'd just heard, Ben couldn't think of anything to say. His body was frozen, as if every nerve and tendon had been replaced by barbed wire.

"Big Ben…," Esau snickered. "That is a good one. Hey, you know what else is funny?"

Ben's heart was racing. His eyes moved to the hammer that was hanging from the strange man's belt.

"We's got the same fingers you and me." Esau held out a hand, splayed and wiggled the digits. "See?"

In Ben's estimation, the man's fingers were about half as long as those of a regular-sized person. It looked like they'd been severed at the second knuckle, but at the end of each was a kind of half-formed fingernail.

"My mama said God don't make mistakes, but every now and then he likes to *experiment* some. You know … tweak the recipe." Esau was smiling. "Did your mama say something like 'at?"

"My mum?" Ben looked ready to spit. "Sadly, no. She didn't stick around long enough to say fuck-all."

Esau just stood there, staring. As if trying to discern whether or not Ben's assertion had been genuine. After a few longer-than-average seconds, he threw both hands up in a shrug. "Okay, well … I guess I'll be seeing ya, then." Wearing a sleepy smile, the strange spooky man meandered around the wagon and back to where the crowd was gathered.

Finally letting go of the breath he'd been holding, Ben shuffled as fast as he could, over to the steps. Reaching out, he snatched up the hand ax and gripped it hard. Then pressed his back up against the last wagon—right beside a wheel that was nearly as tall as he was.

Claws appeared—poking through bars that were covered by the painting of a horrible black beast. The appearance of such an appendage would surely have had a bowel-emptying effect on even the most rough and tumble. But for Benjamin Poole, his friend's paw brought only calm.

RRRRRMMM … came a familiar voice.

"Hey, luv. No … I'm all right." Ben's hands twisted around the ax handle like he was ringing the thing out. "He's gone."

RRRRRMMMPH. The animal in the cage did not sound convinced.

"Ben?" called the voice of Hamlin Blithe. "You back here?"

The tall, scrawny man with the broken nose slid through the space between wagons three and four. Under one arm were three yellowed juggling pins that hadn't been white in a long time.

"Hey, there you are!" Blithe clapped his broad hands on his blue jeans, creating dust clouds. "I'm about to go on. You wanna show off what we been practicing, or what?" He tossed over one of the pins, which Ben reached for but failed to catch.

"I think you've got your answer." Ben sighed and picked up the pin that was longer than his arm. Then he glanced over at the end of the wagon. Almost like he expected someone to appear. Or reappear.

"Aw, shoot. That one's my fault—you weren't ready. Really, you been getting so much better lately."

Ben held up a hand to stop the man from going on. "Better's not good enough, mate. If I'm gonna get those people to see anything but my height, I've got to be *great*." He shrugged. "Loads better than *you*, anyway."

The tall man snickered and shook his head.

"Yeah, yeah. All right." Blithe's expression had turned to one of concern. "Hey. You okay?"

"'Course. Never better." Ben straightened up as best he could. Cast a wary glance at the corner of the last wagon that Mr. Esau had disappeared around. "Hey, uh … Ham?"

"Yeah?"

"Do you remember Santa Fe? When we went last June?"

"Aw, sure I do." He smiled. "Now that was a good crowd."

Ben nodded, but whatever he was looking at was miles away. "There was a woman there—a bit of local color. Loco Lucille, they called her. Do you remember?"

Blithe scratched the scruffy line of his jaw. "Should I?"

"Dunno … I found her a bit hard to forget." He limped over to the end of the wagon, peered round at the gathered masses, searching for a pair of pale blue eyes. "Yeah, on the second morning, I went to buy feed with Mr. Faraday. We saw her screaming about some coming biblical disaster. A flood or some such. Then, when we came out of the general shop, there she was, drinking out of a horse trough like it'd been filled just for her. Loco Lucille, someone pointed out as we passed, as if that explained all." A distant smile flickered on Ben's lips. "She came to the show on the second day—I saw her in the back. I think she was afraid of Li-Mei … or more likely … *Clementine*. Anyway, from what some of the locals told Mr. Faraday, that woman was about as predictable as a buffalo in rut, but mostly harmless."

"Sorry, Ben. I don't recall." Blithe shrugged. "Why you askin', anyway?"

Ben's mind was racing—replaying the brief encounter with a blue-eyed stranger—searching for proof that his current state of unrest was unjustified. With a sigh, Ben shrugged his shoulders. "No reason, I guess. Just thinking."

After tossing back the juggling pin, Ben shuffled over to the skull that he'd caught the stranger with. Suddenly, nervous that he hadn't checked already, he picked the thing up and turned it over. To his relief, the leather pad and the straps and buckles all seemed unmolested.

Blithe cleared his throat. "Seriously, Ben ... you look like someone just walked over your grave."

"I'm fine! Just get out there already! Me and Rosie will see you at the finale. Like last time, I'll leave the lock there, right behind the back right wheel." He pointed. "Just make sure you don't miss your cue again, yeah?"

Despite looking a bit dejected, Blithe nodded before heading back the way he came.

"Oye, Ham...," Ben called. "Bump a nose, all right?"

Blithe turned with a smile and a wink, then disappeared between the wagons.

TWO

As the show rolled on, the people of Nacogdoches responded in kind.

Predictably, after getting a taste of Li-Mei, their cheers soured like milk in the sun when the juggler took the stage. Fortunately, Hamlin Blithe kept an ace up his sleeve for just such an occasion. Once the three pins were traded in for five flaming torches, the crowd began to sing a different tune. Catching the final torch in his mouth might have been unnecessary, but by that point he was hell-bent on making them eat those initial jeers.

Watching from his spot, Ben was grinning. Per usual, he'd caught most of the act through the spokes of a large wooden wheel. It was usually pretty muddy under the wagons but there was a spot under the last one that had a great vantage of the action. To Benjamin Poole, it felt like having his own private box at the opera. Not that he'd ever been to one of those.

As he watched his friend leave the stage area, Ben was glad he'd decided to hold off making his juggling debut. He'd been practicing for almost six months, but he still dropped pins about a third of the time. Blithe was all too happy to let him join the act, but the man deserved better. As performers went, Hamlin Blithe was the real deal. According to Mr. Faraday, he worked for Ringling Brothers, once upon a time. Of course that was before the big bad happened. Ben didn't know what the big bad was and he was pretty sure Mr. Faraday didn't either. Blithe would never talk about those days—at least not when he was sober.

A couple years back however, after a show in St. Louis, the man had gotten himself good and lubricated. After throwing back almost a full bottle of red-eye, Blithe started talking all about the past. He mentioned a man called Jack—said what a crack shot he'd been with a pistol.

Seeing how he'd also been drinking that night, Ben was feeling a might bolder than usual. But when he had asked who Jack was, Arthur Hamlin Blithe had turned sheet-white. Then, without another word on that subject or any other, he simply stood up and shuffled off to bed.

"The great Hamlin Blithe, ladies and gentlemen!" As his star juggler took a bow, Mr. Faraday led the audience by clapping his own large hands. There was no denying it—the man had a way of commanding crowds. As far as Ben could tell, his schtick was one part charisma and one part thunder-voice, but he also had that cane. For a man with such thick fingers, Faraday twirled and spun that thing with the confidence of the leader of a marching band. The topper was solid gold—shaped into the head of a bull, horns and all. In the right light, golden arcs could be painted in the air. The cane didn't just draw the eyes of the crowd, it held them.

"And now, if you don't mind, I believe it's time for me to get in on the fun." Mr. Faraday's smile could be heard a mile off in that booming voice. He picked up a strange-looking string instrument—like a banjo but with a more stretched-out look. "Learned how to play this during my time in the Orient. It's a Chinese lute called a pipa. This one I purchased in a small province called—"

"*Who cares*?!" shouted someone. *"Bring back the snake lady!"*

The crowd erupted in raucous laughter at this, causing Ben to angrily search the faces to see who he needed to kick.

"Very well my friends ... very well. Ask and you shall receive!" shouted Mr. Faraday, dropping not one bit of his smile. "Put your hands together and welcome back the mysterious, the beautiful Miss Li-Mei!"

The crowd went positively wild. Men were throwing their hands up as the Serpent Lady of Shanghai walked out again. This time accompanied by the playing of Mr. Faraday, Li-Mei did much more than strut about the square. Along with a snake called Clementine, the alluring woman who had never been to Shanghai in her life, began to dance.

The pling-plong picking of the Chinese instrument paired interestingly with Faraday's choice of tune. But after two verses of *Oh, My Darling*, the crowd was sufficiently wrapped around Li-Mei's finger ... or *figure*, as was more typically the case. Ben had never gotten around to asking which had been chosen first, the song or the name of the great white snake. Either way, it was a hard act to follow.

But follow Ben did—every time. He and Rosey had worked out the finale themselves and, as vulgar as it was, Mr. Faraday eventually warmed to the idea.

Once the so-called Serpent Lady had taken her final bow, the enormous troupe leader put down his instrument and proceeded to lead the crowd in another round of whistling applause—this one louder and more enthusiastic than the last.

"Isn't she marvelous, ladies and gentlemen? Just marvelous. But if you're getting any ideas, I should probably warn you, the python isn't the only one with poisonous teeth. *You can trust me on that!*"

The audience laughed, though some of the men began to look uncomfortable.

"Now, we have a real treat for you." Faraday traced another arc of gold in the air—pointing past the cow, to the last wagon. The one where the image of a shaggy black creature had been painted. The phrase *Terror of the Yukon* stood out boldly for those who were able to read.

"As you know, we are a traveling menagerie, and that means we have for you, sights that your eyes have never seen before. In our last wagon is nothing short of an abomination. A demon, straight from the wastes beyond Perdition, ladies and gentlemen. Somehow, it escaped—clawed its way into our world, where it took up residence in a small valley in that remote corner of the Great White North known as the Yukon."

Ben's heart was racing. He licked his lips and readied his legs—waiting for their cue. From where he was standing, he couldn't see the crowd … but their gasps and worried muttering were music to his ears.

"Keep your eyes on the cow, but please, ladies and gentlemen, if you value your safety … *stay right where you are!*"

When Ben walked out, he looked very, very nervous. Fearful even.

"I'm sure you all remember our animal wrangler, Big Ben!" The crowd didn't respond. They were too busy staring at the painting on the side of that last wagon. At the burning red eyes and the yellow teeth, long as sabers.

"Do I have to do it, Mr. Faraday?" Ben shouted, trying to sound convincing. "She's been acting funny all day! *Extra vicious-like.* I think maybe she's fed up with letting us keep her in that cage. Do you think it's safe to … *taunt her like this?*"

"Why, of course it's safe!" The big man laughed, smiling extra broadly. Then he turned to address his enraptured patrons. "The bars and lock of that particular cage are made of Tibetan black iron and blessed by holy men from three—count 'em, *three*—continents. Mark my words … not even the devil himself could break out of that wagon." Amidst another bravado-filled chuckle, Faraday cleared his throat. "Just in case though, I encourage you all to stay back."

Trying to hide his own smile, Ben gripped a hidden rope that was hanging from the top of the wagon and gave it a sharp yank. The painted canvas retracted to reveal something large, dark and covered in fur. Heavy breathing was the only sound. The creature inside shifted— turned its face toward the gathered people of Nacogdoches to steal the breath right out of their lungs. Two people fainted and there was an orange-haired kid who went running off. As for the rest of the spectators, most couldn't move at all.

The thing in the cage huffed, then pressed its head against the bars. Two horns protruded—scraping horribly against the thrice-blessed bars. The body was massive—covered in long fur as black as Satan's heart. The front legs, or maybe they were arms, ended in terrible claws, big enough to disembowel a man without much trouble. The face was the worst part of all: pale as bone, with dark gaping holes for eyes and steaming slobber dripping from dark rubbery lips.

"It *is* a demon!" one man squealed.

"Yes … it is precisely as I said." Mr. Faraday's tone had turned grim. He pushed his gold-topped cane toward the thing in the cage. "This unnatural thing was born in the fires of hell, but it doesn't subsist on human souls—oh no. Only meat." The big man winked. "Tell me, Big Ben … are you ready to give the good people of Nacogdoches something they'll never forget?"

The dwarf wiped his brow, then relinquished a nod. Unlike before, his outward nervousness was genuine. He shuffled over to the shaggy cow and walked it within a couple feet of the last wagon. The demon began to pace in its cage. It banged its face into the bars so hard, the wagon lurched—only an inch or two, but enough to cause the audience to back up.

"Hey …" shouted a kid no more than ten. "How come the cow's not scared?"

"Why…?" Faraday laughed to give himself a second more to think. "Why, because of the mesmerism, of course!"

"The what?" said the kid.

"Mesmerism, boy! You know … *hypnosis?* When the monster gets hungry, it puts a kind of magic spell on whatever it wants to eat—mesmerizing its prey so it can't skitter off!"

Looking unconvinced, the kid folded his arms. "Yeah? Then why don't it mem-zerize *him?*"

The crowd turned its collective head to look at the small man with the striped cap.

"Because dwarfs are tougher than belt leather, ain't they?" Ben began leading the shaggy cow back toward the crowd, but stopped about a third of the way there. "Our demon prefers something more tender. Cows are fine, but what it really likes is the taste of loudmouth little boys." He pointed directly at the kid, whose eyes were practically bulging out of his skull.

In that exact same moment, the thing in the cage went berserk. Once, twice, it rammed its pale horned face into the backdoor of the wagon's cage. On the third hit, the door swung open.

The people of Nacogdoches looked ready to run—to scatter like a handful of black powder to the four winds. They wanted to, needed to … but couldn't. And as the enormous hulking thing poured out of the cage that had held it, all they could do was stare. The wagon jumped back when the thing stepped off and swung its hideous pale face toward the crowd and to the diminutive animal wrangler who was far closer.

The two locked eyes, and though the audience was too stricken to notice, Ben offered the thing a nod.

Throwing back its head, the demon belched up a guttural, grinding roar. Tearing the ground with long claws, the thing moved in a strange, shuffling gallop—for his part, the animal wrangler had no chance. On good days, Big Ben's legs were like to complain after a short walk. The crowd could see the panic in the little man's eyes, but they didn't have long to process it. One second, two seconds, then BANG. The demon's boney face shot forward as jaws closed around the waist of the fleeing dwarf.

Benjamin Poole screamed. His stunted arms flailed as the demon carried him back to the only den it knew. The wagon tilted toward its bulk as it entered, then banged back to horizontal. The impact caused the bunched-up canvas to unfurl and hang down again—obscuring what was sure to be a grisly scene within.

The old juggler appeared, already running. Hamlin Blithe rounded the back of the last wagon, located a large lock on the ground and slammed it back on the door. Then he pounded both hands off the wagon's rear and slipped out of sight.

In shock, the men, women and children of Nacogdoches turned to regard the man in charge. The only one whose name was painted on the sides of the four wagons in big circus letters.

To their surprise, and in some cases, disgust … Mr. Finneas Faraday was smiling. Slowly at first, he began to twirl his gold-topped cane. He spun it left, then behind the back, finally tossing it up into the air. The people watched it rise, then fall right back down. In one fluid movement, Faraday caught the cane and pointed that gleaming bull's head at the last wagon.

From the shadows between the wheels, out rolled a very small someone who appeared to be wearing a red vest and a striped bandanna. After rolling for a few feet, the man posed with both hands up in the air and a broad smile on his lips.

"Give it up for Big Ben, ladies and gentlemen!" Faraday's voice rang with pride, but his laughter was swallowed by the eruption of emotional cheers. Hats were thrown, spouses kissed, and children were lifted up into the air.

Mr. Faraday looked at Ben and Ben looked back. No words were needed, but the large man's gratitude was plain.

After the show was through and emotions had cooled, the people of Nacogdoches were invited to ogle the various caged beasts. The performers were all in attendance to say hello and shake hands, but also to make sure no one did anything stupid. There'd been a kid in

St. Louis who'd lost a finger to the Gila monster. As a rule, that kind of thing had to be minimized. The screaming and all the blood could really put a dampner on the day's take.

Hard as it was to admit, the heyday of the traveling menagerie was long past. Now, only one or two such troupes wandered across the country and none possessed the kind of attractions their ilk had once boasted. Animals like lions, tigers, elephants and giraffes were expensive to feed and difficult to replace. And with the success of Bostock and Wombwell in the forties and fifties, plenty of regular everyday folk had been exposed to creatures their grandparents would have called fantastic. The fact was, it was getting harder and harder for smaller outfits like Faraday's to leave a real impression.

When Ben had first suggested the idea of the final act, Faraday had not responded the way he'd hoped. But the little man had developed an incredibly tight bond with the animal he'd named after not one, but three people. Friends he'd lost to the harsh streets of London's west end. Heck, he'd even moved his bedroll from wagon three to the small interior section that abutted the cage in old number four so that every night, he and Rosie Jones Thomas were separated only by a few bars. To see the two playing and training was almost unbelievable. The way she acted, Rosie seemed more of a puppy than a six-hundred-pound grizzly bear.

Mr. Faraday surveyed the crowd with hands on his hips and a not-so-subtle grin. It had been a good show, a good day. Now they were in the winding-down period. After experiencing the spike of emotional duress … the audience seemed content to ogle the smaller caged creatures, as was usually the way.

The Scottish cow called Caboose always got plenty of attention from the younger members of the audience and today was no different. Elsewhere, there was a toucan with a chipped bill, a finger-hungry Gila monster and, of course, Clementine. The massive white and yellow snake was resting comfortably on the shoulders of Li-Mei but blatantly eyeballing the increasingly nervous-looking toucan.

"You see the look in her eye?" The younger of the two Fàn sisters, Susu was trying to remain professional but allowed herself a giggle.

"Tutu is safe in her cage, but in the wild, a python would definitely eat her up."

"Or at least she'd try." The Serpent Lady spoke with a low sultry tone and a crooked eyebrow. "Though toucans are from South America, my darling Clementine here was born in the forests of Burma. Which is just south of China."

A kid with carrot-colored hair stepped forward, looking confused. His lower jaw was agape as if his brain had recently fallen out.

"You speak real good American." He sniffed. "I never heard Chinese people talk so good before."

The Fàn sisters exchanged a wary look. The fact of it was, both girls had been born in the city of San Francisco. Their mother was indeed an immigrant—not from Shanghai, but Guangzhou, China. Until the time of her death, Fàn Hua was owned outright by the man who had, on occasion, caused her to become heavy with child. In Li-Mei's mind, father was an ill-fitting word. Not that it mattered. She couldn't say any of that now. Couldn't tell this snot-nosed kid that she didn't have a Chinese accent because she could barely speak her mother's native language anymore. But then … Mr. Faraday always said that the real story didn't matter. That, to win over the gibbering masses, you had to leave them with something pretty. *Hold on to the fiction*—he'd say—*wear it like armor and they'll never be able to hurt you.*

"Well …" Li-Mei bent closer, which meant, so did Clementine. "My sister and I have worked very hard on how we speak. So as to better communicate with honored patrons such as yourself."

The kid's body was leaning away from the snake, but his feet seemed planted. Suddenly, one of the rusty gears in his brain managed to turn a notch. "Hey, what'd you just call me?"

Li-Mei looked confused, but before she could suggest that the kid poke a finger into the Gila monster cage, he ran off calling. *"Mom! Snake lady called me a pay-trunn!"*

The sisters exchanged some rolling eyes, then settled back into their smiles. There were plenty of people lining up to see the exotic bird or test their manhood by touching the snake.

In front of the last wagon, the dwarf and the juggler were passing pins in a basic routine. Going at about half of Blithe's regular speed, Ben was still self-conscious about juggling in front of a crowd. But doing so like this, as the show was coming to a close, served a dual purpose. Not only was more practice a good thing, it also kept the more curious of the attendees from trying to steal an additional peek at the so-called *Terror of the Yukon.*

Rosie had done a great job, as always. The way she carried Ben, though seemingly violent, was gentle as any mama bear with her cub. The pair must have practiced the act a hundred times before its debut in Little Rock, two years earlier. Six months later, after a dozen performances and countless traumatized women and children, Mr. Faraday had the idea of adding the buffalo skull. Repackaging the finale from a bear act, to something with a bit more *oomph.*

Ben had hated the idea at first, but he owed Finneas Faraday a heck of a lot. Maybe everything. And so, he started whittling away at that skull. Making new eye holes in the forehead for Rosie to see through—removing enough of the bone so it could sit comfortably on her head. Fàn Susu, who had already taken to sewing most of the costumes for the troupe, helped figure out how to attach the leather straps and buckles. After that, for around five minutes per show, Rosie Jones Thomas became a big fierce monster. Even so, Ben always made sure to remove the skull right after she carried him into the wagon. He'd unstrap the thing, tell her what a good girl she was and then slip out the trapdoor that had been specifically made to be too small for anyone but him. And so it had been tonight.

As Ben continued to pass the juggling pins, he smiled. It was always a good feeling when things went off without a hitch. They had to have gotten a healthy take. In the morning he and Mr. Faraday would go into town for supplies for the animals and themselves. Then, they'd hit the trail—move onto another town, another show, another day.

THREE

It had been three hours since the last paying customers had wandered off. After packing it in, the troupe settled back into their respective wagons for some well-earned rest. Faraday clicked his teeth and urged the two Clydesdales to round the wagon train and head off in the other direction. The horses had already been watered, as had the shaggy cow which was once again attached to the end of the last wagon.

He looked up at the dusky sky. It would be dark soon, but they didn't have far to go. His rule was to always park the train no more than a quarter mile from whatever town they'd just performed in. This helped alleviate any potential tensions with the local law, who might take issue with having a real live demon within town limits overnight. But it also kept them close enough to roll back into town the next day for supplies. As rules went, this one had served them well over the years.

With so many hands, camp went up easy. The four wagons created a tight square, with plenty of space for a fire in the center. There was no need to ration their remaining stores, not with all the shops of Nacogdoches opening first thing in the morning. And judging by the grin on Faraday's face when he finished counting the till, a little excess felt more than justified.

As the last of the beans simmered over the fire, Blithe added a few chunks of venison he'd salted earlier in the week. After a healthy stir, he leaned in and inhaled until his eyes rolled back from the aroma. Though they lacked the spices for a full chili, he reckoned no one was likely to complain about this particular supper.

"Another fifteen minutes," he called out.

"Likely to be the longest span of my entire life!" Fàn Susu made a face and pantomimed a bout of crippling stomach pains.

"I'm gonna have to concur with that assessment." Mr. Faraday looked up from tuning his guitar, and threw on a heavy Southern accent, *"Them beans is making quite a racket!"*

Everyone laughed.

Nights like this were what made it all worthwhile. This unlikely band of unfortunates that Faraday had compiled over a life's worth of traveling from here to there. The man had a way of looking through the dirt and circumstance and just seeing the person. To him, their heart was the thing. Sometimes, even if tarnished and bruised or mired in layers of spiderwebs, it could polish up real nice. With enough encouragement and a little purpose, such a heart might even be able to shine again.

Of the lot, Hamlin Blithe was the only one with actual circus experience. Of course that was a long time ago—in another life that had almost destroyed him. Billed as the Amazing AppleJack, Blithe had been more than a juggler, he'd been a trickshooter. Able to blow the legs off a flea at sixty yards—if you believed the posters. Blithe had toured under the AppleJack name for more than a decade with The Ringling Brothers, but the evolution of his most famous act happened rather early on. After all, while shooting what you were juggling made for good entertainment, more pins weren't exactly growing on trees. Apples, though, were another story.

He started with six and tossed them in a standard fountain pattern. For most, this alone was enough to impress. But after some basic showboating of juggling while walking, running and finally, standing on a balance board, it was time for the Amazing AppleJack to give the audience what they came to see. The final trick was to perfectly shoot the apples right out of the air. Every shot was taken when the apple reached its highest point, with his Colt Army Model revolver returning to its holster each time. It'd been said that his hands moved too fast to see. The gunshots came in quick succession—*one ... two ... three ... four ... five ... six.* And then there were none. God, he could still remember the cheers.

He never talked about those days anymore—tried like hell to not even think about them. The end was simply too painful. Back then, Hamlin Blithe could have outshot just about anyone. Thing of it was, though, he was a performer. As such, the barrel of his revolver had never once been aimed at another human being. Not that this fact ended up meaning much in the end. That woman and the little baby pressed to her bosom were still dead. And whether or not the bullet that had torn a hole through both their bodies had accidentally ricocheted off the trapeze didn't change the fact that he was the one who'd pulled the trigger. Not the Amazing AppleJack, but Arthur Hamlin Blithe.

"Ham?" The voice was Ben's. "You okay, mate?"

Blithe inhaled sharply. Then he looked down at his friend. "Oh so now you're asking me?"

Ben shrugged. "Well … I mainly just want to make sure our supper doesn't burn."

"Oh." After stirring the pot, Blithe regarded Ben with a sad smile. "Rosie did great tonight."

Ben nodded. Then he looked over to the last wagon. Between it and him, Mr. Faraday was sitting on a box and strumming an upbeat tune. Clearly enjoying the music, the Fàn sisters were there too—both of 'em dancing in a circle. Just laughing and smiling at the end of a long but fulfilling day. Li-Mei spun over to the large man who was her husband and kissed him on the lips. Mr. Faraday intentionally never advertised that part to the audience because it was none of their damned business.

Seeing them kiss like that made the dwarf turn away fast. On one hand, he was happy for the couple. And yet, deep inside, Ben knew such happiness would never happen. Women had never looked at him that way.

What in the heck is that? he could still hear a man from the audience say.

Ben shook his head. Forced the memory down, underneath the mountain of other miserable shit he carried in his misshapen barrel of a chest. At least he had Rosie.

"So … did it look convincing this time?" Ben asked as if he were afraid to hear the answer.

"Are you kidding me?" Blithe slapped his own thigh. "Real as can be. Shoot, there were two people that fainted after she carried you off! One lady and one fat guy—just keeled over. And that little snot-nosed turd that Faraday had to feed that stuff about mesmerism and such?" Blithe bent down and lowered his voice. "Pissed hisself!"

"No!" Ben punched his friend in the leg.

"Hand to God. Saw it happen with my own eyes." Blithe nodded as he lifted the wooden spoon. Before tasting, he blew on the steaming scoop of beans and meat. "The kid's mama was so mad, she smacked him good!"

"Bloody hell!" Ben couldn't help it. He laughed. "Now that's what I call frontier justice."

Blithe snickered. "Ain't enough of that these days." As he said this, his focus shifted off to the side.

Ben turned to see three silhouettes on the edge of their campsite. After sharing a wary look with the man stirring the pot, he started walking toward where Mr. Faraday was sitting. He didn't rush, didn't force his twisted legs to run—nothing like that. Sudden moves were a bad idea when dealing with wild animals, and he had no way of knowing what sort had wandered so close to their fire.

As he passed, he tapped the big man on the shoulder and whispered something in his ear before continuing on to Rosie's wagon. He wanted to check on her, to tell her everything was okay. But he also wanted to locate that little hand ax he kept around.

Faraday stood up and gently leaned his guitar against the box he'd been sitting on. The man was truly of a rare size.

"Help you gentlemen?" His tone was friendly enough, but the smile he wore during performances was nowhere to be found.

One of the men stepped forward, while the other two held back. The flickering light from the campfire shone on his face. The narrow frame and glasses made the man look like a banker, but there was a massive scar that belied this. The fire seemed to dwell there, on the ragged length of it. The way it stretched from his left ear, all the way down his neck where it slipped behind the man's collar.

"Evening," said the banker, removing his bowler to reveal a startlingly bald head. "My friends caught tonight's show. They tell me it was something to see."

Mr. Faraday took a step toward the men. "Well, that's mighty kind of you to say. Maybe next time you'll be able to see it for yourself."

The banker man smiled tightly, then put his hat back on. "Actually, I was hoping for a bit of a private encore. Not a full production, mind you, just a *taste*."

Faraday glanced over at the Fàn sisters who were starting to look nervous. With a quick gesture of his head, they moved slowly into the second wagon and shut the door. Then, with a hard expression, the big man returned his full attention to the three interlopers.

"Unfortunately, we only do one show a day, friend. We're heading for Beaumont tomorrow. You're welcome to come see us there."

The banker looked down at his pocket watch, than snapped it closed. "That isn't going to work, I'm afraid."

The largest of the other two men chuckled at this. From the look, he had long hair that might have been red. The last one was standing too far back to make out.

"From what I've heard, you have some trinkets that a man I work with would find most interesting. Clearly, the quality of one such item was not exaggerated." He nodded at wagon number two. "Truly, she is a vision."

"That's my wife you're talking about." Faraday's eyes narrowed. His muscles tightened. "Now ... I'm only going to say this once. There's nothing for you here."

"Oh, I see." The banker man looked suddenly vexed, but gathered himself quickly. "My name is Mr. Whimble. *Ethan*, if you prefer. And my associates are hoping to strike a deal."

"No deals here. Not for the likes of you all." Blithe blurted this out. There was fear in his voice, which he despised as soon as he heard it.

"It's okay, Arthur." Faraday held out a reassuring hand. "Why don't you bring some bowls of that fine chili to the rest of the family. I'll handle things out here."

Mr. Faraday had only used the name Arthur twice before and right now it felt like a plea. *Do as I say, and don't say another word* might as well have been Hamlin Blithe's true first name. With a shaky hand, he spooned out three bowls worth of what he'd been cooking and headed for the wagons. In his haste, he forgot to dish out any for himself, though in truth, he was no longer hungry.

Once the interlopers were alone with the leader of the troupe, Ethan Whimble removed his glasses and cleaned them with a handkerchief.

"I truly hope that isn't so, Mr. Faraday. For all of your sakes. I'm told you had a good day today. A *very* good day. It would be a shame for it to end ... badly."

"What do you want?"

"As I said, Mr. Faraday. A taste. My offer is this ... hand over the day's take and that cane with the gold top. Do this quickly and quietly and you have my word that we will leave without incident. No one will be harmed. Not even that intoxicating wife of yours."

The man standing on the other side of the fire was no longer the jovial, ever-grinning ringmaster. Without his ringmaster jacket, Finneas Faraday looked like a savage. Like a half bear, half man berserker out of some viking story. He couldn't remember picking up his cane, but he looked down at it now. The light of the fire was dancing on the golden bull's head, but also in the man's eyes.

"I have a counteroffer," came the low, grim voice of Mr. Faraday.

Finished cleaning his spectacles, Whimble placed them back on his face just in time to see movement. The old carnival barker barreled through the slender man like a steam engine shooting through open air. Whimble was knocked senseless. He didn't understand what was happening as his body began to move through the air.

With a roar, Faraday tossed the bankish son of a bitch over at the next closest man. Pistol already drawn, the large desperado with the long red hair didn't have a chance to fire before the limp body of Ethan Whimble smashed the weapon out of his hand—causing him to fall backwards and directly into the fire.

He began to scream. To tear at and rid himself of his already flaming shirt. But Faraday was looking at the third man. The one who never came close enough to see. He was already at thirty paces and running like he was the one on fire. With a furious roar, Faraday lifted his gold-topped cane and hurled it at the fleeing man. The cane spun end over end, cutting through the air like the blade of a circular saw.

Miraculously the unlikely projectile found its mark. With an audible *ping*, the man went down, careening ass over teakettle into the dirt. Maybe dead—Faraday no longer cared.

He turned to the red-haired man, who was now shirtless and breathing hard. Sections of his skin were black and still smoldering. The burning man picked up Ethan Whimble—slapped him back to consciousness. Through clenched teeth, he said:

"I can take him. Get out of here. See if Campbell is still alive, then you find that *fooken* gold cane and bring it to Dekker. You hear me? Tell him everything!"

"But Angus, I ..."

"Go!" The red-haired man shoved Whimble. After a stumble that cost him his glasses, the small bankish man began to run like he'd never run before. Faraday moved to follow, but the large Scottsman stepped in his way.

The expression on his face was one of madness. His blue eyes looked yellow in the light of the fire and he was smiling. Unlike Faraday, the man was fit—muscular without any padding around the midsection. And he had an enormous pinkish-brown scar over most of his flesh. It looked like a naked tree with leafless branches that extended down from his neck, across his chest and down the left arm.

"That's some scar," said Faraday, a little less hot than a minute ago. "You've been struck by lightning, haven't you, son?"

"I ain't yer son, Grandpa. But yeah, the bolt hit me right in the head." He snickered at the thought. Then he bent down and picked up his revolver. "Though I prefer the term *touched by God.*"

Faraday frowned. He looked at his wagons—at the painted words on the canvas, and thought of the people inside. He'd tried so hard to give each one of them a second chance at life. Li-Mei was his wife, but they were all family. He'd do anything to keep them going—keep them safe. Anything.

"I know you. I've seen your posters around. You're Angus Baines. The Scotsman who runs with Ted Campbell—and is always going on about being *struck by lightning.*" Faraday turned to where the man he'd hit with his cane still lay. Ethan Whimble was much farther out already, and he was carrying a gold-topped cane in his hand. "I assume that's Campbell over there. Looks like your little friend couldn't get him up. For what it's worth, I'm sorry, son. I truly didn't mean to kill anyone. As it happens, I put those days behind me a very long time ago."

Faraday looked at his scarred hands. As they trembled in the firelight, his fingers clenched—becoming fists. The only weapons he needed.

"But you all threatened my wife. You understand? My *wife*. Actions like that ... come with consequences."

The reactions of both men occurred in perfect unison. It was like horses taking off in a race at the sound of the starter pistol. Only this shot was aimed straight for the heart of Finneas Faraday. The big man was already charging forward, too full of piss and rage to feel the impact. And so, for the next few seconds, nothing changed. He swung hard, feeling the Scotsman's jaw crack against his knuckles.

Calling on his pugilist training, Baines tried to cover up, but there was nothing for it. The hands that were coming his way were things of iron. Each hit was a hammer blow and his entire body was the railroad spike. The pain from his fractured jaw was blinding. In desperation, Baines' finger pulled again and again, but the only thing he managed to hit was sky. Ted Campbell had the right idea—clearly running was the only sane thing to do. Then again, Ted Campbell was likely dead.

They'd heard the master of the traveling menagerie was big, but never in their wildest dreams did they expect anything like this. The man was a beast, or at least had once been. There was an adage about sleeping dogs and what you are supposed to do when you find one ... but at the moment, he couldn't bring it to mind.

Ears ringing, all Angus Baines could manage was to put all his remaining strength and will into a final desperate blow. The man's knee shot up, right into the balls of the fully berserk man who was absolutely not going to stop until one of them was dead.

Faraday relented at last. His eyes were all black and bloodshot and there were thick cords sticking out of his neck. With a grunt, he dropped to one knee, riding the waves of nauseating pain exploding from between his legs. It was then that he first saw what he had done to

Angus Baines. The man was so bloodied, so swollen and misshapen, he barely looked like the same person.

He'd done that. His rage had. That beastly fury he'd worked so hard to keep in check for so many years. How far had he gone to escape it? How many seas and countries had he crossed, only for it to rear its ugly head again here? Just outside the oldest town in Texas.

Baines raised his hand as if it were the heaviest thing in the entire world. He was still gripping the pistol. And as he aimed it, Finneas Faraday did not blink. He simply turned to regard his wagons, sparing a smile for what he saw.

The man with the lightning scars leveled his barrel to Faraday's forehead and pulled the trigger. Funny thing was, the only thing that took a bullet was the dirt, about a foot to the left of where he was standing. Confounded at first, it took Angus Baines a second to realize two things—firstly, he was completely out of ammunition. And the other thing …

BANG!

Another puff of dirt exploded—this one right between his legs. He was being shot at!

Baines turned to see the Chinese lady. She was leaning out between the wagons but instead of a snake, she was holding a Winchester Yellowboy. Comprehending the situation in full, the Scotsman put a hand to his busted jaw and ran for all he was worth.

Relief washed over the big man then, but it was a cold sensation. In fact, despite his proximity to the campfire, Faraday was freezing. Confused, he looked down at the patch of shirt about his heart and regarded the dark patch that was spreading there. Had he known? Had he thought that so long as he didn't look down, Baines' one decent shot wouldn't matter? He shook his head, snickered, coughed.

Then he heard them coming.

FOUR

Finneas Faraday looked up and his head felt like it was underwater. People were coming … running from the wagon. Blithe, Big Ben and Susu—but they were all behind *her*. His emerald rose of the Orient. The girl who'd become the most important woman in his whole damn life. When he'd agreed to take the sisters away from their bastard father in San Francisco all those years ago, he'd never guessed how things would turn out. Thinking on this, he smiled. It really was a funny old world.

"Finneas!" cried Li-Mei—tears streaming as she ran.

"No," he said, not loud enough for anyone to hear. "No, you have to …"

Faraday collapsed onto his side and didn't move. A second later, his wife reached him. She slid in the dirt, cradling his head in her lap. Hugging it and leaving kisses in his hair.

"*Finneas*! Come on, darling. You have to get up—for me, okay? We'll get you to bed. You'll be right as rain in the morning. You just need some rest. That's all." She sniffed. Slapping the tears off one of her cheeks. Sniffed again. "Did you still want to go to Beaumont tomorrow? Because I was thinking it might be nice to head back North—up to Oklahoma. If you'd like, we could—"

The presence of the enormous hand on her cheek made Li-Mei stop.

"That sounds fine, darling. Just fine." Faraday smiled, but only for a second or two. "Those men will be back with worse ones. One of 'em said the name Dekker."

Blithe's eyes lit up and not in the good way. "As in *Pete* Dekker? As in the goddamned *Silverfish?*"

Faraday nodded. "Back in Fort Worth, they were talking how he was still in Texas. That he's been calling all the wayward members of his gang down here for some kind of gathering. Don't know what, but … I doubt it's anything good." He was looking into the lovely eyes that had so captured his heart. "They'll be coming, and I don't want to think about what they'll do if they find you. Any of you." He turned to regard the motley band who he'd collected over the years.

The only family he had left—maybe ever had. "You've got to leave me here and go."

"What?" Li-Mei practically shrieked. "Are you *shot,* or completely insane?"

"Why … I'm shot, darling." Faraday smiled. "And I do believe it is of the mortal variety. And while I appreciate that you love me enough not to, you've got to do as I say. I'm too big. Too damned heavy. I can't have you all wasting precious time hauling my carcass back in the wagon. If Pete Dekker really is coming, you need to be as far away as possible. Please …" Tears welled in the man's eyes, then he turned to Arthur Hamlin Blithe, who had removed his hat and was sort of wringing it out.

"Arthur, you're driving from now on."

He nodded. "Yes, sir."

Faraday nodded back then shifted his eyes. "Ben?"

"Yeah?"

"I need you to do something you're not gonna like."

"Anything."

"Caboose." Faraday winced from the pain. "Cut her free."

Hearing this was like a knife in the heart, but Ben understood. With tears welling in both eyes, he too managed a nod.

"I know it's hard, but speed is your salvation. You understand? These men are the worst of the bad, and believe me, they're coming." It was getting hard to talk. Hard to stay awake. "Susu, love …"

The youngest of the troupe was unable to speak due to all the tears.

"I need you to start tossing whatever you can out the side. And that goes for all of ya, tables, chairs, anything heavy. The lighter the load, the quicker the road."

Summoning the last of his energy, Faraday swept another glance over those standing above, ending on his beautiful wife. The sight made him smile. "Oh, my dear ones … thank you for coming on this journey with me. For helping build this show, this life. Just … *thank you.*"

These were the last words of Finneas Faraday, purveyor of want and wonder. As the man's large head slumped to one side, Li-Mei Faraday screamed, collapsing bonelessly on top of her husband.

The traveling menagerie rumbled north—as fast as two Clydesdales had ever pulled four wagons with as many people, a couple of reptiles, a toucan and an enormous grizzly bear.

Though it had almost killed him to do so, Benjamin had carried out the final request of his friend. The man who had taken pity on him so many years before back on Mayfair Street. His family, as it was, had all succumbed to the condition—to the pox of living the wretched life they were born into. Bill Jones, Thomas Hewitt and of course, dear Rosie. They were all gone by the time little Ben Poole had tried and failed to pick the pocket of the largest man he'd ever seen.

And now that one had left him, too.

RRRRRRFF …

The sound was the first the bear had made in a while. She lifted her head, then swung it round to the back of the wagon, where Caboose usually was. The sight twisted the stiletto already in Ben's stomach.

"She'll be all right." Ben lied though mainly to himself. "There's plenty of grass in Texas. Or maybe a kind rancher will come along and bring her home to breed and make lots of shaggy cow babies."

This seemed to agitate the bear. Suddenly, she began to huff and grunt—her face still pointed at the back of the wagon. That's when something terrible occurred to Ben. He stared at the canvas flapping back there, but he had no more ability to see through it than did Rosie Jones Thomas. He grabbed one of the bars and hauled himself up. His back was on fire again.

The interior portion of wagon number four was small—just enough for a bedroll and a small table that Faraday had built into the wall for him.

Ben hated moving between the wagons when they were rolling along at a casual pace, let alone this. But he had to look. Had to know. The door swung open and banged. The opening felt like it was pulling the little man in, or *out* as it were. For a second, the Englishman almost lost his nerve but, grabbing the jamb, he steadied himself—stepped out into the ear-splitting night.

On either side of the door, there was a small place to stand with a railing which, in Ben's case, was at eye level. He moved one hand from the door jamb to the railing, while still clinging to his ax with the other. Then he took a deep breath. Whatever he saw ... whatever happened in the coming minutes, he regretted nothing. Meeting Mr. Faraday, coming to America, purchasing a bear cub from that trapper in Montana ... these were the best things in his life. The moments that all the suffering and gibes and humiliation had paid for. Now, it was simply time to pay a little back.

Gripping the railing as tight as he could, Ben peered around the side of the last wagon. What he saw made his eyes go wide.

Heart racing, he looked at the ground speeding past below—at the rusty old pin that held the wagons together. That was the only step between the cars of what always felt like a train when it was moving. He could do it. His legs would have to be strong enough. There was simply no other choice.

Ben moved back through the door and called to the animal in the cage. "I'll be right back, luv. Don't worry. Everything is gonna be all right."

Then he shot forward like a lead plumb—through that doorway and out to the thunderous night. He jumped and for the briefest of moments, flew. The landing wasn't pretty but could have been a lot worse. On the back of wagon three, Ben grabbed the railing and hauled himself up. His whole body hurt. From this vantage, he could see them better. There were riders coming. About a quarter mile back—all galloping hard in a cloud of moonlit dust and fury.

Wasting none of the time they had left, Ben turned the doorknob and burst into wagon three.

"*Ham!*" he shouted, before remembering who was driving. The cabin he'd originally shared with Blithe was empty but for the man's belongings, some simple furniture and what remained of their feed. A little corn and some oats were all they had left, considering their morning shopping trip in Nacogdoches had been canceled. As his eyes darted about, Ben remembered what Faraday had said at the end.

"The lighter the load, the quicker the road."

He grabbed a stool, a lantern and an empty cage that had been the home of a rattlesnake before it had passed the previous fall. There were things that could be thrown out the side too, but he had to keep going. To warn the rest of the family.

The lantern was the first thing he tossed between wagons three and two—then the stool. The snake cage was a bit heavier since it was made of glass. That took both hands and a little effort. As he watched it hit and tumble—smashing on the passing ground, he hoped it would bring misfortune to their pursuers. Not that such luck had historically fallen in his lap. Too small, abandoned by a mother he never knew, homeless, starving in the rain, lost … but found. The dwarf shook his head. Forced himself to focus on that last part. Mr. Faraday *had* found him, saved him. And for his sake, Ben Poole had to keep going.

After another running start, he cleared the next coupling and limped into wagon number two. The Fàn sisters turned with shock in their eyes.

"*Ben?*" exclaimed Fàn Susu—clearly in the midst of consoling her older sister. "What are you..?"

"*We've got to go faster!*" Ben was out of breath. "The bastards Finneas warned us about … they're coming."

Li-Mei shot to her feet, Fàn Susu did not. Both began to look around the wagon's interior. The younger sister was sitting on a small bed with hinges that could be made to lie flat against the wall. This was her wagon, but she shared it with the smaller animals. The toucan and Gila monster and five empty cages rested on freestanding shelves that Mr. Faraday had built special. Ben's eyes rested on the largest of the empty enclosures, remembering the white-tailed jackrabbit it had once held. Wasn't long ago that all of them had held animals for the show.

The irony was, if they'd been robbed back in those days, the pot would have been a hell of a lot bigger. Until tonight, the show and its performers had managed to evade the ugliest inclinations of humanity. But the good years were long past, and traveling menageries were all but extinct. Hard as it was to admit, shows like Faraday's were relics. They were always meant to bring smiles and laughter—want and wonder, everywhere they deigned to stop. But in a world where things like ugliness and ignorance were not only sewn but cultivated, the currency of joy was getting pretty damn hard to spend.

Maybe it was always going to end this way. Badly.

Ben grabbed the rabbit cage with both hands and pulled. "I've got to warn Ham. You stay here—start tossing anything you can out the side. These cages, and ..." He tested the shelving unit itself with a gentle kick. It barely budged, but it was only connected to the wall by two supports. He slipped out his ax from where it hung on his belt.

"Here." He handed the small chopping tool over to Li-Mei. "Once the empties are gone, we've got to get rid of the shelves."

"What?" Susu was standing now. "But we need them!"

"Not more than we need to survive, luv." Ben looked miserable. "Put Tutu and Albert's cages on the floor for now—they'll be okay. And I'll be right back to help. All right?"

Li-Mei Faraday wiped her cheek. "Go. Tell Hamlin what's going on, just ... be careful."

Ben smiled, nearly overcome with an unexpected swell of emotion. "I will."

With that, he dragged the rabbit cage through the door. It took some effort to lift it over the railing before dumping it, but doing it felt good. Weirdly so. He looked back and the riders were closer than before. He could count five of them, but it was hard to discern much else.

He turned to the gap between the wagons and swallowed hard. God, he really hated this.

Landing on the back of the front wagon, Ben's body was positively screaming at him to stop. But he couldn't stop. He was on a mission—doing maybe the most important thing he'd ever tried. Clenching his teeth, he grabbed the railing and hauled himself up for the third time. There was no reason to go inside the first wagon. That belonged to the Faradays and Ben wasn't about to start tossing the belongings of his fallen friend. But the front wagon had a small walkway along the side, which led to the driver's seat. Being as careful as he could, Ben hobbled and limped along until he had to turn sideways to proceed. Then, after a moment's consideration of the speeding ground only feet away, proceed, he did.

Moving like that wasn't easy—shimmying on legs that were so full of knots they could barely hold him up was not something he hoped to repeat.

"*Ham!*" he shouted up at the driver, who turned with genuine disbelief on his face.

"*Ben?! What in the hell are you doing?*"

"Warning you!" The dwarf pointed behind. "Look, Finneas was right. It's those bastards from Nacogdoches. *They're riding right up our arse!*"

"What?!" Blithe turned to look behind. The riders were hard to see from where he was sitting—concealed by a bad angle and the ample dark. "Shit!" exclaimed the man with a jerk that knocked over a half-empty bottle of rye sitting beside him. "They're right on top of us! Oh my God, oh my God … *what the hell are we gonna do?*"

"The only thing we can do, mate." Ben picked up the bottle, took a swig, then tossed it over the side. "Lighten the load and pray for a miracle. Me and the girls are taking care of the first part; you just keep those horses bloody going. All right?"

The eyes of Hamlin Blithe were just about popping out of his head, but no response passed his lips.

"*Arthur!*" It was the first time Ben Poole had ever used his friend's first name. "Did Faraday own a gun?"

Blithe turned, but still had nothing to say.

"A pistol, a rifle, even a rusty old pea-shooter—anything stashed away somewhere we can use?!"

"I … uh …" Blithe licked his lips, tried to focus. "A single-action Colt revolver. I think he kept it in his wagon. Maybe Li-Mei knows where."

"Be that as it may, she's a whole wagon back and you're right here. Think, Ham. You knew Mr. Faraday longer than any of us. If he held onto that revolver, where would he keep it? *Think*, mate!"

Blithe did think. His mind flitted back and forth over the years—to better times and worse ones. And that was what snapped him back into place. There *had* been worse times than this—one in particular. And all that'd been before he finally found this current life. The latest in a long line, but the first that actually felt like home.

"Finneas had a chest. A small wooden one for some of his old things. Stuff from … before he did his time in Missouri State."

"He *what?*" Ben looked shocked. "Faraday went to … prison?"

"For almost four years." Blithe nodded but kept his eyes on the middle distance. "There's a lot that man didn't want none of you to know. Li-Mei, most of all. Though … we all saw a sliver of that tonight." He hung his head. "Goddamn it, Finneas."

"Hey, what he did, he did for us. So let's make sure it wasn't for nothing. Right?"

Blithe turned to regard his friend and relinquished a sad nod.

"Right then, I'll leave you to it. Just …" Ben turned to look behind them again, hoping to find that the riders had miraculously vanished. They hadn't. "Just promise me … whatever happens, you'll keep driving those horses. Get us to the next town you see."

"Yeah? And then what?"

Ben smiled. "Then … we move onto the next thing. Whatever that may be."

With that, the two men shared a long moment of consideration. Though neither wanted to say as much, it felt a lot like goodbye.

By the time Ben leapt back onto the last and final wagon, he could barely move. His body was so banged up from the tribulations required for someone of his size to get from car to car. Also, he'd done as much as he could to help the ladies get that shelving unit apart and out the door. Over all, they had unloaded just about everything that wasn't either a permanent fixture or was still breathing.

Ben wanted badly to go through that door and see Rosie again, but there was something he had to do first. Slowly, he leaned over the side of the railing, but what he saw made his pounding heart sick. The bastards were still there. A bit farther back, but not by much. The Clydesdales wouldn't be able to keep up their current pace for long, Ben knew. And when they started to get tired, well … the show would be over. With this revelation, Ben could feel the beginnings of true despair creep into his chest.

"There's nothing else!" he bellowed up at the sky. *"What more do you want?"* He kicked one of the metal rails. *"These twisted legs weren't enough? Aye?! This blasted body—this ... all of it? You hate me so much you're gonna end it like this? Take them all for the bargain? Why? Who was I before that you would hate me this much?!"*

With tears in his eyes, Ben hauled off and struck the side of wagon number four with his ax. The blade bit into the wood and stuck there. Fàn Susu had handed it back to him before they started tossing pieces of the shelving. Now he just looked at it. It was just a small hand ax but, for Ben, it had always felt like a measure of safety. A kind of weapon. But that's not what it was at all. An ax was merely a tool.

Slowly, he looked down—considered the pin that hitched the two wagons together.

"Is that what you want?" asked the little man of the great unknown.

The fact was, Benjamin Poole didn't speak to God much anymore. Not unless he was real mad and looking for someone to blame. Still, part of him couldn't help but feel that the world would be better if there was no one upstairs pulling the strings. Kinder, too.

He wrapped his stunted fingers around the ax handle and pulled it free. Then, getting closer to the open places, where the ground felt like a river of death rushing just below, he positioned himself above the rusty old pin.

"Well ... if you were ever gonna do me a favor ... now's the bloody time."

He jammed the ax blade under the lip of the pin and pulled ... pulled ... pulled until it budged at last. Catching his breath, Ben spared a glance up to see the younger of the Fàn sisters standing in the back doorway of wagon number three. Judging by the horror in her eyes and the way her slender hands were covering her mouth, Susu held no confusion about what she was seeing.

"Ben! Don't!"

But Ben didn't respond. He simply smiled, winked and pried that rusty old pin the rest of the way out. As the wagons began to separate, he backed up—grabbed hold of the railing. When he was steady, he looked back at the girl. She was about to throw something.

"Catch!" She shouted before tossing Faraday's pistol. It had been right where Blithe had thought it'd be. In a small wooden chest under a folded military uniform, dark Union blue and covered in dust. But the revolver he had given to the younger girl was now soaring through the air. He reached out and caught it against his chest.

"Ow," he didn't mean to say.

He looked at the shrinking vision of Fàn Susu, meaning to protest. But when the two locked eyes, Ben did no such thing. Because sometimes love requires a sacrifice. It's not a thinking thing, it's just what a family does. And right then, as he watched the girl blow over a final kiss, all he was able to feel was fortunate.

FIVE

The door slammed on wagon number four, causing Rosie Jones Thomas to lift her head. She was lying down in a ball against the bars, and quickly began to make nervous huffing sounds.

"It's okay, luv." Ben hobbled across the floor and dropped beside the enormous bear. Her nearly black fur was sticking out through the bars. It felt good in his hands. Like being safe. Though the little man knew this was not so.

He could feel their speed decreasing and tried not to think about what was coming. It was possible that the men from Nacogdoches would speed stop to investigate. Then again, they might just as well speed right past and choose to stay on the main wagon. And if Ben's gambit paid off, Blithe would have enough speed to get away—hopefully as far as Henderson. In that case, their pursuers would be looking for someone to take their frustrations out upon and would likely double back to the cast-off wagon anyhow.

Ben looked at the single-action Colt in his hand and sighed.

"What if it's the third scenario?" he asked the bear. "What if the load still isn't light enough?"

Wanting to do just about anything else, Ben reached up and grabbed the nearest bar and hauled himself up. Rosie whined, sticking her snout out and nuzzling the back of Ben's head. The saliva made his hair stick up funny, but he smoothed it back down.

"Sorry, luv. Has to be done."

Every joint and muscle screamed as he forced them back to work. Tears were in his eyes when Ben reached the door and stepped out onto the small landing. The wagon had almost stopped as he leaned out again over the railing.

The five riders were barely a hundred yards back and did appear to be about to pass him by. He leveled the revolver at the one who was going to be closest in less than a minute. Then he held his breath and waited.

BLAM!

BLAM!

BLAM!

The three shots echoed out—rolling over the shadow steeped plains of east Texas. And while the rounds hit nothing but open air, they had the desired effect. All at once, the bastard riders began turning in wide circles—some firing back until all of them were.

Instead of slipping back inside, Ben made a quick decision and leapt onto the ground. Then he ducked his head and disappeared between the two stationary wagon wheels. Not inside the wagon, but under it, as a hail of hot lead flew his way.

After what felt like years, the bullets stopped. Fortunately, at the distance they'd been fired, even the ones that had hit the wagon hadn't done any real damage. Ben had slipped through the trap door he used for the big finale and was inside with Rosie. It felt safe, but this was a lie. The canvas walls would be only too easy to move aside—then him and Rosie would be like sitting ducks. Fortunately, he never went anywhere without his keys.

As the riders approached the wagon, they did so with weapons drawn.

"You alive over there?" ,alled a man through clenched teeth. The cloth wrapping that cradled his jaw made it look like he was suffering from a toothache."Which one of you is it?" He hissed. "That old pin-tossing drunk? Or one of those nice China ladies?"

When no response came, another of the riders cantered over to the red-haired loudmouth. This one wore a long charcoal frock coat with a black shirt and red vest—he was tall. As long from head to toe as Faraday had been, though somewhat less vast. On his head was no hat, only a shock of thick hair—fully silver despite the fact that he couldn't be too far past forty.

Upon reaching the side of Angus Baines, the silver-haired man paused—locking eyes before punching the man off his horse.

"Christ, Pete." Baines picked himself up. "Remember my jaw! Might be broken!"

"I remember," said Pete Dekker, in a tone as cold and slick as fish scales. "Who talks first?"

"You do, Pete. Always you. I won't forget again."

Dekker glared down at the man for a few seconds more. "It's important that you don't."

Ethan Whimble straightened his glasses and made a point to not look at the large Scotsman as his horse trotted past.

"Mr. Dekker," he said in a private tone. "There was another member of the troupe. A dwarf. He had a rather thrilling act involving a bear that came out of that wagon."

A strange liquid giggle wormed out of one of the other men. This one was smaller—pale, with heavy eyelids and bulgy light blue eyes. "Weren't no bear," said the man called Esau. "That were a demon. I saw it myself. A demon straight from the fires of perdition. Had horns and everything. Just look at the painting!"

Whimble gently cleared his throat. "It was a bear … with a mask or something. But, its bond with the dwarf was impressive. It stands to reason that he was in that wagon when it decoupled. Also, as I turned I thought I saw something moving under the wagon."

"I saw it. He's wrong. It was a demon." Esau was grinning, giggling. "It was the *terror of the Yuuu-kon*."

"*Shut it up*," growled Dekker. The man's voice was like two stones being rubbed together. "A dwarf and a bear." He snickered, stroking his silver mustache. "Well I think we can handle that before catching up to the rest. What do you say, John?"

All heads turned to the last man of the five. The one with the purple birthmark connecting his eye to his chin. Suffice it to say, the one the posters called Weeping John Wraith was not the man he used to be. Something had happened on the trail. Something bad enough to wipe out his entire gang, though he never said what. In fact, since arriving half-dead in Dallas last month, no one had heard the man utter as much as a single word.

"That's what I thought," said Dekker. "Old John thinks we're wasting precious time with all this jawing. Can't honestly say I disagree." He dismounted. Began approaching the wagon with his Colt Walker ready at the hip. The rest followed suit.

"Is that you, little man?" called Dekker, his eyes devouring the monstrous painting on the side of the wagon. One of the corners had come free and was flapping in the breeze. He tried to see inside, but it was too dark. "Why don't you come out now and we'll talk." He gestured at Baines and Esau to circle round and they complied without a word.

"Just toss out your weapon, and we won't punch any holes in that pretty painting you got. You know, with that in the way, there's no way of telling what we're gonna hit in there."

The Dekker gang was a scant twenty paces from the wagon when he motioned for them to hold their ground.

"Unless, of course, you're dead already. In which case I can assure you of this. Once we catch up and have some fun with your friends, we will come right back here and make easy work of whatever's in that cage. Always wanted to try bear. I hear it's ... naturally spicy."

When no response came this time, Dekker relaxed his arm. Then he signaled to the Scotsman, who was by this time, coming around the other side. Understanding what he was meant to do, Baines approached the back door with the gun that had killed Finneas Faraday held out in front. Then, about ten paces away, he stopped and scratched his head.

"What is it now?" snapped Dekker, no longer seeing the need for subtlety.

"It's uhh ... the cage door, Pete. It's ..."

Already open were the words Baines never got to say.

With an ear-splitting roar, the six-hundred-pound grizzly bear called Rosie Jones Thomas burst out the back of the cage. Baines stumbled, fell. When his ass hit the ground, a lightning bolt of pain shot into his cracked jaw. To him, the bear was as big as the sky. Its rubbery lips seemed to reach for him as the animal's breath stung his eyes. There were also teeth and claws, and though he knew one or the other was going to end him any second, the only impact that came was a headbutt. The bear rolled the large Scotsman, batting him around like a ball.

"What are ye waiting for?" he cried between hits. *"Shoot the fooken thing!"*

"No!" The cry came with gunfire.

BLAM!

The dwarf appeared from under the wagon. He was running, firing at the man with the silver hair, who was the closest.

BLAM!

The last one was the only shot that hit. As it did, Pete Dekker, the man wanted for robbery, horse theft and the murder of eleven men and five women including his own mama, reeled back as if he'd been kicked by a mule.

"Son of a ..." His hand went right to his ribs. "He's empty! Grab him, but don't shoot." Dekker's face was contorted with pain. "This little bastard is gonna pay ... long and slow."

Ben's eyes went wide as the bankish man and the creep he'd found skulking behind his wagon earlier lunged for him. In desperation, he hurled Faraday's revolver, smashing Ethan Whimble in the forehead.

"Ah!" Blinded by pain, Whimble reflexively fired his weapon.

Having tired of her new toy, the bear abandoned the unconscious Scotsman and turned to see someone she didn't know attacking her friend. The man who had been both mother and friend—her constant companion since her earliest memories.

That was when Rosie Jones Thomas stood up and roared, for the first time in her life, in anger. After the bankish man had actually soiled himself, she took off on a run.

Still holding his reddening side, Dekker was the first to fire at the charging beast, but Esau, Whimble and even Wraith followed a half second later. All of their weapons aimed as a very large, completely furious moving target. The small caliber bullets and balls bit into the bear's hide, but they were akin to bee stings.

"Mr. Dekker?" Whimble yelped as he squeezed off two more shots.

The Silverfish didn't answer. He had stopped firing, but was aiming still. Waiting for just the right moment.

"Uhh, Mr. Dekker?"

BLAM!

The grizzly reeled back and fell hard. Then began slapping its face—hammering the ground with its paws.

"Rosie?!" came the desperate cry of the little man, who Esau was having trouble holding onto.

As the bear turned to face him, Ben could see blood. It was starting to pour out of a hole just above the left eye. Again and again, the animal slapped itself, finally dropping to the ground, adding grit to the sticky wet parts of its fur. It looked around desperately. Wounded, scared.

"I'm right here, luv! *Right here!*"

Grinning wide as ever, Esau pulled Ben back—his half-fingers digging into the little man's arm like blunt stilettos. The retaliating head butt came quite unexpectedly and brought things like shock, pain and flashing ghost lights. Staggering backward, the pale bulgy-eyed man let go of Ben's arm to cup his own mouth.

"You! You!" was all he could articulate before spitting out both front teeth.

With no thought for being fired upon, Ben hauled off and ran to his friend. His legs burned—threatening to buckle more than once and at the end, he did fall. But he pulled himself through the red mud and up to cradle the animal's enormous head. The gore was worse up close. His eyes followed the red trickle up to the hole and he knew that the bullet was in her brain.

"Oh, luv." Ben was sobbing by that point. "What did they do? What did they do?"

The bear's eyes rolled and darted, trying to focus. Trying to remember. Then, they caught those of her Ben and for a fleeting breath of a moment, everything was fine.

Then she was out. Her head hit the ground in a wet squelch. And though Ben did scream, he could see the gentle rise and fall of her side.

"Look what you did!"

Ben turned with a sneer of unrestrained hate for the man called Esau. His mouth and chin were covered in blood and his front teeth were missing. He still had his pistol but was gripping it by the barrel. He raised it and brought it down on Ben's rather prominent forehead.

And then there was only blackness.

Slowly, eventually, Benjamin Poole drifted back to consciousness. He tried to move his arms and legs, but they refused.

"Hold her down," came a giggly, high-pitched voice. "I know this fits. I saw it before."

Ben's eyes shot open. He turned, found that his limbs had been tied to four stakes that were currently in the ground. He was splayed. As helpless as a newborn babe.

"Good, he's awake," came a gravelly voice. "Hold on, Esau. I want him to watch."

A long shadow slid over Ben's face as he looked up to the smug face of Pete Dekker.

"You fucking cunt! You shit-eating cock!"

Dekker's frock coat and vest were off, and the side of his shirt was soaked. "Kiss your mama with that mouth?"

"He said he never met his mama." Esau grunted as if lifting something heavy. "Course I s'pose he coulda been *lying*. Just like they all lied about this stupid bear." The man sounded genuinely hurt. "I was promised a demon and, by God, I's gonna get one."

"You want a bloody monster?" Ben hissed through clenched teeth. "I'm looking at one right here." He stared up at the man with the silver hair. "Have a look, boys and girls, it's a walking, talking *silverfish*."

Dekker's smile faded at this and he blinked real slow, only once. After dropping to his haunches, he spoke softly into the ear of his helpless victim.

"Life has dealt you a shit hand, my friend. But even at the end, you're still full of piss and vinegar. I like that. Can respect a man who'll spit in the fire that's burning him alive. What I don't like is being shot. So here's what's gonna happen. I'm gonna leave you in the care of my compatriot over there." Dekker shrugged. "Esau's a few critters short of a stable, but nothing if not creative. Has a thing for working with a hammer and nails. Those long ones they use for roof shingles. To be honest, sometimes things get a mite too gruesome, even for a monster like me." He chuckled. "Anyway—don't you worry. I've told old Esau to have his fun, but to make sure you survive the night." Dekker stood and started to turn. "Best of luck tomorrow. If you'll recall, the sun's been a bastard all week."

As he stood, Dekker winced and put a hand back on his wound. "John, Ethan, you're with me. Baines, you can stick around and assist the man at work."

"But, Pete," said a very beaten, very dirty Angus Baines. "What about the rest of the wagons?"

"Hell with 'em," said Dekker, limping to where they'd left the horses. "It's late. And that is entirely too much effort for a box full of small potatoes."

"But, Pete ... don't we *have to* go? You know, on principle?"

BANG!

Dekker had fired without even looking. And while smoke still leaked from the barrel of that enormous Colt Walker, the Scotsman staggered back a step. Where his right eye had been, a ragged hole now gapped. Baines looked perplexed, but it wasn't more than a second or two before he hit the dirt like a bag full of hammers.

"*On principle*," was all Dekker said.

Ben couldn't believe his eyes. And despite all the horrors still to come, he felt a surge of satisfaction to see Mr. Faraday's killer fall to the ground. He watched Dekker and his men get on their horses and ride south—in the direction of Nacogdoches. Then he turned to Rosie.

Esau was giggling almost uncontrollably. He must have found the buffalo skull when Ben was out, because Rosie was dressed for a performance.

"You know what?" The man repositioned the demon face as if straightening a picture on a wall. "These straps are lookin' a bit worn. But that's okay.... I's got a more permanent solution in mind anyway." He tossed his hammer in the air and caught it again. "You know ... I thought we was friends. Maybe even kindred spirits on account of our same fingers and all. But friends don't lie to each other. No sir. That is not nice. Even warned you about all this, didn't I? Told you something bad was gonna happen tonight. Something *nasty*. And unlike you, *Big Ben* ... Esau ain't no liar."

The dwarf only sneered.

Part of him wanted to ask God for one more favor. To rain down fire and lighting on the demon who was standing above his unconscious friend. To stop him before he could do anything with that awful -ooking hammer. But Ben did no such thing. Because Ham and the Fàn sisters and the rest of the animals were all safe. And that was no small thing.

As he heard the first metallic ping of hammer on nail, the Englishman looked away. Forced himself to remember why he was where he was. And that love, real love, sometimes demands a sacrifice.

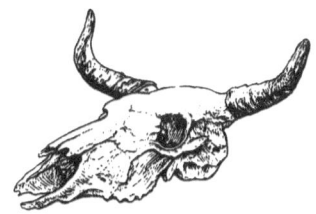

SKUDDA GOOMICH

ONE

Cruelty for no sake but its own was becoming the American pastime. Despite the war being good and over, there were plenty who took umbrage at what the world was trying to become. Typically though, the Owl-Man didn't concern himself with such matters.

He was a passing thing. An errant breeze, too inconsequential for most to take notice of. The man had a crooked nose and only one working eye. That one he kept shut most of the time. He'd lost it long ago—in a violent manner, some thought but never asked.

He wore a threadbare blanket, lined with feathers. On his head sat a wide-brimmed hat with a dented crown. The Stetson had been adorned with a beaded band and the skull of a bird. It was an owl, of course—you could tell by the eye sockets. They were forward-pointing like those of a cat—or a man. No one knew his real name, but that skull was rather conspicuous, as ornaments went. And since it was the one aspect most recalled after his passing, the Owl-Man was what he became.

He didn't mind. Most other folks he was aware of in the way a buffalo might be aware of a signpost. He knew they served some purpose or other, but his role wasn't to ponder the matter. His was only to blow through. To soar soundlessly above and eventually, past. Every once in a while though, the remaining eye of the Owl-Man would turn. Register something it couldn't abide. Ugly things happened all the time. In every corner, under every rock. True cruelty, though, was another thing. Maybe the Indian didn't have a word for it, but he sure as hell knew evil when he passed it on the road.

He'd heard the gunshot from a ways off. Something about it had drawn him, though even he couldn't have said why. He'd already walked the earth for longer than most and had heard his fair share of the white man's weapons. Usually the thunder they made caused him to turn the other way.

Usually.

By the time he crested the hill, the Owl-Man could see the tree and what it had been turned into. His remaining eye narrowed at the three men on horseback. Buffalo hunters, he judged by the distinctive rolled-up pelts burdening their mounts. The rider in back was leading a fourth horse by the reins. Likely hoping to get a few dollars for his trouble—enough for a round of whiskey or other such indulgences.

As he watched the three escape, the old Indian looked as if he'd been carved out of wood. Hard were the lines of his sun-beaten scowl as eyelids flexed, caressing a false eye few ever saw. Right then, all thoughts of blowing through unnoticed were gone. For what is an errant breeze if not the wind in an agreeable mood? The thing about wind … when it becomes impassioned, it can be a terrible thing. After all, tornadoes are passing things too.

The shadow of a large, headless bird passed over the dry ground west of Omaha. Its wings were broad and soundless—they flapped only once.

Arriving at the gallows tree, the Owl-Man looked up at the tragic horrors on display. Not much made him feel a part of the world these days, but this was the opposite of that. This was a whole lot of *much*. There were two bodies hanging there—a black couple. Both had been beaten horribly. Their faces were swollen and bruised, covered in open wounds. Whoever they had been, now they were just this. Bodies on ropes—swaying, leaking whatever was left inside.

The Owl-Man approached the woman first. There was no doubt that she had gotten the worst of it. What remained of her dress was torn— shredded as if by claws. Legs and feet were covered in dirty scratches and her most secret places were laid out on display. The Owl-Man turned from this, narrowing his eye in the direction the bad men had gone. Inside the old Indian, a storm was brewing and that was no small thing.

He reached out a hand, laid it upon the woman's bare foot. Softly, just enough so he could see. As usual, the reaction was explosive. Images came in a torrent—a coursing river of light and sound and memories that weren't his. The spirits always sent them that way.

The Indian's head snapped back as if reliving the horse kick that had broken his nose so long ago. For almost a minute, he stood trembling. Just trying to catch his breath and to make sense of what he'd been given. When his good eye shot open, the white was obscured by the colored part. Not brown but orange. It was the eye of a bird of prey, but only for a second. Steadying himself, the Owl-Man shook his head and blinked until the eye was that of a man's again.

Long gray hair blowing in the afternoon wind, the Indian looked up at the bodies—first the woman, then the man. Saw how they had been hanged from branches on either side of the old tree. He knew them now, and his shriveled old heart ached because of it.

The couple were homesteaders. Lisbeth Goodrow and her husband, Jeremiah. Lizzy, the man called her—had done since the summer of 1872. Lizzy, who loved yellow flowers and bread pudding and making things grow.

Once married, the Goodrows managed to purchase a small plot of land from the government. Just three acres of hard earth—too dry to grow anything real. The first year was more difficult than they'd imagined, but the Goodrows were no strangers to hardship. Both were tough, born and bred. The two shared a bond and a dream that was worth working for. Problem was, no matter what they tried, corn wouldn't take to the land. And because nothing in life was easy, corn was the only seed the local general store kept in stock.

Since Omaha was nearly a day's ride, Jeremiah would have preferred Lizzy stayed behind, but the woman's mind wasn't easily swayed. Thing of it was, she had never been to a city before.

The trouble had come when they were heading home. When they'd passed the hide hunters on the road, both Lizzy and Jeremiah had kept their eyes down—had even given the men an overly wide berth. Last thing either wanted was to be accused of offering a slight, perceived or otherwise. Slights, offenses, trespasses—no matter how small or imagined, were things that became convenient reasons for a certain sort of folk. But when men are bad enough, *want* is the only real thing that enters into it. Those hunters wanted to do what they did. And that was that.

The Owl-Man was very old. Older than anyone brave enough to ask would likely believe. Climbing trees was a young man's game, but no matter how his bones creaked or his joints protested, the Indian kept going. A small flint dagger was the only edge he carried, but with enough effort, it sawed through the ropes. When the woman dropped, the impact hurt his heart, though no words were offered. The man came next, but his longer legs made the drop shorter—perhaps easier to bear. It was hard to tell considering how numb the Owl-Man was. And still there were hours left to his task.

A rock was located and used in place of a spade, but the work went slowly. When finished, two graves lay side by side at the foot of the old tree. They were shallow things—scarcely larger than the bodies they were intended for.

One by one the Goodrows were carried like babes and laid to rest in the cold, hard ground. The husband was first, then the wife—Lisbeth. Lizzy. Before covering her up with earth, the Owl-Man had wrapped her in the old blanket he used for a cloak. She deserved more than rest, she deserved dignity. And yet, even this felt like a poor reward.

Her face was the last bit to be covered and doing so was painful. For a while afterwards, the Owl-Man simply sat rocking and humming softly to himself. Feeling that his task was incomplete, but wholly unsure what to do about it.

A sudden rustling drew his eye as all fell silent. Peeking around the tree, lined in the light of a half moon, was a snake. The rattler looked angry. Furious, even. The animal locked eyes with the old Indian and did not let go. For a long spell, between the two passed a silent palaver. After the snake broke eye contact, it tasted the air three times and slithered off into the grass.

As for the Owl-Man, he understood. Right then he knew what the dead girl really deserved. Not rest or dignity, but what the white men called *justice*.

His face was a wooden scowl as he glared down at the spot where Lizzy's face lay beneath the dirt. Calloused fingers found his bad eye and the lids parted to reveal a polished stone—the surface of which swirled with yellows, golds and a pale green. This he plucked from the socket and pushed without hesitation into the dirt, right above the woman's forehead. The old Indian's humming returned and this transitioned into a soft prayer. A plea to the darkness above and below as a boney finger traced shapes on the woman's grave. The humming in his throat increased in volume until chapped wooden lips parted to permit the release of a single word.

"*Skadegamutc.*"

TWO

Some days, the sun could be a real bastard. Like the whole damn world was sitting inside the devil's stewpot. Days like that, all a man could do was to carry on and try his damndest not to take it personal.

So far, Scott Birdwell had only managed the former. It'd been two days since the incident outside Omaha with the black couple and nothing had been the same since. Or rather everything had. Maybe that was really the problem. He looked up at the sun, wiped a shirtsleeve across his brow. If his two partners bore some manner of guilt for what they'd done, neither had shown any sign. Then again, both were hard men. Confederate men. Originally from Lincoln, Scott had been too young to fight in the war, but these two? Rutherford C. Hardee and Willard Tooms were mean enough to steal the coins off a dead man's eyes. Fortunately for Scott, as well as what posed locally for polite society, most of their frustrations were taken out on the buffalo.

"There!" The voice of Willard Tooms came in a shouted whisper. "You see it?"

Hardee raised a spyglass and aimed it in the indicated direction. Then he smiled.

"Well, boys ... looks like today might not be a waste after all." He chewed once and spit an oily mouthful on the ground. The man's teeth were every bit as brown Tooms's, though he was in possession of a few more in the front. "I only see the one but ... there may be more over that ridge. Hey, Bird ... you take care of the horses, we're going on foot."

The youngest and by far comeliest of the three didn't immediately respond. Never missing an opportunity for a jibe, the pack's alpha dog licked the chaw in his bottom lip and spat again.

"What's the matter, Scotty-bird? You go deaf?"

Frowning, Birdwell picked his rifle off the ground and stood up.

"Aw shoot, Rud, I'm coming." Dusting himself off, Scott moved toward the horses. As he removed some rope and three railway spikes from a saddle bag, a drop of sweat slid right into his eye and stung like absolute hell. "Damn it!" He frantically wiped his face on one sleeve.

"Hey! Quiet up, you idiot. You wanna scare off this one too?"

So far, the men had only managed to bag one buffalo all day. The kill had been Scott's, but the pelt was currently laid out on the back of the only black horse. Rud's horse. The man in charge didn't always claim the first kill, but when a subordinate's shot caused the animal to bleed and holler and run around scaring off the rest of the herd before it finally dropped, well …

"No!" Scott shot back, realizing he was, in fact, being loud. "I mean … *no*," he repeated in a more measured volume. "Of course not. Sorry Rud. It's just so damn hot today, I can't hardly think straight."

"You say that like it's a *today only* problem," Hardee really leaned into his drawl as he said this.

Looking sheepish, Scott continued about his task. As quickly as possible, he tied off a length of rope to the bit of the first horse, than did the same to the first spike. After testing the knot to make sure it was good, he pressed the pointed shaft into the ground using the sole of one boot. When it was good and flush to the dirt, he sighed and started on the next.

"Hurry up!" Shaking his head, Willard Tooms began fanning himself with his own bowler.

As it happened, the hat was of a style worn by the group. A simple bowler was good enough for Rutherford C. Hardee, so it was good enough for all. Despite two being more alike than the third, they all had the same hats, same horseshoe mustaches with three days of beard coming in, and they carried the same weapon. The Remington No. 1 Rolling Block, all loaded with .45 caliber cartridges. Some men went out with rifles that shot ammunition as high as .70 but according to Hardee, that stuff was for greenhorns and bluebellies. The higher the caliber, the louder the blast would be. And that meant the more likely you were going to scatter a dense herd to the four winds. But with a series of well-placed .45s right above each one's temple, you could clear out an entire family group, one at a time.

Back in Kansas when he was working for Union Pacific, that blowhard Bill Cody boasted raids of over thirty per day…, but Hardee and his were catching up. Combined, they'd bagged nineteen on their last good run. Problem was, that was almost four months ago. Sad fact of it was, the plains were emptying out. After the U.S. army sanctioned the wholesale slaughter of the buffalo a few years back, what had already been a lucrative way to make an honest living turned into the next gold rush. Every would-be hunter with a working iron wanted in on the action. But, as many discovered along the way, there was real nuance to the work. A level of skill in dropping a two-thousand-pound hump-on-legs.

"Shee-it!" Scott shot to his feet, launching himself backward. The other two looked where he was looking and saw a small tan snake with copper spots.

Tooms laughed so hard he almost fell over. "Looks like you've finally made a friend, kid!"

Hardee was stone-faced. He stomped on the snake's tail, pinning it. Then, without breaking eye contact with the terrified Birdwell, he picked it up and held it within a foot of the younger man's face. Scott could only watch in horror as again and again, the animal reached back and sank its teeth into Hardee's hand.

"What's the matter, Scotty-bird?" Hardee asked, as if oblivious to the bites he was receiving. "Don't you know pain builds character?"

Still refusing to break eye contact, Hardee snickered. Then he fired the snake at the younger man, who gasped and flailed as it bounced off his chest.

"It's a prairie snake, you idiot." Hardee stepped to within an inch of Birdwell's face. "Ain't no poison in those teeth. Though I got plenty in mine." Letting this suggestion hang, the man in charge smiled a slimy black grin. "So ... them horses anchored yet?"

Scott swallowed hard. Nodded furiously.

"Well, all right then." Both of Hardee's eyes rolled as he turned to face into the wind. Through his spyglass, he could see that the lone buffalo hadn't moved. "Let's go bag number two."

Now, when it came to hunting buffalo, Rutherford C. Hardee had three unbreakable rules.

Stay low, approach on foot and always keep the wind in your eyes.

The breeze blew over the three men—bending the flowering prairie grass they were trying to stay as low as. Scott closed his eyes, reveling in the momentary relief. That's when he heard it. A muttering in that breeze that approximated a human voice.

"... *skade ... ga ... mmutc ...*"

Scott stopped cold in his tracks. He'd heard about the feeling of someone walking over your grave, but until right then, he'd never experienced the sensation.

"*Hey!*" he whispered, as loud as whispers go. "*Y'all just hear that?*"

"*SHH!*" hissed Tooms. Even the veins in his yellow eyes looked mad. "I swear to God, kid, if you don't shut that mouth of yours, I'm gonna put something in there that'll close it for good." As a form of punctuation, the largest of the three shoved the smallest with the butt of his rifle.

Scott was used to the threats and abuse of his two compatriots. They didn't bother him that much. After all, his old man had done a whole lot worse—to him and his little sister both. Compared to all that, what were a few empty death threats or the occasional bruise? Nothing—that's what. And when Rud and Will did bad things, things like Daddy used to do to him and Janey, well ... at least they did 'em to someone else.

At least, that's what Scott told himself in his bedroll, when the nightmares came.

He could still see the black woman's face. How her eyes bulged when Toom's knife sliced her cheek and when the noose was tossed around her husband's neck. The man had already been beaten unconscious by that point so he didn't protest much. Hardee had lifted him into his saddle—positioned him in a kind of slouch while Tooms stabbed at the wife with his other blade. Scott didn't look, but he heard the sounds. Hardee told her what was gonna happen if she cried out. Had she only listened, he never would have pointed his Remington No. 1 in the air and fired.

For three days, Scott Birdwell had tried to shift his mind to anything besides that first scream—or the way she'd kept on hollering after the horse ran off and the rope around her husband's neck went tight. Shit,

Scott knew damn well the couple had done nothin' wrong. Hadn't looked at the group cross-eyed or whatever Rud had said. No—they were just simple homesteaders with the wrong color skin for his taste. Simple as that. Didn't even have nothing worth taking. Just seven dollars and a scraggly old mare they sold for five more in Omaha.

It all happened so fast. So goddamn fast.

And that's just what Scott was. Damned by God and all his angels for once again proving himself nothing but a worthless coward. The snake in his belly was back. Twisting, tying itself into knots over what he hadn't done but should have. The two homesteaders were Janey all over again. Poor sweet little Janey with dandelions in her hair.

"... *ska ... degam ... mutc ...*"

Again came that whisper on the breeze. Before a chill had a chance to travel the length of his spine, Scott saw the shadow of a large headless bird. It was on the ground, passing right over the hide hunters. As it went, Scott looked up, but the sun and sky were too bright. He winced and was left blinking away the green ghost spots hanging in his eyes.

"Skudda Goomich?" asked Scott, of no one in particular.

"Quiet up!" hissed the ugliest and least patient man of the three. "Look how many there are!"

There was a reason Rud's rule insisted they always approach on foot. Now that they were at the crest of the hill, the men could see a whole family group of buffalo were grazing on the other side. Sixteen in total.

Willard Tooms raised his Remington at the buffalo he'd spotted first—judging it at a distance of about one hundred and seventy yards.

"This one's easy, but what about the rest? How d'you wanna play this, Rud?"

Pinching one end of his mustache, Rutherford Clarence Hardee considered the question. Then he spat. Scott watched the long brown stream exit the man—saw how three drops of the chaw juice remained on his chin.

"Same as we used to," the alpha dog said at last. "Now I know it's been a few months since we seen a herd this big ... but we're professionals, boys. If we play this right—pick off the stragglers three at a time, well ... this might just turn into a record-breaking day.

"Sixteen." whispered Tooms. "That's about fifty dollars right there."

"More. You're forgetting the one from this morning. Tannery in Omaha pays three dollars per hide and twenty-five cents for every tongue. That's over fifty-five right there. But ..." Rud turned to glare at the youngest member of the group. "That money's only ours if every kill is a one-shot. You miss the brain? Get them to holler? The rest of that herd will be gone before you can spit. "

Without breaking eye contact, Rud wiped the brown spots off his chin. Then, with the same hand, he half-patted, half-slapped the face of his subordinate.

"You got that, Scotty-bird?"

Scott winced, both from the pain and from the wetness on his cheek.

"Yeah, Rud." He swallowed nervously. "O'course. I ... won't miss again, I promise."

"Better not." sneered Tooms. "I swear, you cost me one more penny, you little birdshit ... it'll be your hide I turn in at the tannery. *Comprende?*"

Eyes wide as windows, Birdwell nodded.

"All right, boys, it's time to meander." said Hardee with a sweep of his rifle. "Start with the old ones, find the leader if you can ... and keep that wind in your eye."

Without another word on the subject, the men parted ways—their focus shifting to the herd of unaware buffalo grazing below.

THREE

The day had been long and hot as hell's cellar. What it hadn't been was a bust.

The trick was to go slow. Pick off three at a time, then do nothing. A patient hunter will see that the American bison is a curious beast. When one of their ranks falls, the others come in for a sniff. Gathering around the dead in small numbers, sometimes small enough to drop straight away ... though other times, more patience is required.

As it turned out, Tooms' original count had been off by three—in the good way. By the time dusk came knocking, twenty buffalo lay in red stains of their own making. Combine that with the cow from that morning and Rutherford Hardee and his band had officially broken their dry streak.

"Sixty-five dollars." Tooms reclined on his bedroll, allowing the heat from the crackling fire to warm his bloated stomach. "Not bad at all."

The day's haul was a good one but the work of skinning so many humps had taken well into the night. By the time they'd collected all the tongues and rolled and tied off the hides, the men were just about ready to collapse. And while all three were fatigued and heat stricken, they were more hungry than anything. Fortunately, there was plenty of meat.

"Just remember, we don't get paid unless we get those hides back to town."

Picking his teeth, Tooms scoffed at this. "Until, not unless. Don't you worry, Rud, we'll get 'em there first thing in the morning. I don't know about you two, but I'm procuring me some whiskey for breakfast. The good stuff. Single malt."

Scott sighed. Nights like these really were the best of times. When both Hardee and Tooms were too blissfully content to remember what mean sons of bitches they were. The end of a hard, successful day of hunting had become his sanctuary. It had a quieting effect on his body, but also those damn unrelenting memories. Daddy ... Janey ... that black couple ...

Scott swore under his breath. Then, folding his arms, he rolled over to frown into the campfire. Sometimes, if he stared hard enough, he could see things. Shapes. Not of the past, just random odds and ends. A leaping deer … a soft bed … a pot of coffee.

"What's the first thing you're gonna do? After we get paid?"

It was a few seconds before Scott realized Toom's question was aimed at him.

"Oh … I dunno." He shrugged where he lay. "Probably get a shave. Maybe a bath."

"Better take two. Take at least that many to get rid of the smell! Ain't that right, *Birdshit?*" Tooms laughed long and loud at his own joke.

"All right, all right. *Enough.*" The voice of Rutherford Hardee had a way of cutting into your bones when it wanted to. "You two sound like a couple of goddamned crows. We load up and ride at dawn, so if you're gonna sleep, now'd be the time."

Scott didn't say anything after that, though he didn't know why he had been counted as one of the so-called crows. With another sigh, he resumed staring into his own private picture show. The flames licked and popped and they lulled. He could see a man and a woman … an old tree … a horned bear … and the outline of a bird with no head.

As he drifted off, Scott Birdwell was vaguely aware of something else in the fire. Not an image but a whisper. Words that didn't make any sense.

As he slept, Scott dreamt of secret shames and regret and of being afraid. But there was something new in the dreaming. A woman. She was walking on the other side of the fire—moving with the care of a stalking cat. She wasn't clothed so much as adorned with strips of fabric. The filthy remains of what had once been a dress flapped in the wind, but there was something strange about the movement. Almost as if the tatters were matching the woman's speed—carried by some supernaturally slow breeze.

The moment the woman turned her head on that wrong-angled neck, Scott knew her. It was the same woman. The homesteader wife from the tree, only she wasn't alive anymore. Her skin was hard and shiny like lacquered wood, and there seemed to be a yellow stone embedded in the center of her forehead.

He could see the gash on one cheek—same one Tooms had put there. The edges of the cut had peeled back far enough that he could see some of her teeth. The eyes were the same as they had been. Or, mostly the same. Difference being the hate there was now so naked, so frightening to gaze into, it made Scott want to pluck his own eyes out.

"*Skadegamutc.*" The word wasn't exactly formed by her lips, though it did slip past as they parted. Holding the terrified man in her dead eyes, Lizzy Goodrow raised a single finger. There was something almost alluring in the gesture as she let it hang for a while before wiping something dark and red from her chin. Something that sure as hell wasn't chaw.

The eyes of Scott Birdwell opened. Still in his bedroll, he sat up and turned to where the dead woman had been standing in his dream. Because that's all it had been—just another bad dream.

He rubbed his eyes, blinked away the weary-sleep. The fire pit had been reduced to embers but was not quite out. Past the feathery wisps of smoke, he could see the broad side of Tooms' back. The man was lying on his side as he slept. Somewhat relieved, Scott yawned and looked to the horizon. The rosy fingers of dawn were already at work, slowly pulling back the curtain of night to usher in another miserable day.

"Morning."

The voice was Hardee's. Being he wasn't ready for it, Scott half jumped out of his skin. A familiar blackened pot was placed onto what remained of their fire. Coffee. Serve with jerky and you've got your typical breakfast on the trail. Right then, Scott decided what he was going to procure directly after his shave. A real meal. The kind you eat with a fork and a knife instead of dirty fingers.

Hardee bent down and blew into the embers around the coffee pot until they kicked up a small lick of flames.

"Where'd you get the water?" Scott asked, rubbing his eyes again.

Already Hardee looked annoyed. "That creek we found last night. One we filled our canteens in—remember?" He clicked his tongue. "I swear, Scotty-bird, another piece of your brain falls out every night."

Scott blinked real slow. *If only*, he thought. *If only that were true.*

"The creek. Right." After pulling on his boots, he stood up. "Sorry, Rud, it's early is all."

Hardee was shaking his head, annoyed at the fact that he was already annoyed. Then he checked his watch.

"It's ten past five. By six, I want to be riding to Omaha."

Scott's eyes flicked to the unstirring form of Willard Tooms. He wanted to suggest that perhaps Hardee should mention his schedule to the one who was still sleeping. Maybe after kicking him awake first. Instead, looking sheepish, Scott just offered a nod.

"You got it."

Hardee pressed his bowler on his head. "Coffee will be ready in ten. Better start rolling those hides. And you better stow 'em good. If one falls off on the way back, it's coming out of your share … *with interest.*"

Scott said nothing at this; instead he just hobbled over to his horse and began doing as instructed. It had been pretty late by the time they'd laid out all twenty hides around camp. They wouldn't be dry yet, of course, but with Rud itching to get them to the Tannery, there was no point in mentioning the obvious. Scott hated this part, but he supposed it was only fair that the task should be his. After all, the other two did most of the skinning.

He always managed a few, but the art wasn't really Scott's forte. Turning them was the hardest part. After finishing one side, a skinner was presented with the problem of getting at the other. The Hardee-accepted method involved pulling at the back legs and holding the hindquarters up high. This allowed a second man to get under the lower front leg and pull and turn and work it until the sometimes two thousand pounds of dead buffalo, flipped over like a pancake.

Scott Birdwell had never been able to do any part of it very well. And so, it was what it was. He was too good a shot to kick out of the group … but too lousy at skinning to deserve help rolling the hides. In the old days, when higher kill counts were the norm, they used to set up camp first and park a wagon there, so they could load up later. But with the herds getting thinner and thinner, such additional precautions had become a waste of time and effort. Stowing a handful of rolled hides back on three horses was usually no problem, though admittedly, twenty might be pushing it.

Reaching down, he lifted the edge of the first hide and shook it like a blanket. He was about to start rolling when he spared another glance over at Tooms. From this vantage, Scott was faced with the man's feet and fat ass instead of his back. But there was what looked like a shadow on his other side. Like a great dark stain on the ground. In the low light, colors weren't yet what they would soon be—but the shadow looked brown. As if Tooms had vomited up a full spittoon worth of tobacco juice while he slept.

Suddenly, Scott remembered his dream.

"Uh …" He swallowed nervously, his voice barely a rasp. "Rud?"

"What?"

"Is, uh … Will okay?"

"What? Sure he is. He's just lazy." Hardee sounded even more annoyed as he walked over to the only hide hunter who was sleeping in. "Lazier than a dog with no legs." With that, he delivered a swift boot to the man. The unmoving body of Willard Tooms didn't protest, nor make a sound. When kicked, it simply rolled—slumping over from side to stomach.

Hardee and Birdwell met each other's eyes then—both seeing how perplexed the other was. Dropping the hide, Scott walked over to where Tooms lay with his face in the dirt. The stain on the ground was a lot more obvious when you were right on top of it.

"Will?" Hardee's voice carried an uncharacteristic lilt. "It's time for us to git. Come on now."

Again, the two standing men exchanged a glance.

"Scott?"

"Yeah, Rud?"

"Turn him over."

"What? *Me*? But I …"

"I said *turn him the hell over*."

Scott removed his bowler and scratched underneath. He looked very nervous, but this was underselling the situation. The snake in his gut had moved from tying knots to knitting a whole damned sweater.

Wetting his lips, he forced his knees to bend. He could see his hand reach out. Bizarrely, as he watched it get closer and closer to the man, it didn't seem part of himself. When contact was made at last, Toom's shoulder felt wrong. It was hard as a rock and just as cold. Right then, Scott felt like he was going to retch. Whatever they were about to see was going to be bad. Real bad. Like something out of a nightmare, only worse because he wasn't sleeping.

"Well?" Rud sounded more nervous than he ever had before. "What are you waiting for? Do it."

Closing his eyes, Scott bit his lip, gripped hold of that rock-hard shoulder and pulled.

The truth of what had become of Willard Tooms hit both men like a kick to the balls. It forced them both backward, causing partially digested buffalo meat to come back up and splash on the ground.

"Jesus Christ!" Scott managed this between heaves. "Agh. What in God's name could have done that?"

The heart of Rutherford Hardee banged in his chest as he searched his considerable experience for a possible explanation for what he was seeing.

Willard Tooms was dead, but that wasn't the worst of it. Half of his face looked to have been eaten away—gnawed at by something. The damage was so extensive the pale bones of his cheek and jaw weren't hard to miss. And then there was the matter of his chest ... of the ragged, gaping hole where his heart should have been.

"Must have been ... a coyote." Hardee said after a while.

"What?" Still on his hands and knees, Scott turned. "A *coyote*? Are you kidding me? You ever seen a coyote gut anything bigger than a fucking rabbit?"

Hardee was backing away by this point. Scrambling for purchase on the flat ground. Without thinking, his hand reached out for the handle of the steaming coffee pot, picked it up and dropped it again when the pain registered.

"I ... I've seen a lot of things." He said wincing—waving his hand as if to cool it off. "Tooms—that grass-bellied son of a bitch, probably fell asleep with a mouthful of buffalo and choked to death without us hearing. Yeah, the greedy bastard. Then something … a coyote or maybe a bear … comes up, smells the meat in his mouth and, well … *got at it*."

The suggestion pushed Birdwell over the edge. His body lunged forward, as his stomach gave up more than it could spare.

"That's not what happened." There was a line of drool connecting Scott's lower lip with the ground. "Weren't no animal that did this. It was *her*."

Hardee's expression remained dazed for a second before turning hard. "What are you talking about? Her *who*?"

"That woman. You know … the homesteader's wife. The one you … we …" Scott's voice hitched, as his body was wracked by another heave— this one dry. "I saw her last night. I thought I was dreaming it, but I saw her right there. Broke neck and all. She looked right at me and … oh God … there was blood on her face." Scott wiped his mouth on one sleeve, and got to his haunches. "Skudda Goomich. That's what she said."

The bootfalls of Rutherford C. Hardee were like hammer strikes as they approached. Before Scott knew what was happening, he was being wrenched to his feet by the collar. Though, whether it was from all the purging or the general shock of the moment, the young man didn't have the usual sense of when to shut up.

"You ever heard talk like that before, Rud? *Skudda Goomich?*" Scott spat with wide bloodshot eyes. "You think that's Arapaho or Cheyenne or something?"

A broad hand slapped the kid's face so hard, his ears were left ringing.

"Listen close because I ain't in a repeating mood. You and I are going to load up all twenty of those buffalo hides … then we are going to take them to the tannery in Omaha and get paid. After that, this little business venture we got going is over. And if you ever mention any of this or anything about that peanut-gallery whore again, so help me, I will find out." A large knife appeared—its blade streaked with dried blood. "And if that happens, well … I'm gonna cut so many pieces off you, Scotty-bird … old Will here is gonna look pretty by comparison. *Comprende?*"

FOUR

The ride back to Omaha was as quiet as it was sobering.

Seeing as how conversation was out of the question, Scott Birdwell used the time to think. Not just about the hideous demise of Willard Tooms at the hands of an undead, apparently cannibalistic ghost witch … but also about what he was going to do now that he had to find a new job. At least he would have a little money in his pocket to start out this latest time of financial uncertainty. Enough for that bath and a room for a few days, anyhow. Though he was probably going to skip that fork-and-knife meal.

It really was over. The partnership yes, but also their way of life. As much as it hurt to think about, the Great Plains were nearly empty—the buffalo all but gone. The simple fact was, while that herd they'd cleaned out had been their second biggest of the year, twenty humps were still shy of the numbers that made Bill Cody famous. But those days were gone. The thing of it was, Hardee and his ilk had been so successful when times were good, they had accidentally put themselves out of business. As a concept, the buffalo hunter was becoming obsolete— though extinct was probably a more fitting term.

The two men rode into the city of Omaha at just past eight o'clock on Sunday morning. Over the course of his short life, Scott had been to plenty of towns across the territories, but none with more than a single horse—as things were measured. Omaha, on the other hand, had three general stores, two tailors, a barbershop, and an impressive livery stable with a big corral out there, which, depending on the day, was packed with horses. More importantly though, it had Lady Fairfax's. Providing you didn't mind using someone else's water, a man could get a nice hot soak for a quarter. Granted, the soap and towel would run you another twenty cents, but it was well worth it. There was nothing like a bath to make you feel like a new man. And that's what Scott Birdwell was aiming to be—whether he had a say in the matter or not.

Eyes turned as the two men passed. For the second time in four days, Rutherford Hardee was cantering into town with more horses than men. But that wasn't really what had caught their attention. The hides were rolled up like blankets and strapped to the backs of the three horses. Scott's was bearing six out of the twenty as well as the bag of tongues.

For a minute there, he had nurtured a hope that they'd be splitting Will's share. But all that ended when Rud loaded up the dead man's horse himself and promptly hitched it to his own. Part of the young hide hunter wanted to say something about that. To stand up for himself and make a case for fair being fair … but the rest of him wanted to keep breathing.

He was trying real hard not to think about Tooms.

There was certainly no love lost there, but the facts surrounding his death were *worrisome* to say the least. He could still see the ghost woman's eyes. How bright yellow the white parts were. How unnaturally textured and wooden her skin looked. Whether it had happened for real or had really just been the result of his own buried guilt that'd come rearing its head in dream form…. Scott couldn't get that face out of his head. The way her neck was bent all wrong from where the rope had broke it. And how she'd held up that one slender finger.

There must have been something up there she'd wanted him to see. That had to be it. If only Scott hadn't been so frozen with terror, he might have inclined his head. Maybe her husband was up there … still swinging on that rope Hardee tossed around his neck.

Scott slapped his hand to his face and pressed hard as the snake that lived in his stomach stirred some more.

Why did the worst things always come back? Hadn't he always tried to be a decent man? He'd have never hurt those poor homesteaders. Hell, the only black folk Scott had ever known were free to begin with. And if Hardee and Tooms had such closely held Confederate views then why had they set up base in a Union-aligned place like the Territory anyhow?

Of course, Scott already knew the answer to this. It was a simple matter of economics.

"Where go the buffalo, so goes the buffalo hunter." The words came with a snicker. Dropping a hand from his face, Scott had to blink through the spots he'd put there.

Him and Rud were passing the corral in front of the livery on the right.

Omaha Transportation Co. read the big white letters on the side of the main building. Just below this were three words more … *Livery, Stables, Sales.*

The buildings were situated in a very central, very unmissable spot. A kind of four-sided almost-triangle surrounded by dirt roads on all sides. Being the only livery in the whole city, its twelve stables filled up fast. And that meant most of the horses they took in were out front in the famous corral. It was like having a wide store window with the best wares on display for potential customers to ogle as they passed. And ogle they did.

Scott had seen the pen full before, but not like this. There had to be three dozen in there. Normally the animals were free to roam about, but as it was there was barely enough room to stand. Those horses were packed tighter than cattle before a drive. And yet there was one that caught the eye of Scott Birdwell.

It was light brown all over, with a slightly paler mane and a pink muzzle. The animal's aspect was unremarkable but for a distinct splotch of red over one eye. It was the same horse that Scott had personally sold to the livery just three days prior, for the sum of seven dollars. The horse was looking straight at him. Its dark, bulbous eyes were utterly locked— following the youngest of the remaining hide hunters as he trotted past.

This sent a shiver up Scott's spine. Lowering his bowler, he looked ahead at Hardee. His old boss looked as stone-faced as ever though. His head turning no more at the sight of the horse they'd stolen and murdered for than he would for a fly.

Suddenly, Scott had the distinct feeling of worms crawling under his skin. The idea that he'd allowed such a man to shape not only his day-to-day but his appearance as well was suddenly enough to make him vomit all over again. Right then, he needed that bath more than ever. And after that, a new hat and a shave.

He didn't care how much it would cost.

Eighteen dollars for the six pelts and another five for the bag of tongues. Scott counted the money three times, lamenting the half of Toom's share that Hardee had kept for himself. After a quick reminder of what would happen should Scott ever muse on certain topics out loud, the two men parted ways. And while Scott headed for his hot bath and shave, his former boss was leading Toom's horse back in the direction of the livery. By Scott's estimation, the sale of the animal was going to put another ten or more dollars in Hardee's pocket. It was a notion that made the younger man even madder than he already was. There was no two ways about it—the three-year partnership of Hardee's hide hunters was officially dissolved.

As Scott stomped down the street, that snake in his gut began to turn again. It did what it always did, kicked up things that he should have said—actions he should have done. Because a real man would have stood up to the likes of Willard Tooms or Rutherford C. Hardee … or to a half dozen other men who'd treated him like so much shit on their heel over the years. And really, all those bastards had all been the same one. The original.

As he walked up to the side door of Lady Fairfax's, dirty tears streamed down the face of Scott Birdwell. Driven by instinct, he moved a hand to wipe these away, then stopped. Decided the tears were fine where they were.

FIVE

Ever since entering the city of Omaha, Lizzy Goodrow had been afraid to blink. There was so much to see. So many stores and signs and of course, people.

To say the least, she wasn't accustomed to that sort of thing. In broad terms, Jeremiah was the only person she saw anymore. Her parents were gone—sisters too. Had all been taken within nine months of one another by cholera back in '71. Now, Jeremiah was all she had left. Though kind of a string bean, the man was kind, devoted and smart ... heck, as far as she was concerned, the man's biggest flaw was never looking good in hats. The two had been in love in one fashion or another since childhood. And, as it happened, there was no one in the world Lizzy would rather spend her days working a two-acre plot of dried-out silt with. After all, they were still young. There'd be time enough for little ones later. Three, she reckoned. Two girls and a little boy whom they could name Miles, after her daddy.

"Where are you at, darlin'?" The voice of Jeremiah pulled Lizzy from her thoughts.

"Hmm? Who, me?" Lizzy turned with a secret smile that quickly bloomed. "Why, I am right here—in this big beautiful city with the handsomest man around."

Jeremiah couldn't help but smile too, but he quickly put the expression away. Cleared his throat. "So tell me ... was it worth the saddle sores?"

"Well I will be sure to let you know as soon as they stop screaming." She readjusted herself, then looked to a sign to their right. Big white letters had been painted on the main building there and, while she did not know how to read, Lizzy was positively transfixed by them. After a few seconds, her eyes moved to the roadside corral. "My goodness, Mr. Goodrow, have you ever seen so many pretty horses in one place?"

"No ma'am. I don't reckon I have." As he said this, Jeremiah was scanning faces. Taking in the kinds of looks they were receiving from the citizens of Omaha, he pulled out an old brass pocket watch and frowned at the time.

"Just after one o'clock." He offered grimly. "Trip took eight hours."

"Well …" Lizzy shrugged. "You said it'd take ten."

Jeremiah nodded, continuing to absorb their surroundings. "That's still eight hours home. I figure … so long as we head out by two o'clock, we can be back by ten."

"One hour?" Lizzy sounded somewhat devastated. "We come all this way for one little hour?" She looked up, scrunching her bottom lip in that way that Jeremiah had so much trouble saying no to. "Way I see it, Mr. Goodrow, if we can be home by ten, then we can also be home by eleven."

Jeremiah gave a disapproving look, but it was promptly dismissed.

"Besides, I'm sure Earle would appreciate a longer break. *Wouldn't you, Earle?*"

The horse did not reply, though it did not seem to mind when the woman began scratching behind one ear.

"*See?* That's him saying yes."

Jeremiah shook his head in that defeated way he was so practiced in.

"Besides," Lizzy went on. "If you are *that* worried about making time, we could always find a room somewhere and just head out in the morning."

Jeremiah's expression sank. Then after stopping Earle at a communal trough, he dismounted. As the horse began to drink, he helped his wife down. Then he began to remove the saddle.

"I don't think that's a good idea. Staying overnight, I mean." Jeremiah's tone was soft but firm. "But I suppose you're right about staying an extra hour." After undoing the last strap, he placed the saddle on the ground. "Earle could use the rest."

Lizzy's eyes lit up. "We could leave him at the stable back there! I'm sure they'll take good care of him while we meander."

As the Goodrows stood there in the middle of the street, the faces, the looks, the feeling of being watched and, worse, *weighed* were not lost on Jeremiah. And yet, these felt like small prices to pay. Beyond the hope of finding better crops and supplies, he knew what the day trip meant to his wife. The both of them so rarely left the homestead anymore, and never for anything like the city of Omaha. For her, this was an adventure. Lizzy wasn't seeing those looks or glares, only faces.

"I don't know." He frowned, thinking of the money roll in his left boot. "Fifteen dollars is all we have."

"Yes, yes, Mister Raincloud, I know." Lizzy looked a little crestfallen as she stroked Earle's neck. "But it's only for a couple hours. Shouldn't be more than twenty-five cents."

"For them, maybe."

At the sudden voice, Lizzy almost jumped. There was a man and a young boy walking their horse towards the same trough. They were both wearing fur-covered boots and the boy was fumbling with a length of wire that ended in a loop. It looked like a snare for some kind of small animal—a rabbit, maybe. More interesting than what they were wearing though, was the color of their skin.

"My apologies," said the man. "Didn't mean to overhear. But for you or me ... a stay for even an hour or two at the Transportation Company over there is going to be a dollar at least."

"What?" Lizzy sounded outraged, for mathematics was not so elusive to her as reading. "Four times more? But why?"

The two men and Jeremiah shared a knowing look, though neither looked inclined to answer the question.

"Because they can," the man said at last.

Jeremiah shook his head in knowing disbelief. He wanted to leave—not just the conversation but the whole city. Wanted his horse to be done drinking so they could get back on and ride home to their little patch of dried-up slice of untillable heaven.

"Aw, come on, boy!" The man tried to take the wire away from his son, but it was pulled back. "Not like that. You're gonna get it all tangled!"

"No, I ain't." The boy fired back, than hung his head. "I mean ... no, I'm *not*."

Lizzy bent down and offered the kid a smile. "What's your name?"

"... Dwayne."

"Dwayne—I like that. Nice and strong. I'm Lizzy."

"Okay. It's, uh ... nice to meet you," said the boy, not really meaning it.

"This is a snare, right?"

The boy nodded his head. "Yeah, it's our spare one. The rabbit we caught this morning got tangled real bad. It kicked so much, the wire wrapped around its belly and was cutting it." Looking suddenly sad, he sniffed. "Now it's all messed up. I'm trying to fix it cuz we only have one other good one."

"Oh dear. I'm sorry to hear that, Dwayne." Lizzy looked positively motherly right then, as she cupped the boy's cheek. "Do you mind if I have a try?"

The kid looked up at his father, who smiled and gave a nod.

Lizzy accepted the snare and began turning the loop—unwinding it. "You know something? I used to make these when I was little."

The boy's eyes lit up in disbelief.

"You did? But ... you're a girl."

"*Dwayne!*" snapped the father.

"No, it's all right," Said Lizzy with a smile. "You're absolutely right, Dwayne, That is exactly what I *am*. Fortunately, my parents taught me how to do a few things anyway."

When she winked, the boy smiled back. Once the misshapen loop had been fully unwound, she wrapped the length of old wire around a nearby post and began twisting the two ends together again. Dwayne watched as the new neck of the snare grew. And when the woman slipped the loop up and off of the post, it held its shape.

"Wow, thanks!" said the kid, taking the snare back to show his father. "Look, Pa! It's okay!"

"I can see that, son," Said the man with a smile. After clearing his throat, he tipped his hat and said, "Much obliged for the help, ma'am."

Lizzy waved this away, then looked at her husband. Jeremiah had watched the whole scene with equal parts disbelief and an admiration that went all the way into his core.

"You seem familiar with the city. Mister...?"

"Jim," said the man. "And yes, we are. Dwayne and I are about these streets most days. Whatever we catch that doesn't go into the stew pot goes to that butcher shop there." He gestured toward the building with the cow sign. "So … what brings such a fine couple to Omaha?"

"Supplies," said Jeremiah. "Lizzy and I have ourselves a little plot of land, but the trading post near Beaver Lake only sells corn seed. We're looking to try something that grows with a mite less moisture. Beans, maybe."

"Beaver Lake?" Jim raised an eyebrow. "Why, that's near thirty miles from here. Did you really come all that way today?"

Jeremiah nodded, "And we're gonna go back all that way again as soon as Earle here rests up."

"I see." Jim said, turning to look down the street. "Well … if you're aiming to buy dry goods, the one you want is down that way. Can you uh … read?"

"We *can*." Jeremiah answered a little too quickly.

"All right then," said Jim. "You'll want to skip Omaha General—trust me on that. When you see it, just keep going … take a right at the post office and look for Dunbar's. They got a few hitching posts out front for Earle here, and if Joe is working, he'll give you a free handful of oats." The man patted the horse on the neck.

"Yeah," nodded the boy. "All you gotta do is ask. For a white man, Joe is really nice."

"Dwayne!"

"What? He *is!*"

Jim was shaking his head—his hand already pinching that space between his eyes.

"Appreciate the help," said Jeremiah, offering his hand.

"Likewise." Nodded Jim, shaking it. As he looked at the woman one final time, a coldness crept up his spine. He wasn't sure why, but he had a bad feeling about the couple riding all the way back to Beaver Lake, especially at night. For a fleeting instant, he considered offering his cabin, but the idea was quickly dismissed. "Come on, son. Let's leave these two nice folks to their business."

"Okay." Dwayne did not sound happy at the prospect. He started chewing on his bottom lip. "It really was nice to meet you, Miss Lizzy."

"Why, thank you, Dwayne; it was nice to meet you too. You know what? Here ..." She bent down again, then unclasped a cord that was around her neck—hidden until that moment by her hair. "If it's okay with your daddy, I would very much like you to have this."

When Jim indicated that it was, she placed the cord around the boy's neck. On it hung a crucifix. Nothing valuable, just a little stamped piece of tin.

After turning the gift over in his hands, the boy looked like he might cry. He lunged forward and wrapped his arms around the woman's neck. Being as Dwayne's mom had been gone since he was three, the boy couldn't remember her face anymore, but as he hugged Lizzy—felt the warmth of her neck on his cheek, the feeling of being completely safe came rushing back all at once.

"*Thank you.*" He sniffed. "And also for fixing the snare. I wouldn't have thought to untie it and start over like that."

"There was this saying my daddy had." Lizzy smiled. "Sometimes things need to be undone before they can *become*."

"Become?" The boy looked confused. "Become what?"

Lizzy raised a finger, held it in the air for a second, than she bopped the kid on the nose.

SIX

The woman's face was with him. Scott could see how it had been, right at the end. Contorted—stretched over the enormous wrong she and her husband were being forced to endure. It was a face that, for the first time in Lizzy Goodrow's life, knew what it was to hate.

The barber's razor was cold against Scott's cheek. It had been a long time since he'd had a proper shave, but no matter how hard he tried, the kid could find no more relief in that chair than he had at Lady Fairfax's bath house. Every time he closed his eyes, the woman was there. The homesteader's wife—waiting with her hideous naked hate.

Already she'd come for Willard Tooms. Scott knew because he'd seen it. Whether with his own eyes, or through the spyglass of a dream, somehow he *had* seen it. How she'd turned her bent neck and those dead eyes. Cracked lips had parted to say words that made no sense. A ghost tongue not spoken by living. And yet, he had understood. *Skudda Goomich* could mean only one thing.

I'm coming for you, Scotty-bird. You, most of all.

The sound of a woman's shriek caused Scott to flinch so hard the barber's razor entered his flesh.

Twenty-four minutes later, Scott stepped out of the barber shop. A large white bandage was covering the left side of his face as well as some very hurried stitches. Miserably, he glanced over the striped pole beside the door and was reminded what the red was for.

"Goddamn it," he grumbled—wincing at the numb tightness that wasn't there before. Why had he done that? Lunged at the sound of a ... a what? A memory? No. The shriek had sounded so real, so *close*. Like someone had snuck up right behind him before screaming directly into his ear. And yet, no one else had heard it.

"You're losing it, Birdwell." Scott mumbled this to himself with a joyless snicker.

With one hand on his bandaged cheek, he turned to walk further into town, then stopped. People were rushing past in the opposite direction. Not one or two, but a crowd. And yeah … now that he was paying attention, he could hear a commotion.

Deciding that breakfast could wait, he began to march back up the street. Wooden heels banged the ground with every step and throbbed in his cheek. Worst of all was that damn snake that lived in his belly—the thing was writhing something awful.

He craned his neck, but couldn't tell what was going on. Only that the crowd was gathered in front of the Omaha Transportation Company.

Panic and curiosity rose in his throat as Scott pushed his way through. Unfortunately, all he could discern was that the horses out front were all riled up. Stomping and snorting and squealing like someone had dropped a sack of rattlesnakes in the middle of the corral.

"I never seen nothin' like it before."

Scott overheard someone say. He turned to see a burly man wearing a buckskin coat.

"Yep. He was running, shouting behind him like he was being chased by something. Thing is, there weren't nothing there. I was standing right here. I saw him coming up this way and I'm telling ya, that street was empty."

"Yessir, I saw it too." said a man wearing furs. "That bastard was running so fast, he tripped—went tail over teakettle into the mud there. When he got back up, I saw his eyes—they was crazy like them horses in there. I thought he was gonna keep going, but he changed direction and came this way. It was like he wasn't running from just one thing. Like everywhere he looked, he saw the devil himself."

"Or ghosts," offered buckskin.

"Ha!" scoffed a third man. "Only spirits that sumbitch saw were at the bottom of a glass! Clearly the man was drunk!"

"No, no … all y'all are wrong." said a man wearing a straw hat. "I seen this same thing happen to a cousin of mine. Silas—*God rest his soul*—he always had the night terrors, y'know."

"Night terrors?" Exclaimed the man in the furs. "But it's not even lunchtime."

Straw hat looked nearly overcome with emotion. "All I can say is that my poor cousin got so bad, he started having them terrors when he was awake. Yes sir. Hand to God's honest truth. One time, we was in the cornfield and Silas just started screaming something about a stampede!" The man removed his straw hat and held it to his chest. "Ran all the way to the road and got himself runned over by a passing carriage."

At this the man in furs and the one wearing buckskin looked at one another, then began to laugh uncontrollably.

Frustrated at being the only person apparently in the dark, Scott pushed the rest of the way up to the corral fence and then began moving along it. There were numerous employees of the Omaha Transportation Company, trying to calm the horses, but it was a fool's errand. There were too many animals for an enclosure of that size. Going in would be suicide.

A few sections down, Scott came to a small girl who was standing up on the bottom rail and just staring inside. She couldn't have been more than seven or eight years old. Her hair was pulled back into wiry braids and her little brown hands gripped the top rail.

"Hey kid," Scott said stiffly, with another wince of pain. "You see what happened here?"

The girl nodded her head, but did not turn.

"*Well?*"

"A man come running up the street. Running like the devil hisself was chasing him."

"Yeah, I heard that part." Scott was getting frustrated, but also afraid for some reason. He didn't know why, but the snake in his belly told him he needed to know what the hell was going on and fast. "So? *What happened to him?* And what in the hell is wrong with these horses?"

"The man was running like he gone crazy." The little girl spoke in a slow drawl. "He come running this way. Tried to go round this fence here, but kept changing direction. Back, forth, forth, back. You ever seen a rabbit caught in a trap, mister?"

"What?" Scott was flustered by the question. "Sure. Of course I have, why?"

"That's just what he looked like. As for the horses, well ... they're scared of the same thing he was. I think they were the only other ones who could see her ... besides me."

As the snake in Scott's belly sunk its teeth in, the jolt almost doubled him over. He licked his lips. Forced out a question he dearly did not want to ask.

"What do you mean … *her?*"

"Oh, the dead lady," said the girl, still refusing to look at the strange man she was talking to. "I knew right away she was dead because of how she moved. I ain't known a living person to slide through the air like that."

Scott stumbled backwards. He felt faint.

"The man had nowhere else to go," Said the little girl in her slow, uninterested drawl. "He hopped the fence. Tried to get to the other side—to the road over there. But the dead lady didn't like that."

Finally, the girl hopped down and turned to look at Scott.

"She opened her mouth so wide. More than alive people can do."

As Scott listened, his eyes stared into the center of the corral. It was hard to see through the waves of panicked horses, but there seemed to be something on the ground in there with them. In his ear, he could hear the faintest, most gentle of sounds that somehow seemed to drown out all else. They were munching sounds. Like something being chewed, crunched, and gnawed.

"Mister?"

The voice of the little girl startled Scott almost as much as the phantom scream in the barber shop had done. He looked down, his heart pounding like a drum in his chest.

"Do you want to know what she said?"

Just then, from the center of the roiling horses, something shot up into the sky. The thing that had once been Lizzy Goodrow hung in the air. Her tattered clothes flowing too slow, her eyes burning with fear—just not her own. Her mouth opened wide and wider still—stretching like a snake's before swallowing something bigger than its own head.

"*Skudda Goomich.*" Scott mouthed the words, but soundlessly.

BANG!!

The unmistakable report of a Remington No. 1 Rolling Block exited the mouth of the thing that had been Lizzy Goodrow. It was loud. Like ten shots rolled into one—or fifty. And yet, no one seemed to hear it. None save for one little girl, the doomed man she was talking to, and the horses.

The gunshot that wasn't sent all of the penned animals into a second round of panic. This time, a large chestnut bay hammered its way through one of the sections of fence, allowing the squealing mass to pour out onto the street. The employees of the Omaha Transportation Company were shouting, pointing, fumbling with their lassos as they tried to take charge of the fear-mad animals. Citizens of Omaha leapt and dove and ran from the stampede, but not Scott Birdwell. He was standing on the other side, frozen in place—just staring at the trampled, broken body in the center of the now empty corral.

Rutherford C. Hardee had never been called handsome, but what was left of the man was a full assault upon the eyes. His arms and legs had been broken so many times, they looked like red snakes with hands and feet instead of heads. The back of his head had been smashed as well, and Scott was pretty sure that the shiny wrinkled thing he could see hanging out was the man's brain.

"He tried to get to the other side," Said the little girl in that far away drawl. "He tried, but she wouldn't let him. Her voice is like a gun, Mister. Do you know why that is?"

In shock, Scott took a few seconds to understand the question. He looked down at the little girl, but didn't know how to answer. To tell her that he did know. That the sound the dead lady made was the same that had been used to spook her own horse. To make it run when her husband was on its back … tied by his neck to a tree by the very man before them. No—Scott couldn't say any of that.

"I don't know either," said the girl. "But it's kinda funny, don't you think?"

Scott looked up into the air where the dead woman had been hanging, but she wasn't there anymore. His breaths were coming too fast, too deep. As he whipped his head around from side to side, the edges of his vision were getting dark. But if Scott passed out now, he'd never wake up again.

"She hates you most of all, you know."

The words cut to the core of Scott Birdwell. Stopped the whole damned world from spinning.

"What did you just say?" His voice was a thin raspy nothing.

"The other men were worse. Was their hands that did all the hurting. But you're the one she blames."

Scott swallowed, looked left, right and up, but could see no sign of the homesteader's wife. He swallowed again, winced. His throat hurt. Not in a getting sick kinda way, but as if something were around it—squeezing tighter with every passing second.

"But … why? I never meant to hurt anyone! It's like you said, I didn't lay a hand on either one of 'em two! That was them! Not me! That was Rud and fucking Tooms!?!"

As he said this, Scott was backing up. Suddenly, his heel hit something that caused him to fall backward in the mud.

"Why?" He could feel the cut on his cheek as a thin line of pain. "Why would she hate *me* more than *them*? I didn't do *nothing!! Not one goddamned thing!!*"

Stepping forward, the little girl leered down. She was cast in silhouette by the late morning sun and looked enormous.

"Yeah … but you could have." The little girl's voice sounded older. "*Should* have. You knew what was gonna happen and yet … you did nothing. *Not one goddamned thing.*"

"No … no, no no …" Scott was shaking his head, backing up like a crab in the mud.

"You could have stopped them, Scott. Your daddy, too. Maybe, you could have saved us all. But you didn't even try."

Suddenly, the little girl flickered like the flame of a candle, and was gone. Blinking in disbelief, Scott scrambled to his feet. The corral was empty save for the dead woman and a single horse. It was light brown all over, with a slightly paler mane and a pink muzzle. The woman walked over and put her shiny wooden hand on the animal's face. Then, after regarding what was left of her second victim, she fixed those dead yellow eyes on the one she hated most.

Scott's chest was tight, his breath practically strangled in his throat as he watched the homesteader's wife raise a hand and extend two fingers. That's when it hit him. When he'd seen her the first time, this dead thing, this ghost witch—she hadn't been pointing at all. She'd been counting.

"*Skadegamutc.*"

He heard the word as a loud whisper on the side of his head that nearly made his heart stop. This time, Scott knew that previously he'd been overcomplicating the translation. All Skudda Goomich really meant was …

"*Run.*"

SEVEN

Oh, how Scott did run.

Up the street and out of the city of Omaha and then past it. The sun was fully awake and seemed intent on being a real bastard again, but Scott couldn't worry about that. He had to keep doing this one thing—that same thing he'd been doing his whole miserable life. Running from his troubles, from his fears. Running because it was all he knew.

"She blamed you, Scotty-bird. Blames you still."

He turned to look back and the dead woman was in the sky.

"That snake in your belly? The one that tells you what a worthless yellow sack of shit you are? She's the one who put it there."

"No!" Scott shouted into the wind. Banging his ear as if to get something out. "You shut up! You can't know about that! I never told anyone."

"You didn't need to." The woman flickered and appeared directly in front of him! So close, he saw the yellow stone in her forehead throb!

The toe of his boot caught, sent him wheeling into the dirt. Scott hit hard and spat out a mouthful, wiping the earth from his eyes. There was something white in the dirt—his bandage. Touching the exposed wound with the back of one hand told him the stitches had let go, too.

His eyes darted a couple times before stopping on the dead woman. She was standing in the southwest, about a hundred paces back. And yet, when she spoke, he could feel her fetid whisper-breath blowing inside his ear.

"I'm in your head, Scotty-bird. Everything you know, so do I."

"I'm sorry!" Scott was crying now. Really sobbing. "I loved my sister."

"And yet ..." came the terrible brain-whisper. "On those nights your daddy stopped at your door ... and kept on walking. Her pain was more than your secret shame ... it was your respite."

"*No!*"

"Oh, sure it was. Because why should you have to bear the whole brunt of your daddy's ... *inclinations?*"

"I was only nine!"

"And *she was six* … and I was nineteen. But numbers only matter when the bill comes due. You left her there. Alone … with *him*." The dead woman was shaking her head. "That's not love, Scotty-bird. That's just plain fear. Seems to me your whole life has been ruled by nothing else. Fitting it should end the same way. So go on. Fly, little bird."

The woman raised a hand and counted on long, slender fingers.

1 …

2 …

3

With a wink, she put both hands together and dove into the dirt as if it were the surface of a pond. For a second, she was gone, then something worse appeared. Scott's eyes shot wide and with tears still streaming down his face, he began to run for the last time.

Behind him, undulating in and out of the earth, was an enormous thing. A serpent in shape, but monstrous in size. Its body was made of dirt and roots and had dark cavernous hollows for eyes. It leapt out of the earth and crashed back down like a breaching whale, though Scott had no such point of reference. All he knew for certain was that he was tired of running.

He stopped, turned. Blood had cascaded out of his cheek and was coloring his neck, soaking the collar of his shirt. The same shirt he'd purchased only because it was the same style worn by Rutherford Hardee. Now he was glad the blood was ruining it.

The dirt snake was coming. Swimming like a sidewinder through the hard packed ground. When it was close enough, it leaped into the air and he let it come. Watched as a third cavern ripped open and yawned, revealing the thick broken roots it had in place of fangs.

Before the impossible thing hit, before it swallowed him whole … Scott Birdwell spat out the last thing he'd ever say. A lifetime of regret in a single word.

"Janey."

EIGHT

Cruelty. It had a way of spreading like a pox. Those who were transformed by it would never again be the same. As the Owl-Man walked, the feathers on his threadbare blanket twisted and fluttered. On this day he felt remorse. Maybe for the first time in two hundred years.

The ugly mound of dirt was nearly as tall as he was. Just existing in the middle of nowhere, as if dumped off the back of a wagon. Only this mound had features others didn't. Amidst the popped strings of root, the surface held the repeating texture of scales. Also of note was the shape. How here and there, the eye would catch a curve—the indication of a sculptor's hand. In all, the mound looked like the tightly coiled body of an enormous serpent. Even if the features were already crumbling away.

The Owl-Man walked around the inexplicable thing. His eyes followed the coils, trying to find a head. As he did this, he almost stepped on something that moved quickly out of the way. The rattlesnake looked angry but offered no retaliation. It simply stared up at the man and soundlessly offered what it knew.

In somber response, the old Indian gave a single, barely perceptible nod.

After that, the snake returned to its usual business and slithered away.

With a weary sigh, the Owl-Man lowered himself to one knee, then he closed his good eye. A hand was extended and made to sweep over the mound. As he searched, the Owl-Man took steps around the thing, while taking care not to touch. Finally, he stopped, opened one eye. It was dark, burdened with many lifetimes of sights that could not be unseen. Without a sound, the searching hand was plunged into the dirt, causing a portion of it to crumble away.

There was part of a face there. The side of a nose and mouth, the distinct curve of a jaw. Whoever the buried man was, he looked placid in his rest. Surely he had seen the end coming, and yet no look of fear contorted the line of his mouth. The Owl-Man did not know if this was a good thing or not, but such things rarely colored his actions. Good, bad—right, wrong. Ugly things happened all the time. In every corner, under every rock. And that was exactly what the dirt mound was—an ugly thing. *His* ugly thing.

From within the earthen flesh of the mound, something small was excavated. A tiny roundish stone. The Owl-Man held it between his thumb and forefinger—turning it so the dirt fell away. The yellow turquoise was a fragment of something older. A shared point for the worlds of spirits and men—one of many. Its surface swirled with yellows, golds and a pale green, but also a kind of magic. Without hesitation, the Owl-Man pushed the thing back where it belonged.

As he shut both eyes, a low humming began to rumble deep in his throat.

Then it stopped.

Abruptly, he turned east. In the direction of the tree and the two shallow graves he had dug with his own hands. For a moment, the Owl-Man considered going there. Though, in the end, he was but an errant breeze. And the wind does not always choose where it goes.

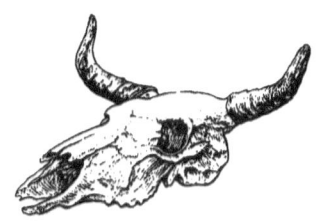

SEWING BEES

(One for Dianne)

The summer was winding down. Soon the leaves would begin to change colors and that would bring other things. Shorter days, cold winds and of course, snow. Anne liked the last part just fine, but the rest gave her stomach that upside down feeling. Winters were hard on the Willamette river. Though not as hard as what had come before.

The Breen family was originally from Nebraska—a place which Anne only knew from stories. She had been a baby when the family made the harrowing trip along the trail across two and a half states and into Oregon. Mama hadn't survived, but Daddy never talked about that. All Anne knew was that she was buried somewhere in Idaho—in a quiet, pretty place with a view of the Rocky Mountains. She hoped to visit the spot one day, though she wasn't sure if she would ever be able to find it. Dennis said he knew how, but Dennis said a lot of things.

Like that, Daddy had decided to move the family because he wanted to be a gold miner, but that wasn't true at all. How could it be? Daddy didn't dig for gold; he worked at one of those big new mills in the city. And every night when he came home, he would talk about how the family was going to move again someday real soon. This time, to the city, so he didn't have so far to walk home every night.

Anne hoped this was true. She loved her little house by the river … but some days, Daddy didn't get home until really late and last night, he didn't come home at all. Dennis kept saying that she shouldn't worry. That Daddy must have slept at the mill so he could start work early today. He said that was how grown-ups made more money when they wanted to save enough for things like a house in the city, or a horse to ride there. To Anne, this sounded true enough. After all, she had wanted a horse for as long as she could remember. Maybe longer. And yet, all day she hadn't been able to shake the feeling that something was indeed wrong.

She kept telling herself that the upside-down feeling in her stomach was because of the weather. Because her favorite time of year was ending … and maybe that was part of it.

For now, she was trying to concentrate on the Willamette. On the silvery fish that swam and lived there. Despite being almost as big as she was, the steelhead were hard to see until they turned. Dennis called that *catching silvers*. Sometimes it hurt to look at them, but it was always fun to see how many big flashes she could count in an afternoon.

"Ah!" she squealed, rubbing her eyes.

"How many was that?"

She turned for the second surprise in a row. "Oh, it's you," she said glumly.

"Well, who else would it be?" asked Dennis, not really expecting an answer. "So how many you got?"

Anne rolled back onto her stomach and plopped her chin back down in her hands. "Four," she said.

"That all?"

"Was almost five, but …" She took a deep breath and huffed it out. Then scanned hungrily the surface of the water.

"But what?" Dennis folded his arms and grinned. "You scare one away with your farts?"

Anne turned in her best impression of being horrified. Her mouth was agape, but she managed to compose herself before responding.

"Only one who does *that* is you."

Dennis laughed and sat down. "There's one." He pointed.

"Aww …" Anne sounded upset. "Don't count if you see it first."

"I know." Dennis's tone was a little softer. He decided to just watch for a while. Even kept a few silvers he caught to himself.

"You worried about Dad?" he said after a while.

Anne's lower lip puffed out, than sort of swallowed the top one. After a few seconds, Dennis could tell she wasn't going to say anything back.

"He's on his way home right now."

She turned fast. Looked her brother right in the eye. "How d'you know?"

"'Cause I do."

Anne rolled her eyes and looked back out over the water.

"You don't know anything."

"I do so!" Dennis rolled on his back. From the way he was facing away from the river, he could see some woods. Just a small thicket that had caught fire the previous summer and left a barren, blackened patch of nothing good.

"Then prove it." Anne pressed. "How do you know Daddy's on his way. Or …" Her voice fractured suddenly. "Or that he's coming back at all."

Dennis frowned. Sat up and glared. "Hey. What'd I tell you? Don't talk like that. Not ever. All right?"

After a few seconds, Anne wiped her cheek and nodded.

Dennis let out a big sigh and laid back down, just staring at those black sticks that had once been trees.

"I know because of what he told me about … the bees."

"What?" Anne looked unconvinced. "What do honey bees have to do with Daddy?"

Dennis put a hand in his pocket, feeling the spool of thread he'd forgotten to put back after mending the seat of his pants.

"Not honey bees, *sewing* bees."

Anne just stared for a couple of seconds. "What are sewing bees?"

"Dad told me not to tell you. He said you were too little and that you'd be scared."

The little girl scrunched her face up. "What? But I'm seven!"

Dennis appeared to consider this. "Yeah … that's true. Maybe you are old enough now. But … I don't want to hear about how you can't sleep for the next week because of nightmares or somethin'."

"You won't." There was a note of excitement creeping into the girl's voice. She crossed her heart with one finger. "Promise. What's a sewing bee?"

With an exaggerated sigh, the boy of fourteen sat up and tossed a glance back at the blackened grove behind them. "They live there. In the burnt-up trees. After the fire last year, Dad warned me about them—said they made a nest. We didn't have them back home in Nebraska, but they got 'em here."

The boy checked to see if he'd captured his sister's attention, finding her positively enraptured. He tried to suppress a smile.

"What Daddy said is ... they find a place that needs mending and then fix it up right again. Like a needle and thread with a torn shirt. That's why they made a nest over there. Get it?"

With wide, wonder-filled eyes, Anne indicated that she did.

"Well anyway." Dennis went on. "According to Dad, sewing bees can be a kind of omen. On the days that they're working, nothing bad is allowed to happen."

"Oh, come on."

"It's true!" The boy threw his hands up. "No rain, no stubbing your toe, or any bad news at all—so long as the sewing bees are working. Mending the world and such." He shrugged. "It's just how it goes."

"Really?"

"Mmm-hmmm." Dennis was nodding and looking a bit smug. "Yup. So there's no way anything bad can happen today. Not to Daddy, or anyone else. *That's* how I know he's on his way."

"Oh." Anne accepted the information with a solemn pout. After almost a minute's worth of churning the story over in her head, she looked over at the blackened grove.

"What do they sound like?"

Dennis seemed startled by this. "What does *who* sound like?"

"The *sewing bees*, dummy." Anne was squinting now, trying to bring into focus details from the thicket she might have been missing. "If you know they're working today, you must have heard 'em. So? What do they sound like?" She shrugged. "Maybe I've heard 'em too—just didn't know it."

"Oh well, you know how regular bees have kind of a humming sound? Well, these are more of a ... a whistle."

170

Anne's eyes widened. "Really? Like a train whistle?"

"More like … the wind over the roof at night. Yeah," One corner of Dennis' mouth tried to get the other one to make a smile. "That's probably why some people call 'em *whistling* bees."

Anne scrunched up her nose. "I like the first name better."

"Me too." Dennis smiled in full. "But … *yeah*, I heard them this morning. You know, when I went fishing for our breakfast. They was just working and whistling away. Sewing up the world, I guess."

Anne sniffed, wiped her nose along the length of one forearm. Then she stood up. "I wanna see 'em."

Before her brother could protest, the girl was off. Running across the patch of green where you could just see the road to Oregon City, straight towards the woods. The part that had burned was only about a half acre. The rest of the trees were still healthy, even if the green leaves had already started turning orange and yellow. Daddy had warned her to never play in that bad section. He said that there was no way of knowing if a burnt up tree was ready to fall until it was halfway on top of you. But this time was different because she wasn't going to play.

As she ran toward the blackened grove, Anne couldn't help but wonder why Daddy hadn't told her about the sewing bees. If all they did was fix things, why would she need to be old enough to know about them?

"Anne, wait!" The boy wasn't fast enough. He shouted again. "Hey! *Dianne Matilda, you come back here!*"

Dennis' calls felt like a low priority. The girl kept running, slowing down only when she'd reached the edge of where she was going. Her breath came fast as she scanned the ugly charred lot. The fire hadn't spread far, but it must have burned hot, considering the skeletal sticks and charcoal dirt before her. If there really were sewing bees, she wondered how long it would take them to fix something like this.

"You gone deaf or somethin'?" Dennis pulled her back. He looked mad. "You know you can't go in there! Ain't safe! Dad told you a hundred—"

"I wanna see the sewing bees!" Anne's expression matched her brother's. "Or hear 'em at least." Tears were welling up in her eyes. Big angry dewdrop tears, just hanging in the corners—swelling, threatening to fall. "I wanna know that Daddy's okay!"

For the next few seconds, emotions hung in the air—flitting between the two young siblings like fireflies. Eventually, Dennis took a deep breath.

"Listen ..." The boy looked around, warily. "There's something else you need to know about the bees. I was gonna tell you before you went running off, but ..." He was still a little out of breath.

"Well?" Anne put both hands on her hips. "Tell me then."

"I'm trying! If you just ..." Dennis licked his lips, his mind again going to the spool in his pocket ... and the needle that was tucked in with the thread. "There's another reason why they call 'em sewing bees. You know how a spider can make its own thread?"

"Yeah, of course. Comes out of its butt."

"Right." Dennis tried not to smile. "Well, sewing bees can do the same thing ... only I don't know where it comes out of. Combine that with their stingers, which are extra long and curved ... and you got yourself some needle and thread. See, that's how they mend stuff."

Anne's expression softened a little. "Makes sense."

"Right. Well, the thing is ... sewing bees aren't too smart. They see an opening and they sew it shut. Now this could be a split section of tree bark, or it could be other things. Things like ... little mouths or even eyelids."

Speaking of eyelids, at that moment, Anne's went wide.

"That's right." Dennis leaned in. "Hearing them working from a distance is one thing, but if you get too close ... if they see your little eyes and mouth and nose holes? Well ... the sewing bees are gonna do what sewing bees do."

Anne swallowed hard. "Even nose holes?"

"Nose, ears ... everything." Dennis nodded.

Now Anne's eyes were practically bugging out of her head. *"Everything?"* She took a step back.

Dennis folded his arms and sighed. "That's why Daddy didn't think you were old enough to know. He said you wouldn't be able to sleep for a whole week."

"And no wonder." Anne and Dennis were both startled by the sudden third voice. "That's one scary story you got there, kid."

The siblings turned sharply to see a strange-looking man emerge out of the green section of the woods. If not for his hair, he would have looked pretty young. Twenty at most. But the hair was all they could see. It was still black on the sides, but the rest was a shocking gray. Gray on its way to becoming full silver.

"Bees that sew your eyes shut?" Gray-hair stepped into the blackened grove on long legs, his boots producing dry crunching sounds with every fall. "You ever heard of anything like that, Snake?"

Suddenly, there was a second man, or boy—because that's really all they were. This one had dark hair and only the very beginnings of a mustache. He looked only a couple years older than Dennis did.

"Can't say as I have," said the boy called Snake, as he shot Anne a smile that froze the blood in her veins. "Sounds scary though."

"That's what I said." The boy with the gray hair snickered. "Dangerous, too. Sounds to me like we all ought to get inside, just to be safe." He scanned the area around the river, but there was nobody else around.

Snake stepped forward, and there was a flat box labeled *crackers* under his arm. As Dennis noticed this, he was aware that the boy had noticed where his eyes had just been.

"You eyeballin' my crackers, kid?"

"What?" Dennis stepped between the still approaching boys and his little sister. "No. Course not."

"Goddamned *sewing* bees." He snickered, the boy with gray hair. "If that ain't the stupidest thing I've ever heard."

"It's not stupid!" Anne snapped back. "My daddy told Dennis all about 'em. They're here to fix the burned part of the forest! You just can't get too close, is all. Because they'll sew you up too on account of they don't know no better."

The two older boys looked at each other, then broke into a round of side-splitting laughter. The dark-haired one was wracked so hard, he dropped the box under his arm. When it hit the ground, the sound was more like coins than crackers. Or maybe bullets.

"*Careful, you idiot!*" Gray-hair looked suddenly murderous. The other scrambled to pick up the box—dusting it off as he did.

"No harm done! See? Didn't even come open." He was grinning the way a little boy grins at his mama when he's done something wrong and hoping not to get whopped.

"Good. See that it don't." Gray-hair's fists unclenched. He took a breath. "Hey, where do you think you're going?"

Dennis and Anne froze in their tracks. They'd only gotten a few steps from the blackened grove.

"We uh ... gotta get home. It's getting late and all. By the time we get back it'll almost be time to make supper." Even as he said this, Dennis knew he was talking too much.

"Supper, aye?" said gray hair, "Well that sounds pretty good to me. What do you say Snake? Shall we accept this gracious invitation?"

"Be happy to." Snake was smiling as if the near-altercation had never happened. "Heck, with how rude that little girl was just now—correcting you and all ... I say they owe us some supper at *least*."

Anne squeezed her brother's arm.

"That's not gonna happen." said Dennis in his bravest voice. "N-now, I don't mean to be rude or nothin' but ... I only caught enough trout for three—that's us and our father. He'll uh ... be coming down that road any minute. We was just waiting for him." Dennis glanced hopefully back towards the road to the city but there was no one on it. He put his hand on his sister's back and ushered her away.

The boy with the gray hair started shaking his head. Then he spit. "Y'know, Snake ... I get the distinct impression that our new friends here are not being completely forthright with us."

"No?" said Snake, pretending to know what the word *forthright* meant.

"Well," shrugged Gray-hair, "Way I figure, *either* they was waiting here for their daddy to come down that road ... or they gotta get home and cook supper for him. Can't rightly be both, now can it?"

Dennis' stomach sank as he heard his own contradiction laid bare. He dared not look down at Anne—not now. Now he had to be strong. To be the protector. If there was only one boy, he'd tell his sister to run home. But with there being two and both being older ... he had no chance. Heck, one would probably make short work of him while the other chased down Anne.

"So ... it's you who's doing the catching *and* the cooking?" The gray-haired boy started walking around the younger kids. "That sounds a lot like providing to me. Almost as if you got no mama waiting for ya."

Dennis turned in a flash of anger. "Just helping where I can. That's all."

Gray-hair leaned in close and he wasn't smiling. In fact, he looked downright insane. "Don't change the subject. I asked about your mama, boy. You got one or not?"

Dennis' face scrunched up, contorted by rage and pain. It all flushed so quickly, he had no power to stop the tears from tracing lines down his dusty cheeks as all the various hurts he had forced down over the last few years were suddenly released in a single naked glare.

"That's what I thought," said Gray-hair, moving even closer and whispering so only Dennis could hear. "My mama's gone too. In fact … you wanna know what's in that box?"

Dennis couldn't help but glance over at it—just for a second. He did want to know, but he shook his head like he didn't.

"That's all her jewelry in there. Well, all the good stuff anyway. Me and Snake just took it. Gold necklaces, pearls, diamond rings, emeralds … all sorts of stuff."

"Y-you … stole from your own mother?" Dennis' words were scant, weightless things.

"Well, yeah, but that was after I found this in the kitchen and put it in her neck."

A thin curved knife appeared. Dennis recognized it as the kind made for slicing fish. He knew because he'd always wanted one—though he definitely didn't want one now.

"The blade was still slick with fish guts when I grabbed it out of the cook's hand. You should have seen her eyes when I did it. I swear, they were like two dinner plates. She tried to talk—probably wanted to point out how my hair wasn't the right color or how I wasn't standing up straight enough while I stabbed her all those times. But … all she could do was stare and make this kind of gurgling sound, ya know?"

Dennis' eye hung on the tip of that filet knife. "Why?"

"Why'd I do it?" the boy with the gray hair practically purred.

"No, I mean … why are you telling me all this?"

After a deep sigh, the boy with the knife stood up straight and shrugged. "Felt like someone ought to know, is all. Someone besides Francis."

"Aw, come on," protested the other boy. "I told you, it's *Snake* now."

Suddenly, Dennis understood something. A notion that might have been well beyond his fourteen years. However old they were, these were bad men. And Mama used to say ... bad men are always gonna do bad things. What you gotta remember is, a lot of 'em aren't very smart.

Dennis cleared his throat. "My sister and I ... we don't care what you done, or what you got in that box. But I won't say that if you let us go, we won't tell nobody about this. Not only would that be a lie, I don't think that's what you want."

The gray-haired boy looked somewhat flabbergasted by this. "And how the hell do you know what I want?"

"It's plain." said Dennis standing a little straighter himself. "You want to be famous. Feared, maybe. My daddy says that's half the reason why folk do bad things in the first place. To get their stories told."

"Yeah?" Gray-hair was frowning, but his posture remained relaxed. "And what's this smartass daddy of yours say about the other half?"

"Well? I guess that's your business. But the thing about a reputation ... it don't build itself. So come on ... let us *help* build yours."

The gray-haired boy was so taken aback, knocked so utterly off his tracks, all he could do was stare and blink. Part of him still wanted to plunge that fillet knife into the smug little bastard in front of him ... but another part, the vainest part, had reservations.

"Dennis, look!" Anne was jumping, pointing at the road. She sounded like it was Christmas morning. "At the top of the hill ... those men—I think they're the sheriff's! And, look! *Look!*"

Dennis turned and he saw the most beautiful sight he could ever have hoped to see. His father was riding beside Sheriff Bill Morgan and two of his men. It didn't look like Daddy was in trouble, but rather being escorted.

When Dennis turned back to the other boys, the dark-haired one had already run off, though the one with the almost silver hair looked like he was still deciding what to do.

"Come on, Pete!" came a shout from through the trees. *"Let's get outta here!"*

Gray-hair looked at Dennis and his expression softened. "Sewing bees," he said, shaking his head before disappearing into the woods.

Anne and Dennis ran straight for the road and waved at their father, who pointed them out to the sheriff. Smiling broadly, he enthusiastically waved back. One of his legs was wrapped up in white cloth. This made Anne turn with a sharp gasp.

"Daddy's leg!" she said, cupping both hands over her mouth.

"I see it," said Dennis, feeling cascading waves of emotion he was trying not to show. "He got hurt—at the mill, maybe. That's why he didn't come home!" Dennis sighed in relief. "Well, whatever happened, I'm sure he's got a story to tell."

Anne's smile was so wide, so pure ... it was as if the previous fifteen minutes had been spent catching silver on the river. And yet, when she looked up, the smile was gone.

"Dennis?"

"Yeah?"

"Should we tell Sheriff Morgan about those boys?"

Dennis stared at the lawman coming down the road, then he looked back to his father.

"Naw." He waved a dismissive hand. "They seemed dumb, but not so dumb as to stick around here with the sheriff on his way. I figure we can't stop 'em from getting famous, but we don't need to help, neither."

The little girl thought on this, then nodded in apparent agreement.

"Dennis?"

"Yeah?"

Anne threw both arms around her big brother and hugged him just as hard as she could. "You were right about 'em. The sewing bees."

"I was?"

"Uh huh. Okay ... maybe I didn't believe you *at first,* but you were right. I know, because nothing bad happened today."

LAST STAND AT THE GRAIN ELEVATOR

The black man and the Mexican may have shared a name, but they weren't kin. At least, not in the traditional sense.

As the two men galloped down the dusty road out of Tulsa, the sun was getting low. And right then, Dwayne Chavez wished he was about anywhere else. His crucifix had worked its way out from between shirt and skin and was flapping on its rawhide cord. It was keeping time—counting every beat of his heart before the big finale. Reaching back, Dwayne caught the stamped tin icon on the first try and gave it a kiss before tucking it away.

He spared an over-the-shoulder peek, keeping his body flat against the silhouette of his Appaloosa gelding. They were still there but, closer than before. Just seeing them made Dwayne's asshole clench. The riders were railroad men—paid enforcers so relentless they almost made one miss the Pinkertons.

"Brother!" called the other Chavez in his native Spanish. "These damned goats aren't giving up! I think this is it. We're out of time."

Steweson Chavez was right about the not giving up part. But the riders weren't goats, they were bulls. Union Pacific's own personal gang of deputized zealots. In Dwayne's experience, they were poorly trained, thinly scrupled, and fully prepared to ride into Hell's own gullet, providing it pleased the rail gods.

With a muffled curse, Dwayne felt the one thing he had long ago promised himself to never feel again. Regret. The taste of it was an acrid burn in his chest, but he savored every fiery lick. After all, what was happening was primarily his fault.

"Holy shit!" called Dwayne, also in *Español* as was their custom. He was pointing in the direction of the setting sun—past a lone cottonwood to a vast swath of prairie. "You see that?"

Stu turned and he did see. Standing there, cast in silhouette by the dying light was a structure of some kind. "Is that a church?" He laughed. "I think the time for prayers has passed, my friend."

Dwayne ignored this. Just kept on staring. The jostling of the ride made it hard to focus, but he was pretty sure what it was.

"There's always time for prayer." He said. "Shoot, I think one of mine has just been answered."

With that, Dwayne made a clicking sound and pulled at the reins. As instructed, the gelding turned from the dusty road to gallop across an equally dusty expanse. Stu followed directly, though his mustang didn't seem happy about the new destination. It shook its head and released a loud fearful squeal.

"I think Juanita wants to stay on the road."

Before saying anything, Dwayne checked once more at the posse who was now damn close to firing distance. "That'd be a short ride, I'm afraid. In another half mile, those bull bastards are gonna be right on top of us. But ... if that's what I think it is," He nodded at the steepled structure. "We'll be able to take some high ground. Maybe even pull one last miracle out of our collective ass."

"*Maybe*?" Stu didn't sound very reassured. "I don't think I can stomach another one of your famous maybes, brother."

Dwayne shrugged. "Well ... I'd say a good *maybe* beats definitely being run down like dogs."

As the so-called Chavez twins thundered past the cottonwood, only one of 'em spared it a glance. The leaves were solid yellow. In a few weeks, they would start falling and that meant the frost wasn't far behind. The year from hell was winding down; Dwayne just hoped he and Stu would live long enough to deliver 1894 a firm kick in the ass.

Just one on the way out. Then he could be done with this feeling. This damned regret.

Now that it was full in his mouth, Dwayne realized he'd been tasting the sensation for months ever since they had joined up with a man by the name of John Wraith. Of course they'd run with outlaws before, but this was different. Few alive had the reputation of old Weeping John and for good reason. He was a real killer. As cruel as they come. The Chavezes had only been with the Wraith gang for six months and Dwayne made sure that he and Stu spent as much of that time out with their snares as possible. The fact of it was, aside from rabbits and opossums and such, neither Chavez had a taste for killing. But facts are facts. A man takes up with someone like Wraith, even gloved hands are liable to get dirty. Maybe too dirty to ever come clean again.

Fortunately, the association had been terminated over the summer, but … the less Dwayne thought about that particular evening, the better. Most nights, just before sleep, that goddamned reek would return. He'd never smelled anything like it before. That inexplicable black maggoty rot inside the bellies of those rabbits. It'd been just about enough to make a man go proper *loco,* and God knows Dwayne had come close.

After another five minutes of hard riding, the two men could plainly see what they were riding towards. What had appeared somewhat like a church complete with steeple looked very different up close.

"A grain elevator?" Stu exclaimed as both horses cantered to a stop.

"You're damn right it is!" Dwayne kissed his tin crucifix. "An honest and true sentinel of the prairie. Come on!" After dismounting, he slipped his 1862 Spencer repeater out of its holster. The man's grin was enormous. In the near dark, his teeth and large eyes practically shone.

His own rifle in hand, Stu looked up at the broad side of the structure—at the words painted in white. They were too weatherworn to make out, but that hardly mattered. He'd never learned to read English, anyhow. Scratching under his hat, he gave a perfunctory glance around the complex. He'd seen such places before, but never in a state like this.

Dwayne was already tying his horse to a hitching post. With a sigh, Stu led Juanita over to do the same, but she fought him every step. At the last second, the mustang reared up, lashing out with her front hooves.

The hit to Stu's shoulder was glancing, but it also hurt like hell. As he stood, gritting his teeth, all he could do then was watch his horse gallop away, in the direction of the setting sun.

"Don't worry. We can round her up later, but first …" Dwayne turned with a maniacal look in his eyes. "We gotta survive the night."

Stu looked back the way they had come. The posse of railroad bulls should have been in sight by now. Should have been, but weren't. He could see the tree they had passed—could see the bare, leafless branches in the last light of what was likely his last day on earth.

"Where are they?" he demanded.

Dwayne turned, and his wide eyes narrowed. "Not far, I can guarantee you that. Maybe in the low light, they didn't see us veer off the road, but they're apt to get wise fast. Come on—you want to waste the couple extra minutes we've been blessed with, or what?"

Stu didn't answer that. He was too busy staring at that cottonwood. At its bare, leafless branches. "Something about this place is off." Stu rubbed his throbbing shoulder. "Juanita could tell. She's never acted like that before."

"Juanita is a *horse!*" Dwayne scoffed, storming off toward the main structure. "Horses get spooked all the time."

"Yeah … sometimes by things that men are too stupid to see. Rattlesnakes in the grass." He trailed off.

Dwayne turned on his heel. "You want to follow your darling Juanita? Huh? Well, go on! I'm staying right here and fixing this mess."

"This mess?" Stu's frustration over the follies of the last hour was rising. "You mean the decision to steal a payroll box off the desk of a Union Pacific foreman without even consulting your partner of seven years? Deciding on the spot that the Chavez twins were gonna add train robbery to the list of crimes we're already wanted for? Tell me, *brother* … is *that* the fucking mess you're referring to?"

Dwayne grabbed Stu by the collar and pulled him close. For the next few seconds, the two so-called twins stared each other down, though ultimately, neither one had the stomach to do actual violence on the other. The Chavezes were kin. If not by blood, then by chance. Like it or not, they were all each other had.

"Shit." Dwayne relinquished his hold. "Look … I've made some questionable decisions this year, I'll grant you that. But if you ever trusted me in the past ... trust me now. Just one more time." He pointed to the top of a building that looked like the bastard son of a church and a barn. "There's always a ladder that goes to the top. You see that window?"

Frowning, Stu nodded.

"That's where we'll make our stand. In this light, them bulls won't even see us until it's too late. And if they want to come up and get us, they'll have to use the same ladder we did to get up there. It's the perfect bottleneck!"

Stu's grimace lessened. He sighed. "Okay, okay. It's not the worst plan you've ever had."

"Better than staying on the road?"

"I guess."

Forgetting what had just happened, Dwayne clapped Stu on the shoulder then immediately felt bad.

"Shit. Sorry!"

Right then, the scowl on the face of the Mexican looked deep enough to strip paint off the side of a barn. Through clenched jaws, he hissed, "What if they light the place on fire?"

The question hung in the air for a few seconds. Long enough for Dwayne to look back at the road. There was still no sign of the posse.

"Well ..." Dwayne licked his lips. "Then we will most definitely burn and die. But as last stands go, I'd take that over being run down by a bunch of white folk. We're *free men*, brother. Free to live and die on our own terms and no one else's."

"Our terms?" In Stu's voice was a note of sadness. After another sigh, he made a flourish with the end of his rifle. "Well? Lead the way, *boss*."

That last word, *jefe* ... it was one Steweson reserved for special occasions. It was a gibe—a well-earned, tailor-made curse word and its recipient recognized it as such. Right then, despite all his bluster and bravado, the man could feel a familiar feeling creeping again. That damned regret was scritch-scratching right at the base of his throat. It wanted his full attention.

"They weren't all white. Not all of 'em."

Dwayne turned with a look of confusion.

"The bulls," Stu went on. "One of them was an Indian. Biggest one I ever saw."

For the next several minutes, Chavez didn't say a thing.

Whatever Dwayne wanted to admit, the dilapidated complex was unsettling as hell. As the men drank in the wooden structure more and more questions arose. Fact of it was, the thing looked a hundred years old. This was, of course, impossible, since grain elevators of this type had only been around for closer to thirty. Still, there was no denying their lying eyes. The wood was sun-bleached and had gone to splinter. Then there was the paint.

Dwayne looked up at the faded letters, and quite without meaning to, his mind began to drift back home to Omaha. Suddenly, he missed his father more than he had in years.

A second-generation fur trapper, Jim Chavez was a decent man and had taught his son how to ride and hunt and how a simple stick and length of wire could be turned into rabbit stew. More importantly, though, Jim had taught his son how to read, and how the painted letters on a grain elevator always spelled out the name of the company that built and ran it, along with the nearest town. Glorified signposts—that's all elevators were to Jim Chavez. And it had gotten so you couldn't go ten miles without seeing one.

"Do you know what it says?" asked Stu.

Dwayne shook his head. "It should say TULSA somewhere but, nothing looks close. I don't know. Maybe it—" He stopped talking.

Beneath the distant panicked cries of Stu's horse seemed to be another sound. A rustling, muffled, scratching sound. Something about it was deeply unsettling.

"You hearin' that?" asked Dwayne.

Stu licked his lips, gave a nod. Then, in a low voice, he said, "When I was a boy … my family worked on a farm in Nuevo León. One summer … some rats got into the silo. Ate all the corn. It was many weeks before we discovered this. I've … never seen so many in one place before." He shuddered in disgust. "All those rats … they sounded just like this." Stu looked back to the road and went silent for a few seconds. "Brother?"

he said in a low voice.

"Yeah?"

"Where the hell are the goats?"

Dwayne turned to look back the way they had come. Part of him wanted to browbeat his friend for having the nerve to complain about what was surely supernaturally good luck. Instead, he offered a simple, deflated response.

"I don't know."

And that was the God's honest truth. For the life of him, Dwayne Chavez couldn't imagine why their pursuers weren't halfway up their asses already. Right then a cold sensation ran up the man's spine. Suppressing a shiver, his eye hung on the cottonwood. Under the moon, he could plainly see that its branches were bare. Just as bare as anything.

"Come on." He said. "Let's stick to the plan. If the bulls don't catch up to us by morning, I'd say we're in the clear. Maybe then we can keep going north. Make it to Nebraska." He paused for a few seconds. "I ever tell you that's where I was born?"

Stu smiled. "Once or twice."

"Right." Dwayne looked at his boots, scratched the back of his head. "Be nice to see it again, is all."

Like all of its kind, the main building was divided into two parts. Most eye-catching was the tall, two story structure that from far off had approximated a church. This, Dwayne knew, housed a vertical conveyor belt, lined with scoops that went all the way to the top. It was this marvel of modern engineering that gave the elevator its name. Connected to this was a smaller section—a single-story attachment just large enough to drive a wagon through.

"I worked at an elevator one summer—back in Omaha. Was probably just twelve or thirteen at the time. You see those?" Dwayne pointed out a series of deep grooves in the earth. "Wagon tracks. Farmers from all around would come in like this—just drive right in through here." He nodded at the interior of the smaller building—right through the gaping entrance. "They'd stop at the far end. That's where I'd be. My job was to help shovel out all that hard-grown merchandise out of the farmer's wagon and into the … the …" He thought for a second. "I don't know how to say it in Spanish. Hole? Ditch? We called it the *pit*."

This last word was said in English.

"*El hoyo.*" Stu offered.

"*Hoyo*, right." Dwayne switched back to Spanish again. "Well … the pit is kinda like a basement, but it's got a sloped floor. The incline is so all the grain will naturally gather at one end, allowing the scoops to—"

For the second time in so many minutes, Dwayne fell sharply silent. The men were inside now and that rustling scratching sound they'd first heard outside was louder than ever. The men approached the far end of the small building and looked down. Into a large section of the floor, a metal grate had been installed. Beyond this, only two things could be determined. Beneath them was a perfect sort of darkness and the sound. The Chavezes looked at each other and then back down.

Looking rather green, Stu backed away. "I told you, brother. It's just like in Nuevo León. Rats … they must have gotten into the grain." The corners of his mouth turned in disgust. "Probably thousands down there."

Dwayne crossed his chest, shook his head. "Can't be." He said. "No way, grains only last six months—a year maybe. *Look* at this place! The last crop this elevator moved must be decades gone. If that sound is rats … what the hell have they been eating all this time?"

As the unanswerable question hung in the air, the distant screams of Stu's horse slid into the moment like a cold knife. The Chavezes backed away from the pit in unnerved silence.

Moving almost completely in reverse, they meandered back to the center of the room. On the inner wall, there was machinery—rusted metal scoops all mounted to a thick vertical belt that ran up into the top level of the structure. Next to this, a ladder led to the second floor via a narrow shaft.

Dwayne turned—his large eyes shining like twin moons. "See? What'd I tell you? A perfect bottleneck." He looked up and tested the first rung. "I just hope these are strong enough to hold."

As Dwayne ascended into the darkness above, the Mexican rubbed his aching shoulder.

"Sí," he answered distantly.

The fact was, Stu and Juanita had been together almost as long as the Chavez twins had. She'd always been pretty hard to spook, but here? It was like the whole damn place was a snake on the trail. And where in the name of God and the devil were those railroad bulls?

Back on the road, the men couldn't have been more than a half mile behind. Even in the weird light of dusk, there was no way those trigger-happy sons of bitches could have missed seeing where him and Dwayne went. The prairie was wide and it sloped down to where the elevator stood. A blind man would have seen them make for this place. This dilapidated grain elevator in the middle of nowhere that had apparently made his horse go insane.

None of it made any sense. Cupping a hand over one ear, he listened for the mustang's cries, but could hear nothing beyond the now omnipresent chatter coming from that damned pit.

"All right. I'm up." called Dwayne from above. "Your turn."

The ascent on the ladder was a slow, stressful, claustrophobic affair. More than once, Stu thought the rotten old rungs were gonna break off in his hand. By the time he made it to the top, his fingers and palms had collected an impressive amount of splinters.

"I keep telling you to get some gloves." Dwayne was already at the window, just looking.

Stu scowled, then began working a splinter with his teeth. "Yeah, yeah." He spit. "Is there anyone coming?"

Dwayne took his time in answering. "I don't see a thing." He said, almost dejected. "Except Speckles."

The Appaloosa was right where they'd left him and seemed no worse for wear. In fact, he was lying flat on the ground. Sleeping soundly as if he were in the most familiar place in the world.

"There's something wrong with that thing." said Stu. "Horses don't sleep like that."

"Well, Speckles does." Dwayne sounded defensive. "Sometimes."

"Sometimes as in by a campfire or in a livery, sure ... but *here*?" Stu scoffed. "Seems *Speckles* is the only one who doesn't sense how off this place is."

"Maybe, he just knows something we don't."

"Yeah? Like what?"

Dwayne scratched at his unshaven jawline. "Can't believe I'm gonna say this, but I think we lost those railroad idiots. Somehow they must have missed us changing direction and just kept going. Hell—they're probably knee-deep in Bird Creek by now. I can't explain it, brother but ... I think we actually got away."

Looking unconvinced, Stu spit out another sliver.

Dwayne's smile faded. He couldn't see the road due to the slope of the land, but he could picture everything just as it had been. Tulsa, that foreman's desk, the cash box. Suddenly, a color flashed in his mind's eye. Bright yellow. The chosen hue of lemons and flowers and the plump yolks of chicken eggs. Leaves turn that color sometimes ... just before the frost hits.

Dwayne craned his head out the window but the angle prevented him from seeing the tree. Suddenly, he had to know. Which was it? Covered in yellow leaves or naked as a Jewish whore on Christmas? It couldn't very well be both.

"Let's, uh ... look around." Dwayne dragged himself from the window. "Maybe there's something up here we can ..."

The way it hung there, Stu couldn't tell if the statement was finished or not. After a while, he decided that it was.

The second floor was small. In the center, a massive pulley system had been installed which took up most of the space. Stopping at a control panel, Stu pressed the green button and then the red—neither did a damn thing.

"Probably hasn't worked in years," said Dwayne, already standing behind the only other notable object in the room. The surface of the desk was covered in strewn papers, but there were a few drawers.

"Anything good?" asked Stu.

The last drawer was slammed shut in a puff of dust. Dwayne held up an old pocket watch, indicating that he had. The brass surface was mired in tarnish so thick, it took effort to pry it open.

"It's busted." Dwayne tossed the timepiece, which landed on the wooden desk in a loud, jarring *knock*. "Seems the only time in this place is that which we brought."

This seemed a pretty weird thing to say, but Stu was in no mood to say as much. Spotting a map on one wall, he meandered over, placing his hand on the old paper. Even if he'd learned to read English, the ink was even more faded than the paint outside. Along the bottom there was what looked like a logo, but it didn't look familiar. Fingers began to trace the lines that might have represented state lines of maybe railroad tracks.

"Is this even Oklahoma?" Stu stepped back, narrowed his eyes. "Nothing here looks familiar."

Dwayne shrugged. "Who knows? All these papers must be older than dirt. I can't read a one."

Just then a distant horse cry peeled out of the outer dark. The men looked at each other, then pretended to be looking anywhere else.

"Hearing her carry on like that ... is *killing* me." Stu said, meaning every word. "It's like she snapped. Like this place made her go insane. Is that even possible?"

"Doesn't matter," Gripping his repeater with both hands, Dwayne plodded back to the open window. "What *does* is that from all the way out there, we can hear her just fine."

Stu looked less confused than wounded.

"What I mean is," Dwayne went on. "If a posse of railroad bastards rides up on us in the middle of the night, we're gonna hear them too. Even from up here. Make sense?"

Not particularly wanting to, Stu nodded.

"All right then, here's what I'm thinking. The two of us take a cue from Speckles down there and snag some shut eye. We'll do it in shifts. Two hours at a go. Whoever's awake doesn't leave that window. You gotta piss? Use the window. Gotta shit? Figure it out." Before going on, Dwayne produced a brass pocket watch and tossed it to Stu. "First light, we head north. We'll stay off the roads and take our time until we cross into Kansas."

"Kansas?" Stu checked the watch, than snapped it shut. "No sanctuary in Kansas, brother. Or did you forget that the Chavez twins are wanted there too."

"Not for robbing a Union Pacific bankroll, they ain't." Dwayne's expression turned regretful. "Look ... I've screwed up a lot this year. I know it. But don't we always end up okay?"

No response.

Pursing his lips, Dwayne took out his crucifix and crossed his chest. "Hell with you. Jesus knows I'm right. He's been watching out for us all night. I can feel it."

"You always say that."

"Well it's true! How else do you explain this miraculous getaway? Huh?"

When no response came again, Dwayne spit out the window. "You know what? I hate when you get like this. We should be in a full blown firefight by now. Now that's just the facts. Instead, we're looking at a quiet night of rest and all you can do is complain!"

The silence which stretched after this grew for a while, though it was eventually cut by the distant squeal of a mustang.

"You call *that* quiet?"

Dwayne had *had* it. His eyes were so wide, they looked ready to bulge the rest of the way out and plop onto his cheeks. He kicked something that skidded across the floor. Then, bringing out the grip of his 1862 Spencer repeater, he looked about as far away from Steweson Chavez as was humanly possible.

After standing with his arms crossed for a couple of minutes, Stu shook his head. Here they were again. "Fine," He said after releasing a sigh. "But I'm taking the first shift. You always fall asleep."

"I do not!" Dwayne fired back.

"Yeah, okay." Stu snickered. After picking up an overturned chair from behind the desk, he walked it over and set it down by the window. "All yours," He said as another distant cry twisted in his gut. "I'm gonna be awake anyway."

Dwayne looked down at the chair, desperately wanting to turn down the offer. Then he glanced out the window. He'd never admit it, but it was a bit strange seeing his horse lying like that. All sprawled out and flat on the ground. In fact, it almost looked like the animal was …

"All right …" Dwayne shook away the thought. "I'll have a sit. Just for a minute, mind you. But if you're up, I'm up."

Five of those minutes later, Stu was listening to the familiar grinding noise that had plagued his nights for the past seven years. It was a sound not unlike those big two-man saws lumberjacks use to cut down trees in the pacific northwest. Or at least, what he imagined they sounded like. Truth was, he'd never made it that far.

It didn't take long before Dwayne was dreaming strange dreams.

He could see golden leaves, no—golden *hair*. A woman he'd known years ago in Redford. The prettiest he'd ever been with by far. He could see her plump face and easy smile—still smell the wildflowers in that vase on her side table. Thing was ... they smelled wrong. Not like flowers at all, but closer to the sharp odor of a freshly nicked intestine. Jarred by this thought, Dwayne looked at the woman again, but she was no longer such. Standing there in that quaint Missouri bedroom was a woman-sized rabbit, standing on long womanly legs. It was hairless, skinless. Worst of all, the foot-long gash in its belly was leaking black oil and maggots which, he supposed, accounted for the smell. Dwayne stood frozen in that small bedroom of long ago. Watching helplessly as the hideous rabbit-thing opened its mouth to cough up a single word.

"*Dwayne!*"

Someone was shaking him.

"Hey look!" Came the elated voice of Stu Chavez. "Wake up! Look, damn it!"

In one fluid motion, Dwayne fell, landed hard and shot fully back to his feet. His eyes were wide, his heart, galloping like a crazed mustang. Blinking the weight of sleep away, he glared out the window, focusing on what Stu wanted him to see.

"She's come back!" Stu was so excited, he was all but in hysterics.

Sure enough, standing like a rodeo statue beside the slumbering appaloosa, was Juanita. The buckskin beauty with a black mane and black legs was staring out into the darkness—transfixed by the rolling plains beyond. Dwayne had never seen a horse stand so still in all his life.

"Hey, where are you going?" He turned then, realizing that Stu was about to climb down the ladder.

"Where do you think?" Stu hit back, smiling. "I have to see if she's okay. Maybe she'll let me tie her to the post this time!"

"You think that's a good idea?" Dwayne sounded like he, for one, did not. "What if those railway men come and—"

"Come on now. You said it yourself. Those motherless goats are probably miles from here. Besides, if they magically appear in the next ten minutes, I still got you up here, don't I?"

No response.

"Well, don't I?"

Dwayne frowned. "Yeah. I mean … of course you do."

"Then quit complaining! I'll be right back."

Not wanting to, Dwayne gave a nod and watched the closest thing he ever had to a brother disappear beneath the floor. The hollow sounds of boots on wooden rungs grew steadily more distant, until they stopped.

"Damn it."

Licking his lips, Dwayne rushed to the window and waited. After only a few seconds, he frowned. Spat outside and watched it fall. Why was he so damn nervous? Hell, the window was facing northeast— same direction the road went. And things were just like Stu had said … if those railroad bulls did show up, he would probably see them coming.

"Though it'd serve you right if they rounded the place and approached from the south, you goddamned idiot." Dwayne began picturing the tin box he'd shoved into his saddle bag back at the railroad encampment. "Who do you think you are, making off with a damn payroll box in broad daylight without even the slightest notion of a plan? That sounds more like Jim Jack *Hodge* than Dwayne Chavez."

With a long, weary sigh, he pinched the bridge of his nose and blinked down through the window. Juanita had yet to make a sound or move as much as a single hoof. She was still just standing there with her back to the grain elevator.

"What the hell are you looking at out there?" Dwayne wondered this under his breath, then shouted, "Hey! You down there or what?" He didn't like this. Not one damned bit. "Come on. How long's it take to walk fifty feet?"

But the moonlit yard did not answer this or any of the man's questions. Instead, it kicked up an unrelated rumble of thunder. Rain—that was about the last thing they needed.

"Damn it!" Dwayne kicked the wall. Then, a few seconds later, he kicked it again—hard enough to free dust from the rafters. In the fury of the moment, he raised his Spencer and took aim at the mustang. "Damn it, *Juanita*." After lowering the weapon, Dwayne thought of something his old man used to say about times like this. Times it seemed every uncontrollable thing was conspiring against you.

Just breathe. Good air in, bad air out. Control what you can.

Dwayne took a deep breath, than slowly let it out. To his surprise, the act made him feel better. After repeating this a few more times, he opened his eyes with new clarity.

"Aw hell," he said with a sigh. "He's probably just takin' a shit."

As he said this, Dwayne's words felt not only true, but *obviously* so. Of course that's where Stu had gone. To go take care of some business he'd probably been pinching off for the last hour. And, considering his track record, the man could be gone for twenty minutes or more as he dealt with the matter at hand. Feeling markedly better, Dwayne sat down in his chair, leaned back and put up his boots.

He never meant to shut his eyes. Couldn't even remember doing so. And yet, the moment he opened them, Dwayne could feel a very familiar sensation in his bowels that told him he was missing something. Time had assuredly passed and he had no idea how much.

He stood up fast, sending the chair back across the floor. Hands padded pockets, but then he remembered. Stu had the watch. He had taken it with him when he went down to check on his stupid horse.

"Stu?" he shouted. "Steweson!"

Outside looked much as it had with one notable difference. Juanita remained just as still as if she'd been carved out of marble but she was facing the other direction. Now standing directly over the prostrate appaloosa and glaring directly up at Dwayne as he returned the favor.

"*The goddamned bulls.*" He started trying to piece together a scenario that made sense. "They must have come up real quiet and nabbed him." Dwayne's eyes redirected to the hole in the floor which he knew to be the only way out. "Now they're just waiting for you to come down *because they know that climbing that ladder would be suicide.*"

He rushed over to the opening. Tried in vain to pull out some kind of information out of the shadows below.

"I know you're down there!" he shouted, this time in English. "Listen! The money is in the Appaloosa's saddle bag."

No response.

"Just take it and go. Hell, take the horses too, for all I care. I give my word as a Christian, I won't shoot, all right? Just leave us be."

Still nothing.

"I swear to God, If you've hurt my brother, I'll gut every damn one of you like a ..." But Dwayne trailed off. Couldn't decide what he was gonna gut 'em like. A fish? A snake? A horrible skinless amalgam of rabbit and whore?

It didn't matter. Words seldom did because actions were the thing. Especially the sort that led you to an untimely end at some old prairie sentinel over a matter of a hundred dollars. Less, maybe. Fact was, in his haste, Dwayne hadn't had the chance to count.

Holding onto his Spencer repeater, he dropped onto his back so one ear was right next to the ladder shaft. That's when it reached him. The sound. That rustling, muffled, scratching sound. The same one that'd reminded Stu of rats when they'd heard it earlier. Now it was so loud, it sounded like waves crashing on the seashore.

Only it damn sure was no such thing.

Again Dwayne looked down into the unknown. Whatever else, Stu was down there somewhere. And he and Stu were family. Brothers. All the posters even said so.

The ladder was not so much climbed as it was taken. Dwayne landed hard on ground level as a tin- stamped Jesus dangled on the outside of his shirt. Right away, he moved flat against a wall, trying desperately to use the diffused moonlight to its fullest. Every second that passed seemed to last whole minutes as he went. Stepping closer and closer to the same end of the structure that he and Stu had come through originally.

Upon reaching the opening, Dwayne poked the end of his rifle out first. After no shots were fired, he peeked his head out—fully expecting to see Steweson bound and gagged with the end of a rifle to his head. But there was no one else around. Neither of the horses looked to have been disturbed, but he'd check on them later.

About halfway down the backside of the grain elevator, he noticed something on the ground. Grooves, like those carved by wagon wheels he'd pointed out to Stu earlier, but nowhere near as old. In fact, these looked damn near fresh—almost like something had been dragged from one end of the building to the other. Dwayne's eye followed the inexplicable lines—saw how they rounded the corner up ahead. It was then that a distant flash caught his eye.

Way out in the middle distance, a bolt of lightning had struck out over the plains. And a few seconds later, it happened again. Only these discharges weren't shooting down at the horizon but rather, along it. Parallel to the earth itself. And if that wasn't enough, the light also happened to be a startling blood-red.

"Well," Dwayne shook his head as a peel of thunder rumbled through his bones. "I guess that figures."

Just breathe. Again came the voice of Jim Chavez. *Good air in, bad air out.*

Dwayne almost laughed at this. He wanted to tell his daddy that in this damned place, the regular rules didn't apply. That here, bad air was the only kind there was. But Jim Chavez was dead.

Dwayne followed the grooves to the end of the wall practically in a trance. For some reason or other, caution no longer seemed a worthy use of time or energy. Regret was pointless too and so he spat the last of his out. After turning the corner, the incessant rustling was so loud, Dwayne could feel it pressing into the soft spots of his skull. He looked left, then right—checking ahead, behind and even above, but there were no damned railroad bulls. Just him, some sideways lightning and *that goddamned sound.*

Of that maddening racket, he didn't know if it was being made by rats or worms or hands sifting through wet maggots. All Dwayne could say for certain was that it was filling him up. Souring every finger, toe and testicle like week-old milk. The repeater fell slack, swinging around on its strap as hands were raised to the man's ears.

Shambling like a man only half awake or maybe half alive, Dwayne Chavez made his way to the edge of the grain pit. Hands pressing on the sides of his head, he squinted down and sneered. Something was definitely moving down there and, by God, whatever it was had taken Stu. Dwayne didn't need to look at the man-sized grooves or where they led to know that. Right then his eyes were rimmed both with veins and the fires of righteous vengeance. They bulged as Dwayne's hands flew from the sides of his head. In one fluid motion, those large, calloused hands wrapped around a swinging 1862 repeater and fired over and over again into the pit.

The thing about Spencers was the rate of fire—even said so in the catalogs. While your standard muzzleloader could discharge one to three rounds a minute, a Spencer Carbine .50 caliber could easily fire twenty or more. As Dwayne unleashed everything he had, the bitter regret he'd been tasting for months was gone. In its place was something worse. Something hot and fiery. A need for revenge.

Of what had made its home in the pit of that old grain elevator, the man only received glimpses. Brief flashes of hideous, incongruent things no sane mind was built to endure. There were bulbous eyes the size of billiard balls. Too many to ever count, with oblong pupils like those of a goat. And there were snapping things too, like noseless dog jaws mounted on the ends of long pink snakes. Again and again Dwayne pulled the trigger as the muzzle flashes revealed more of what had taken up residence in that old grain pit. In the time it took the man to fire nine rounds, he came to understand that all the unspeakable things in the pit were actually just *one thing*. One ugly, goddamned son-of-a-bitching thing. The smell of it was in his nose—all black and maggoty and familiar, though right then he couldn't place why.

If there was one bit of good news, it was that he didn't have long to bear his terrible discovery. Because, after nine bullets were fired into the darkness, that tenth one banged off the metal grate and went straight into his brain. As blood dribbled out the back of his skull, the eyes of Dwayne Chevez were wide as windows. Perhaps by the grace of God himself, the man was dead before he hit the ground.

Sensing its moment, the thing in the grain pit wasted no time. Lashing out and latching on with those dog-faced tentacles, it pulled on its second meal in so many hours.

Bathed in the pristine light of morning, a pair of riders crested a nearby hill. The larger of the two thrust out his hand, causing his partner to redirect his gaze. Without a word, the men urged their horses over to the ramshackle old building complex.

The smaller man (who was actually quite tall compared with most who weren't his partner) climbed off his horse, then began to approach the structure. At first, it was hard to tell what the building had been. There was no longer a roof—just some framing, part of a couple walls and not much else.

"A barn?" inquired One Horse Tom.

"I suppose," whispered Patch Briar, absently scratching the hidden line of his jaw. In the months spent working for Union Pacific, his beard had adopted some gray around the edges. "Not that I can see the sense in erecting one in some remote valley with no room for crops or livestock. But ... I don't rightly know what else to call it."

The large Choctaw man dismounted, responding with another of his typical grunts.

"Where do you think we are?" Patch called back. "I figure it's been about an hour since we all split up at Bird Creek. Must be pretty close to Arkansas by now."

"Mmm." Tom squinted at the surrounding hills. "This is Cherokee land."

Without another word, the men wandered off in different directions. Both taking in what remained of the ghost structure. Patch continued on inside, his eyes darting about—attempting to decipher what exactly they were seeing.

"Hey, there's some machinery in here," Called Patch. "But I'll be damned if I know what kind. Everything here looks not just old, but

… too old."

One Horse Tom turned with a raised eyebrow.

"Well," Patch went on, "Even left to the whims of the elements, it'd take this stuff a long time to reach a state like this. Hundred years or something. Shit. One kick and what's left of this good Pennsylvania steel would probably turn to sand. I call that a mite inexplicable—you?"

No response.

Pushing some boards aside with the toe of one boot, Patch revealed a rusted grate in the floor. "Also," he said, mostly to himself, "this is no barn."

Once enough debris had been cleared off, he could see the grate was of a decent size. Six feet across by his guess. Bizarrely, a corner of it had been torn open, as if someone had left a lit stick of dynamite there just to see what might happen. The hole was ragged and ugly—big enough to crawl through. Scratching the line of his jaw, Patch bent down and peered inside.

"*Patch.*" The booming voice of the Indian caused Patrick Briar to flinch. He was glad no one was around to see.

"*Yeah?*" His voice cracked as he shouted back.

"Come see," Said Tom. "You're not gonna believe this."

Patch stepped outside, not sure what to expect. Tom was standing there, stroking the neck of a horse he did not immediately recognize. It was a mustang—buckskin with black mane and black legs. She was wearing a saddle and was just standing there, leaning into the attention. Patch's eyes lowered then and went wide.

"What the hell?"

The second horse was mostly white with black speckles on its hind quarters. It was lying flat on the ground, all rotten and covered with flies.

"Jesus H. Christ." Patch adjusted his hat. "These are their horses."

"Mmm." One Horse Tom nodded.

"Same ones we were chasing last night."

"Looks like."

"So how come that one looks like it's been dead for a damn week?"

Instead of answering, Tom began checking the saddle bags. First the mustang, then the Appaloosa. "You see anyone in there?" He asked.

"No one." Picturing the man-sized hole he'd uncovered, Patch's hand slid to his still holstered Colt Paterson. "Ain't nothing round here but stories we're better off not knowing."

"Hmm." From the Appaloosa's bag, Tom pulled out a tin box with the word PAYROLL printed on the side.

"Well, holy shit." Patch slapped his own forehead. "Is it all there?"

Tom handed the box over for Patch to count. After doing so twice, he closed the lid, latched it. After a few seconds, his jaw was still hanging open.

"One hundred and seventeen dollars. And you wanted to double back to Tulsa."

The Indian gave a shrug. Then he stood up and led the mustang to where his own horse was waiting.

Sparing another glance for the fly-riddled corpse, Patch Briar couldn't help but shudder. Though there was no grasping the how, it truly was the same animal he and the other railroad men had nearly ridden down less than twelve hours earlier. Right before the animals and their riders had disappeared into thin air.

He looked down at the payroll box. The coveted prize he was being paid so poorly to return. If they left now, it would be early afternoon by the time they reached Tulsa. Then again ... the Arkansas line couldn't be far.

"Hey, Tom,"

"Hmm?"

"You ever been to Fayetteville?"

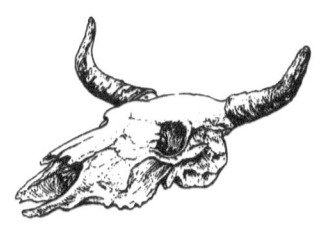

THE REST OF
THE WICKED

ONE

In the last light of a blood-red day, two men stood before five graves. One speared the head of his shovel into the ground and proceeded to lean on it like a crutch. The man's heart was still running—still pumping poison lightning into his limbs. As it happened, the day had gone about as wrong as any he'd known ever had. Just about the only blessing he could count was that he and his partner were, miraculously, still above the dirt.

The man had one of those names you either couldn't quite recall, or remembered forever. Theseus Nil had a long face and dark hair that was even longer. He had stubble that started at his upper lip and traveled all the way down to his neck. Right then, as he leaned on his shovel, he started musing on how badly he wanted a shave and a bath. To wash off what had happened, and then dump the water in a hole six feet deep, or twenty-six, or a thousand. Problem was, the ordeal wasn't over. He and his partner had to go back and claim what was theirs. Otherwise the men they'd just put in the ground had died for nothing.

"Theo."

The voice came from up high. Theo turned—squinted into the sun and let the silhouette of his oldest friend come into focus. Bram Ramsey. The second man was about the same height as the first, but thicker around the arms and across the chest. He wore a dirty plaid shirt, red suspenders and a black beard that was going gray in the middle.

The two men went all the way back to Huston, where they'd been deputized on the same day by Sheriff Hank Dunner. Admittedly, it was strange to see Ramsey already in his saddle. Though that felt like a small matter considering where he was aiming the barrel of his Winchester Yellowboy.

"Sorry to do this to ya, buddy."

Theo narrowed his eyes and sneered.

"It's been a good ride. It has. But … I can't do this anymore."

"Bram," Theo could hear the unsteadiness in his own voice and hated himself for it. For not being stronger in this of all moments. "What the hell are you doing?"

"What I gotta." Ramsey smiled, but there was no joy in the expression. "Now come on. Don't make this any harder. The last thing I wanna do is shoot you, but I will."

"Is that a fact? What for?" Theo's mind was still reeling. Still trying to make sense of a situation he never could have predicted. "The *money*? That's what this is about? You pointing that iron at me over a goddamned payday?"

"Not just money, Theo—a gauldurned *fortune*. More than we've ever seen before or are like to ever again. Don't you get it? This payday is *a way out*. Out of Texas, and of this whole dirty son of a bitching life we carved ourselves into the side of. But … only if it's split one way."

Theo's face was a mask of naked outrage. "If events had gone to plan, we were gonna split everything seven ways. What? Were you planning on betraying all of us? Shooting every man we just spent the last three hours putting in the ground?"

"No," Bram answered regretfully. "No, I was not. But … a man can get a lot of thinking done in three hours—especially if he goes through what we just did. And you should know, buddy … if it were any of them boys standing where you are now, I wouldn't have bothered with this conversation."

"Well, ain't that just *damn* brotherly of you." Theo frowned, casting a glance over at his horse and the Spencer repeater holstered on the side.

"Don't even think about it." Bram's voice was grim as he raised the business end of his Yellowboy. "All right. Here's what's gonna happen next. You see that ridge?" He reverse-nodded at the distant rock formation. "You keep that to your left. There's a town out that way. If you start walking now, you should reach it by morning. When you do ... I suggest you do us both a favor and forget all this."

"Forget?!" Right then, Theseus Nil looked mad enough to roar, but his voice was low. "You're telling me my only reward for over three years of hardship, tracking and having to smell your farts every night is to get robbed blind ... and you want me to just forget it? I saved your hide twice, you son of a bitch—*and that was just today.* You want me to forget all that too?" Theo spit on the ground. "Naw ... you ought to shoot me now because so long as I'm breathing, I'm thinking of nothing but this. Nothing but you, *Abraham.*"

Ramsey looked dejected. With a sigh, he looked down and pulled out a revolver. The cylinder was flicked open and six rounds were banged out into his hand. These he considered carefully, almost seeming to weigh them. A few seconds later, he tossed the empty revolver, which landed with a dull thud in the dirt. Then, after putting half the rounds in his pocket, he closed his fist on the rest.

Making a clicking sound with his teeth, Ramsey urged his horse over to Theo's. Taking the reins of his former friend's animal in hand, he turned halfway back to the man who was standing, seething in a fog of betrayal and rage. Ramsey fished out something from one of the saddlebags and tossed that in the dirt too. When it hit, Theo sneered at his own half-empty canteen, but had nothing to say about it.

"Hey," Ramsey said as if he were reminiscing about better times. "What was that thing your daddy used to always tell you? Something about some Greek monster. What was it? The myna bird?"

"The *minotaur,*" Theo growled back the word.

"The minotau, right. Body of a man with a bull's head on his shoulders." After Theo gave no response to this, Ramsey shrugged. "Sounds like the original *cow*-boy to me."

"It's just a dumb story." Theo's voice was calm, but trembling around the edges. "Don't know why Pop liked it so much but he did. Said I'd find it one day—that great ugly monster and kill the thing." He snickered, shook his head. "Course, being as minotaurs are beasts of the fictional variety, I always assumed old Pop was being metaphorical. Now, though? Seems I've been riding beside the damn thing for years without even knowing it."

"I ain't your *mine-a-tour*, Theo." Ramsey rounded his horse back in the direction they'd come, while holding the reins of the other. "Look—that money ain't yours no more. All right? Just … let it go. And remember what I said. Keep to the right of that ridge and you'll be fine."

Ramsey tossed the ammunition he'd been gripping. Theo watched the cartridges spin and fly through the air like silver dollars—hungrily noting where each one hit the dirt.

"For the coyotes." The voice echoed over the distance that had grown between the two men. It reached Theo's ears just as the other man urged both horses into a gallop.

After snatching up the pistol by his feet, Theo dashed forward. The first two rounds he found quick enough, though the last one took longer. He thumbed all three into the cylinder and snapped it shut. Then he drew back the hammer and aimed … but as much as it wanted to, his trigger finger did not squeeze. Ramsey was already too far away and all Theo could do about it was get more mad than he already was. If he'd been aiming his trusty Spencer Repeater that would be a different story, but the son of a bitch had taken that too.

Lowering the pistol, Theo watched his betrayer shrink into the distance. Bram Ramsey had been his partner, his brother in arms. And now he was nothing but another double-crossing sack of sidewinding dog shit. As he mused on this, both corners of his scowl reached for a line of unshaven jaw.

Then he turned, picked up his canteen and started walking.

TWO

The moon was overhead. Had been for more than an hour. And the first licks of coyote songs were just reaching his ears. The animals were pretty far off, but close enough to know a man was crossing their land. Just one stupid man.

Suddenly, Theo was racked by a shiver. Each hand was already wrapped around the other arm—trying to hold onto as much heat as possible. God, he wanted a fire. That would make everything all right, even if just for a while. The only viable kindling seemed to be the dried-out sagebrush, which was admittedly in no short supply. Of course, even a big heap of that would go up and die in less time than it took to gather. Still, with cold seeping through his coat and into his bones, respite of any degree was starting to sound worth the effort. Problem was, the point was moot, since Theo had no actual way to start a fire. Unless …

The man looked around—teeth chattering, mind cursing every decision made over the last fifteen years. He'd seen a man start a fire by rubbing two rocks together twice in life. But every occasion Theo had tried out the method himself it had ended the same way. His hard work bearin' nothing but ample frustration and swears. Then again, maybe this was the night. The one time he needed it the most.

Two decent rocks were located and brushed off with a trembling hand.

Then, after gathering a small pile of sage, Theo dropped to his knees. The ground felt like the strike of a hammer, but he hardly noticed. With hungry eyes, one stone was scraped against the other. He tried fast and then a little slower. He tried different sides and angles and even threw a half-hearted prayer on the back fifty tries. In the end, he was exhausted—warmer than before, but not in any way that helped.

After scraping through just about the worst day he could remember, Theseus Nil only needed this one thing. A simple mundanity he'd always been able to take for granted. Starting a fire. Now the deed seemed about as likely as reaching the fabled golden city of El Dorado.

"Isn't that the way?" Unable to do much else, the man laughed in his throat. "In hell, the damned are always begging for ice water."

As he sat there, shaking his head, close to delirious, a flash of memory hit. It came with the sudden ferocity of lightning and pulled Theo's addled mind back to where everything had gone sideways. Back to where him and Bram had tracked those bottom-feeders out of Dallas.

The Silverfish himself, Pete Dekker and his dirty gang of murderers, rapists and thieves were about as wanted an organization of notorious bad men as ever there were. And they had taken up camp in the place where the earth had cracked open and a little of hell itself was said to have leaked out. There was a local name for that desolate gorge with the bone-dry ravine. One that inspired most to avoid the area at all costs.

It had all happened within the span of a couple heartbeats. Three at the most. But as everything went to hell, all Theo could think about were the stories he'd heard about that remote place men called the Devil's Claim. How one day, the earth had supposedly cracked open and how that crack swallowed up the river that once flowed. In its place was said to be a rotten smell—the sulfur-breath of a demon, they said. An unnatural thing what crawled straight out of perdition's own womb and claimed the place for its own. Twenty feet tall with claws like cavalry sabers, crowned with the curved horns of an ox.

Now, despite being named after a mythical storybook hero, Theseus Nil was a practical man. He didn't believe in what he couldn't see and that included El Diablo. And yet, back in the Claim, he'd seen that old Devil—seen him with his own two misbelieving eyes.

The bullets were already flying by that point and he'd just finished dragging his former partner behind some cover. That was when something had drawn his attention to the other side of the ravine. A deep rumbling growl, like the warning of a lone wolf. It seemed to cut right through the gunfire and pierce the center of his brain. Hearing it, Theo glanced in the direction of the blazing sun and for the briefest of moments, he saw a hulking shape. Something that stood up on two legs and took note of the ruckus. The thing was enormous, with what very much looked like arms and a pair of curved horns on its head.

Ramsey was white as a sheet. For a second, Theo had the idea that he'd seen the whatever-it-was too. But as another round of lead plums came buzzing past, he forgot to ask. Minutes or decades later, the gunfire came to the punctuation of its proverbial sentence. One of the bastards pulled out a stick of dynamite and held the fuse to the cigar in his mouth. Aside from leaving ears ringing, that explosion set off a chain of unintended events.

Theseus Nil sat, shivering amidst the sage. With no fire, no partner and nothing to punch directly in the mouth, he let out a sigh.

He hadn't thought about it in hours, but now, that shape was fresh in his mind again. The hulking silhouette on the other side of the ravine. With those curved horns, the resemblance to a certain mythical beast his father had fixated on was hard to ignore. But that was, of course, preposterous.

"*Minotaurs*," Theo scoffed, then forced himself to stand up. His feet felt like lumps of iron in his boots. "About as *actual* as the devil himself." The man's words shook as he said them and he tried rubbing some warmth back into his upper arms. "Goddamnit, Abraham."

He turned. Cast a look back in the direction of the Devil's Claim. And right then, Theo hoped that the shape he'd seen stand up hadn't been a mere trick of the light ... but something real. Something actual. A beast every bit as terrible as its outline implied.

As far as he was concerned, Bram Ramsey deserved nothing less.

The town was visible from a few miles off. Theo could see it nested there between nothing much and not a whole hell of a lot. In truth, the sight stung a little.

And while the sun hadn't shown up yet, the sky had that telltale underglow. That rosy hue that for some reason made a man feel calm. It was a magical time of day and Theo had always cherished it. Now, while shuffling on, he tried to recall how that felt. The man had walked all night—and fought his own half frozen legs for every step. The fuel in his belly was what Ramsey had left him—a tepid stew of negative emotions and bile. Heeding the warning of that back-stabber had been hard to swallow, but Theo had been stretched too thin to throw out the only advice he had. So, when he came upon that ridge, he had kept it to his left. And now he could see that, about one thing at least, Ramsey hadn't been lying.

There really was a town.

He blinked. Then again—forcing his eyes to focus on what he thought he was seeing. There was a lone rider out there. Moving away from the town—away from him. Right quick, Theo's mind went to the revolver that was his now. Being as the coyotes had kept their distance all night, there were still two beans in the wheel. It took real effort, but he pulled the weapon out of his belt and pointed the hundred-pound thing into the air.

PANG!

The rider slowed their horse and turned in a circle. Then they just stopped and looked. Again Theo's finger pulled.

PANG!

That was it. The very last of what he had.

Theseus Nil dropped. And though it was cold and hard, the ground felt good. There was dirt on his lips, but he didn't mind it so much because the rider was coming his way now. They were still a ways off when he shut his eyes for the first time—and then they was closer. He could see something long in their hand. A rifle? No—he looked again—more like a fishing pole.

"Hey!" The voice was that of a woman and it was music. "You okay, mister?"

Theo tried to answer, but all he could manage was to open his eyes one more time. Though dressed like a man, the woman getting off the horse was just about the most beautiful thing he had ever seen.

As it happened, he dreamt about nothing else.

THREE

The eyes of Theseus Nil snapped open like his boots were on fire. He sat up—looked around and blinked his surroundings into focus. He didn't recognize where he was. The bedroom was small and plain with not much in the way of decor. Aside from the bed he was occupying, he could see an end table and a window with faded yellow curtains swaying in the breeze.

Beside the table were his boots, but laid out on top were fresh clothes. Throwing the blanket off, Theo swung his legs over the edge of the bed. That's when he discovered two things. One—his body hurt like he'd been run over by a mile-long stampede, and two, he was no longer wearing pants. Suddenly, more disturbed about that than anything else, he reached for the clothes.

On top was a black shirt—clean and folded like it was for sale. Just beneath were suspenders and a pair of tan trousers. Though none of the items looked familiar, Theo wasn't one to look gift horses in the general area of the mouth. As he began to pull on his boots, he noticed how clean they were. It was at this point that he realized that his own person had been likewise freshened up.

He tried to think back. To search his addled mind for something that might explain his current situation. He remembered the Claim and the horrible horned shape. And then, with a sneer, he remembered his former partner. The dirty face of Bram Ramsey was clear as day in his mind. Theo's jaw clenched and the skin between his eyes made a fist. Wherever he was, he knew what had to be done.

Footsteps in the hall drew his attention. Thoughtlessly, his hand flew to the place where his revolver usually was. Finding nothing, his eyes shot for the door. As the knocks began to sound, Theo's muscles tightened. He'd never known a threat to knock first, but then ... he apparently couldn't smell one of those when it had ridden right beside him for the last decade and a half.

"Hello? Mister?" The voice belonged to a young woman and was vaguely familiar. "Are you awake in there?"

Unable to do much else, Theo dumbly blinked his eyes.

"Thought I heard you moving around. Sorry. Not trying to pry or nothing, it's just ... well, the walls in this place are thinner than paper. Are you ... you know ... *decent?*"

On the surface, the question felt too philosophical to be asked through a door. Then Theo remembered the clothes he'd just put on.

"Oh, *decent*. Uh, yeah ... you can come in."

The door creaked open, revealing a woman who appeared in her early twenties. Funny enough, she was dressed like a man. She wore a wide-brimmed hat, dusty trousers and a blue flannel shirt—the last few buttons of which were left undone. The skin of her chest was smooth and just as bright as the sun. It took real effort not to stare at. Theo swallowed hard and looked the woman in the face. She looked Chinese, or half, anyway.

"I hope the clothes fit." The woman smiled nervously. "Not too many options when it comes to the size."

A voice called from a distance away. It sounded as if it were coming from below, giving Theo the impression that he might be on the second floor. As the woman turned her head to respond, a long black braid fell over her shoulder, reaching almost to the middle of her belly.

"Hold your horses, I'll ask him!!" she whisper-shouted behind the door, before reappearing with a slightly lop-sided smile. "You like fish, Mister?"

Unprepared for the question, Theo continued to stare and blink.

"We got some from yesterday morning." The woman went on. "There's a creek about a mile from here just full of catfish this time of year. Them things are ugly, but my sister cooks 'em up pretty nice."

"Ma'am? Right now, I could just about eat my own boots."

"Well, I'm hopin' it don't come to that." The woman winked. "It's Susanna, by the way ... *like in the song*."

"Pleasure," said Theo. With his body now more or less unclenched, he managed a smile. "Thank you for the offer ... and the clothes." He looked at the floor. "Also, I think somebody might have cleaned me up some."

"Was my sister who done that part. She *insisted*."

Theo couldn't tell if the woman was serious or just pulling his leg.

"So are you gonna tell me *your* name or do I have to guess?"

"Oh! No, you don't have to." Embarrassed, Theo scratched at his jaw. "Theseus Nil, ma'am. Deputy U.S. marshal for the Eastern District of Texas."

"Well, Mr. Nil … it's nice to make your acquaintance." Susanna smiled demurely. "Come on down when you're ready."

And with that, the door was closed and the woman was gone.

As Theo stood in that unfamiliar room, pondering the implications of a stranger undressing his unconscious self … something fell into place. The young woman—he'd seen her before. Hell, he'd dreamed just about nothing else for hours.

As he stepped out into the hallway, the echoes of Theo's wooden heels sounded enormous. He could see three other doors, all of 'em shut tight. These he proceeded past, trying to announce himself as little as possible. The hallway terminated at the top of the staircase which was reached without incident. For a moment, he rested his hand on the railing and tried to just breathe. So much had changed since they'd hired those five men. That'd been what? Nine days ago? More?

Suddenly, Theo realized he didn't know what day it was, or how much of a headstart that backstabbing snake Ramsey had. Greed—they'd both seen it change people. Seen how it could twist and corrupt both a man's mind and his morals. Not that, in his experience, most folk had an abundance of either.

With a deep breath, Theo leered down the staircase—all the way to the bottom. Whatever or whoever was waiting for him down there was anyone's guess. And while he had a mighty need for answers and food, Theo also had a lot to do and precious little time to get it all done.

As it happened, the first floor of the building was mostly empty—though every eye abruptly turned to the same spot. For his part, Theo felt like an infected carbuncle at the end of an otherwise perfectly good nose. There was an old timer hunched over his glass at one end of the bar. He turned with a glare, revealing a long mustachioed face and thoroughly broken nose. At the far end of the bar were a couple of well-dressed gentlemen who immediately stood up. After nodding at the old man, one finished his drink and ushered his friend out the door with a hand on the small of his back.

While the batwing doors swung, a Chinese woman appeared from behind the bar. The sister Susanna had mentioned, Theo presumed. The woman was tall and slender, with circles around her eyes that did little to spoil her enchanting beauty. Her hair was black and pinned up in a tight ball, leaving her long neck exposed. Recognizing that the scowl on her face was for him, Theo looked elsewhere as she cleared away the glasses left by the two gentlemen.

The only other person in the room was a twitchy fella who was wearing a dirty old soldier's cap and picking at an empty plate. Most notable were the man's eyes ... or rather, lack thereof. Two hollow sockets were pointed directly at Theo. Glaring like they could still see.

"Hey, there you are!" The familiar voice was welcome but it hit like a bucket of ice water. Theo turned from the eyeless man and was hit by the bright smile of Susanna. She had also appeared behind the bar and was setting down a dinner plate just two seats down. Whatever was on that plate smelled exactly like heaven.

"I figured you could use some water too." She put down a glass before waving her guest over. "When I found you, your canteen was empty. Come on, now. Sit. Eat."

Slowly, Theo crossed the room. His joints, his bones, even his hair—it all hurt. Briefly, he spared a glance for the bartender woman, but she only turned and stormed into the back room. Trying her best not to notice, Susanna smiled on.

"Don't worry about her. She just don't like strangers is all."

"I see," said Theseus Nil. "I'm sorry about that, but you all have me at a loss. Truth is, I'm not sure how I got here. Or even where *here* is."

"Well, Mr. Nil." Susanna produced a fork and set it beside the plate. "If you sit and you eat, I'll tell you what I can."

"Please, call me Theo." He inclined his gaze down at the steaming plate of fish. On the side were some cut-up beets and carrots. "I can't...."

He started, then stopped—wincing at the mule kicks his stomach was managing. "I can't pay for this."

Susanna put her hand on her hips and gave an expression that made Theo wonder if he'd said something stupid. So he sat, and he ate—trying his best not to devolve into a man-shaped hog at the trough.

"Careful, son," said the man with the broken nose, as he stole a mouthful from his glass. "Those bones'll get ya."

Theo nodded as he forced himself to slow down and chew. After a few swallows and his first of many glasses of water, he started to feel better. Still a carbuncle, but one that was a might less swollen.

"This is *delicious*. Much obliged."

"I told you my sister was a good cook." As Susanna said this, a loud bang was heard from the room behind the bar, like something had been thrown. Possibly in anger. "Now, as for where you are ... none of us are sure what the original name was. None of the people who built it bothered to leave a sign. We called the town *Lazris*. You know, after the Bible story of that man Jesus brought back to life. You know the one?"

Theo pulled a thin bit of bone out of his mouth and dropped it on the plate. Then he gave a single nod.

"We're not on any maps. Not yet. But I figure word gets out about Lee's pepper fish and we'll have to build a second hotel." She set down another full glass of water and pushed it forward. "Anyway, you wanted to know how you got here, so that means you don't remember me from this morning. Not upstairs, but ... when I found you out there."

Theo's brow clenched as he tried to remember. But before anything pierced the fog, the young woman went on.

"I was on my way to the creek when I heard the shot. Then I saw you. No horse, just you ... standing out in the desert. At first I thought you might be a product of my imagination ... but then you shot a second time. That's when I realized you weren't just actual, Mr. Nil ... you were in peril."

Theo chewed slowly, swallowed a mouthful of beets. The taste was sweet and earthy. "I ... don't remember that," was all he said.

"Can't say I'm surprised," said Susanna with a wry half-grin. "Judging on the way you passed out, I reckon you were walking all night. But there's nothing out that way. Not for tens of miles."

"There's one thing." The old-timer's voice was a gravelly rasp. He swallowed what was left in his glass then lowered it with a surprisingly steady hand. "The place where dead men grow."

The room went quiet as Theo took a slow sip of water.

"Oh, Arthur, now come on. He doesn't need to be hearing your campfire stories."

"No, it's all right." Theo nodded. "I've heard the song."

The old-timer wiped his mouth on one sleeve and turned in his seat. He was wearing a large yellow-gray mustache and a weathered expression. The man's face and neck were covered in days-old stubble and he smelled like the bottom of a whiskey jug.

"The Devil's Claim is twenty miles due west, or thereabouts." The man croaked, raising an eyebrow. "And I can tell from the look in your eye, you already knew that."

Theo just kept chewing.

"They say it used to be green and good once—with a crystal clear river, blue as the sky. But that was before. One day, if the stories are to be believed … the earth shuddered, cracked wide open and let out a monster. A horned demon all covered in fur and teeth." The man eyeballed Theo, judging his lack of disbelief. "The river and grass are gone of course. Now the only thing that grows in that place are the number of bodies. Dead men, Mister … Null, was it?"

"Nil," corrected Theo. "Theseus Nil."

Now it was the old-timer who wore the look of disbelief. "Can't say I've ever heard that one before."

"Yeah, well … as I said, Theo is fine. Back to the Claim—what do you know of this *monster*? Is it … *actual*? Have you seen it?"

The old man considered this, then absently scratched a spot on one shoulder. "I have not." He said at last. "Met a man who did though. And now I'm thinking, maybe I've met one more."

Theo narrowed his eyes. Then he glanced over at Susanna.

"You really walk all the way here from the Claim?" she said, with obvious reverence. "What in God's name were you doing out there?"

"Just working. Finishing up a job I started a long time ago." Theo finished his third glass of water and sighed. Though finally quenched and sated, satisfaction was still a long ways off. "You folks ever heard of a man by the name of Pete Dekker?"

FOUR

There were multiple gasps—even the blind man in the back stopped fidgeting with his plate. At the mere mention of the name, the older sister reemerged from the room behind the bar. Her face, a mask of warring emotions.

"We are intimately familiar," said the old man.

Suddenly, Theo felt as though he'd stepped in something foul.

"We thought he was dead for a while there, you know. Hoped he was, anyway. There was a blissful period of about seventeen months where no one saw or had their lives interjected by that slimy son of a silverfish." Theo sighed. "A while back, my partner and I got word that he'd appeared in Dallas. That he had sent word to every piece of murderous trash that had ever run with him over the years, to gather at his side."

The two sisters exchanged nervous glances as the elder one put her arm around the younger.

"Well," Theo went on. "We figured ole Pete was planning something big; A job that'd put him in the history books or some such. Never learned *what*, because by the time we got to Dallas, the Dekker gang had scattered to the winds. And so we hit the trail and hit it hard. Tracked him for weeks and then months ... day and night until we lost the scent. Then a few weeks later, we'd heard something—pick up his stink and start tracking all over again. Fortunately for us, the evidence of his passing was *always evident*."

Just then, there were fires burning in the eyes of Theseus Nil. Things he'd seen that were far too horrible to recount. Though his hand was clenched and trembling, when another was placed on top, it went still. Susanna's expression brought a wave of emotion for the man. It'd been a very long time since he'd been consoled—even silently.

"Anyway ..." He pulled back his hand. "It went on like that for three years. Just when we thought we had him, Dekker would find a way to slip through our fingers. Somehow, every time, the bastard would elude and evade. Like he was vanishing into thin air."

"Dekker." The word was spoken with such dripping disdain, it fell like poison on the ears. The older sister, Lee … she leaned over the bar. "Do you know where he is now?"

Theo wiped the corners of his mouth with one hand. Narrowed his eyes and said. "Not just him. His whole damned organization. Last night we found where they'd been holing up, but … things went bad."

Theo hung his head, staring deep into the wood grain of the bar. It seemed like it hurt to keep going.

"Went bad for Dekker too. He's still there. In the one place most regular folk are too afraid to go."

"In the Devil's Claim," said the old man, his eyes moist and trembling.

Theo nodded.

"And Dekker? You say he's there still?"

Hearing this, Theo considered telling all. Recounting the firefight, the gravedigging and the bitter betrayal which followed. He could still picture him and Ramsey taking cover behind that large rock as one of Dekker's men held up a stick of dynamite. He'd felt helpless watching the son of a bitch light the fuse. But this turned to shock when the man was hit in the neck by a shot from Ramsey's Yellowboy. In his mind, Theo could see it all replaying clearly now. How the stick tumbled through the air, landing back in the same wagon it'd come from. Time seemed to move real slow after that. At least, until the world was filled with sound and light and heat—all in quantities he'd never thought possible.

The explosion was enormous. It was like a second sun had winked into existence, right there on the ground. The force shot through Nil and Ramsey and the five additional men they'd hired. Sound was gone, as were things like standing or thinking straight. When Theo came to his senses, the first thing he did was cast his gaze across the ravine. To see if the devil was pleased with the show. But, just like all the members of the Dekker gang, the thing was just gone.

"Mister … Nil?" The younger woman's voice tugged him out of his thoughts. "Theo?"

Back in the present, the deputy marshal inhaled sharply.

"Oh, Dekker's still there," he said. "I'd say old Pete and his ain't goin' anywhere. Not for a while. We just need to pick up what's left."

The sisters exchanged a conversation in a single look. Then Lee spoke up again.

"What do you need?"

Theo took his time making eye contact. "You really want to know?"

The woman reached under the bar and pulled out a rifle. A Winchester Yellowboy of all things, as well as a box of .44's. "Providing this concerns the final fate of Pete Dekker, you're goddamned right I wanna know."

Hearing this and understanding what was being offered, Theo could feel the sides of the room closing in. He'd already gotten five men killed. Hell, the dirt from digging their graves was still under his fingernails. The collective bounties at the bottom of that ravine were worth thousands. But it wasn't about the money, or finishing things with Dekker. Not anymore. Now, Theseus had found himself a new purpose. A new kind of *minotaur* by the name of Abraham Mathias Ramsey.

"I'll need a wagon—the biggest in town. And a couple of horses to pull it. Send me off with that, some rope and as many horse blankets as you can spare."

Again, the three discussed the proposal in their silent language.

Susanna looked thoughtful as she walked around to the customer side of the bar. "I think we can oblige."

Theo nodded. "What about that rifle? That for sale?"

Susanna snickered. She had moved to within an arm's length of the stranger who'd wandered into their lives. From her back, she pulled out a familiar pistol and slammed it on the bar.

"So that's a no on the Winchester, then?"

Lee smiled. "Yes, Mr. Nil. *That* is a no." She patted the rifle's distinctive brass receiver. "Even if you could *afford* her ... this here's my baby girl. Only way she's going with you is in my arms."

Visibly disappointed, Theo picked up Ramsey's pistol. Then he checked the cylinder and sneered at the remaining round.

"There a place to stock up on ammunition in this town?"

The sisters exchanged looks.

"There ain't much in Lazris." Lee went on. "Those clothes you're wearing might look fresh off the shelf, but they belonged to a former resident. Lucky you happened to be of a similar size."

"Yeah, we're mostly self-sufficient here." Susanna interjected. "But that rifle is just about the only weapon in town."

"Just *about*?" Theo sounded hopeful.

"Well, I could get you a pitchfork if you think it'll help." Susanna smirked. "Hold on ... what about Mr. Morrow?"

As if put off by the current conversation, the old-timer sneered, then noisily slid off his stool. After pushing down his hat, the man hobbled straight out of the building. The batwing doors swung out then in, out then in, and stopped. When he was gone, there remained an awkward silence in his place.

Lee spoke up. "Ignore him. It's a good suggestion, Sue." She turned to Susanna. "But Heathcliff Morrow isn't like to be as hospitable as we are. Do you have *any* money, Mr. Nil?"

Immediately, Theo pictured the almost sixty dollars cash that was sitting in his saddle bag.

"Not on me." He forced himself to say. "But here are the facts. Pete Dekker has a price on his head of one thousand and one hundred dollars. Combine that with the other notorious bad men he surrounded himself with and you've got yourself a small fortune. More than enough to go around." He stood up. "I know you all have no reason to take the word of a stranger but ... if you can get me the supplies I need, I'll consider us equal partners. Hell, I don't even care about the money anymore. I just need to finish this."

Again, the sisters traded glares.

"As it happens, Mr. Nil ... you aren't the only one here with unfinished business." Lee bent down, disappearing behind the bar. For a few seconds, Theo could hear what sounded like wood sliding and then fitting back into place. When the woman reappeared, she had a wad of paper money in her hands. Based on her body language, the woman wasn't fully comfortable with the situation.

"Tell him we ain't buying. There ain't enough for that."

Susanna accepted the money with a solemn nod.

"I'll go after Arthur," said Lee, "Providing I can get him to help with the horses, we can have the wagon ready within the hour. That work for you, Mr. Nil?"

Theo was taken aback. "I believe it does."

"That's good, because we are coming with you."

Hearing this, Theo just about spit.

"That's right. Susanna, myself and that skinny old grump out there." Lee brushed a strand of black hair behind one ear, then put that hand on her hip. "And protesting ain't going to change anything, so don't bother. Unless you want to walk out that door and cross the desert the other way with those same boots ... this is the price. If Dekker is going to be ushered unto his final fate, the three of us need to be there to see it. Is that understood?"

"Yes, ma'am. I do believe it is."

"Well, all right then," Lee turned back to her sister. "Just get him to loan us a couple of rifles for a day or two. That's all we need. Might as well take Mr. Nil—he might serve as further persuasion, should old Heathcliff not be in one of his more neighborly moods. Just ... don't offer that man anything you don't have to, all right? You know how he gets."

FIVE

In forty-three years of living, Abraham Ramsey had done quite a few things he wasn't proud of. Most of those he'd been able to push past, but every once in a while, a particularly bad decision came back to bite him in the ass.

About a half hour prior, he'd managed to squeeze into a gap in the cliffside. It was narrow, but deep enough that the thing outside couldn't reach him. That said, he could still hear it out there—bellowing, growling in short cough-like bursts. Sucking breath in through his teeth, Ramsey looked down at his leg. The boot had taken some of the damage, but not enough. He could already feel the blood pooling around the heel—soaking into his sock like it were a sponge. If there was enough room to get the boot off, he thought he might be able to rip off a piece of his shirt—maybe bind the wound.

But there *wasn't* enough room.

Under his breath, the man strung every swear he'd ever heard together into a single unbroken curse. Whatever the beast actually was, it had appeared out of nowhere—just as Ramsey was starting to load the second body onto that pale mare.

He had discovered seven horses not long before that. They'd all been ground-hitched about a quarter mile from where the shootout had happened. The idea had been to load up as many of the dead men on as few horses as possible and then lead them all back to Fort Davis where Bram Ramsey would become a rich man.

It was a simple enough plan and it should have worked. How was he supposed to know that all those idiotic stories about the Devil's Claim were true?

By the meager light of the half moon, the thing was hard to make out. For a split second, Ramsey had been aware of sound and movement, but little more beyond an enormous shape. The most distinct part was the head. Much lighter than the body, it looked to be floating—bobbing up and down as the beast ran. The fact of it was, if the mare hadn't been between him and the thing, Ramsey would have been the one torn to shreds. Truly, whatever other blunders the man had made in life, chief among them was returning to this place alone.

Again, he heard one of the thing's guttural coughs. The sounds were getting louder—*closer*. Though his open leg was screaming, Ramsey scrambled to move backward, but this only resulted in a flash of light and more pain, as the crown of his head connected with a rock. Unable to stop himself, the man cried out. Teeth clenched, he frantically blinked the tears away just as something dark passed before the vertical opening.

"Shit!" He whispered into the hands cupped over his mouth. "Son-of-a-shit-cunny-whore-cow."

The arm—for he didn't know what else to call it, appeared again. The first time the thing had done this, he'd tried to kick at it. But those claws were long—sharp too. That pretty much explained the leg. That's why this time, Ramsey resolved to simply press himself against the far wall and think flat thoughts.

After the longest twenty seconds of his life, the pitch-black appendage disappeared. Through the gap, he could see the face. It was smooth and pale, and there was a black pit of an eye. Not in the front like predators have, but on one side, like a deer, or a cow.

Just then, Ramsey did just about the only thing he still had full control over. He decided to laugh. The sound started low, but rapidly increased in volume and in pitch until it became the shrill cackling of the insane.

"On second thought...," he spat the words between breaths as the laughter went on. "Forget what I said, buddy. All that money split two ways is fine by me. Just ... how about we bring us a priest—maybe some holy water too. Seems the Devil's Claim is in need of a good old-fashioned *cleansing*."

The mad guffaws had an unexpected effect on the thing outside. Almost like they were hurting it somehow. Without warning, the beast banged its face against the side of the cliff. Once, and two more times. Then, with a strange howl that sounded a lot like a question, it ran off.

That was when the cackling man stopped making noise. He waited, practically afraid to breathe for ten seconds, then thirty more. Another hour passed before he dared crawl to the opening. And in that time, Ramsey's mind did some wandering.

When that wagon full of dynamite was made to roar, the force was tremendous. The five gunslingers they hired in Fort Davis had mostly been shot to death by that point, but that last one did meet his fate in that explosion. That fiery roar. His limp body was thrown back where it broke upon the very object two other men were using for cover. These men, these old friends—were it not for that particular bit of rock, would have met the same fate as all the rest.

Being that their backs were to the drop-off, the Dekker gang was thrown in the opposite direction. Most were cast right over the edge of the three-story ravine. By Ramsey's own count, Dekker had twelve men in his camp—almost double what they'd expected to find. And almost all of them died in a flash. One single colossal blunder, set off by a perfectly placed bullet to the neck. As Ramsey thought of it again, he couldn't help but picture the dime novels that would one day recount the exploit. The illustrated covers which would surely depict the best, most important shot he'd ever made.

The man with the dynamite was definitely Standish Poghkenny—a man who started out blasting holes through mountains for Union Pacific, before he decided that robbing their payroll was a safer way to make a living.

There were others he recognized too—none of which had a bounty under three hundred dollars, per his best recollection. Before the firefight commenced, he spied no less than Edwin Kurtz, "Brushfire" Mason Wood, Doc Blamire, Old Ollie Hughes, Dean "High Card" McLinty, "Uncle" Joe Landsbury, Esau Vander Hoeg and, judging by that birthmark, none other than Weeping John Wraith. Like flies, all of them had gathered round the man with the silver hair. The vile son of a bitch, whose reputation had only grown over the years—perhaps in direct proportion to his gut. Peter Morgenthau Dekker. Six and a half feet tall if he was slouching, and meaner than a two-headed rattler. A man so depraved that, before the age of twenty, he'd gutted his own mama with a goddamned fish knife.

They were all there, in the Devil's Claim. Them and at least three more Ramsey didn't know. Scheming, plotting whatever notorious bad men scheme and plot about. And now they were, all of 'em, dead.

Probably six thousand dollars worth or thereabouts, just waiting to be loaded up and turned in. For the likes of a deputy U.S. marshal for the Eastern District of Texas, it was a life-changing amount of money ... providing it was only split one way.

"Oh God, Theo. I'm such an asshole."

As he said this, the eyes of Bram Ramsey stared at the vaguely vaginal opening to the space he'd crawled into. Through that vertical slit, dim moonlight could be seen. Part of him wanted to wait until morning, just to be safe. But he couldn't wait that long. He had sent his only real friend into the desert on foot. Betrayed fifteen years worth of trust and brotherhood, and for what? For some *money?*

Devil or demon, or just some overgrown badger, the thing out there wasn't going to stop him anymore. Ramsey was going to ride out into that desert and rescue his friend. Save him from a fate he most assuredly had not earned. And then they would ride back here together, as God intended. And together they would shoot that devil-whore-shit-beast until it died.

With the salty twang of fear on his lips, Ramsey pushed his head out into open air. He looked left and right and straight ahead. There were shadows everywhere, but no sign of any white-faced demons from hell. His mind raced. Tried to remember where exactly he was and how he'd gotten there. Then he scrambled out and onto the ground. Again he looked all around, and again he saw nothing but rocks and the darkness what coursed between them.

Moving as quietly as he knew how, Ramsey moved along the sheer walls of the ravine, eventually making his way to the slope that he'd come down earlier. Another ten minutes of stealth brought him to the top and eventually to his own horse, Adelaide-June. Named for the strawberry-haired girl who'd made him a man back when he was fifteen. With a swell of emotion, Ramsey patted the animal—accepting the enthusiastic headbutt without protest. Then he stepped into the stirrups and up into his saddle. For the briefest of moments, he felt good. Free and just and full of righteousness and redemption.

Then he heard the sound. Not a roar, but something lower. Like the angry grinding huff of a steam engine coughing back to life. Ramsey turned, but that smooth, bony head was so close, it was all he could see.

SIX

In the oppressive sun of a white hot day, four horses pulled their burden.

The largest two were hauling a rickety old wagon. It was a simple buckboard style, with plenty of room for hauling supplies and a bench up front for the driver. The wagon would serve for the grim purpose ahead, but it wasn't exactly the sturdiest thing. The way the wheels wobbled and the flatbed creaked did not inspire confidence in Theseus Nil. As such, the group moved quite a bit slower than he would have liked.

He squinted over at the driver. Holding the reins was the old drunk, whose name was Arthur Blithe. In the past couple of hours, Theo had managed to learn a bit about the town called Lazris and the people who knew it as *home*. It seemed to him they were all misfits in their way. That the ghost town they'd claimed and renamed was their attempt at creating a place to belong.

That Blithe shared Lee and Susanna's animosity toward the man called Pete Dekker was as plain as the broken nose on his face. As was his boundless devotion to the pair. The man had a serious aversion to firearms though, and that wasn't exactly helpful. Even now, as they rode straight for the Devil's Claim ... the most volatile thing the old man had on his person was whatever he kept in his pocket flask. And that, he only seemed willing to use on himself.

Sitting next to Blithe was the elder sister, Lee. She was wearing a long dress—dark blue and adorned with little flowers. The woman really was striking—a vision of exotic beauty, the likes Theo had rarely seen. She also seemed *haunted*. When she wasn't doling out orders, Lee's eyes always seemed to find the middle distance. As if whatever she was looking at was a hundred miles away. Few enough details had been offered but, when Theo had accompanied Susanna to *borrow* a couple of beat-to-hell old rifles, she made mention of a man called Big Finneas. She'd been smiling when she said it, but this faded almost before the name left her lips. After that, Susanna went quiet for a few minutes before admitting that the man had been her brother by

225

marriage ... and that whatever she'd been about to say was not her story to tell.

Theo turned to look at the young woman now. Like him, Susanna was riding on horseback. And while a wide-brimmed hat kept the sun out of her face, there was fire where it touched her braid. Blazing colors amid the long, perfect black—shining so bright, the deputy U.S. marshal didn't know whether to look away, or stare forever.

Like it or not, Theo was drawn to Susanna. There'd been thoughts swirling around his head since she'd appeared at that upstairs door. Thoughts that he'd been trying to explain away as due to him being on the trail too long, or maybe as simple gratitude. After all, she was the one who'd hauled him off the desert, where he'd so ungracefully collapsed.

Those arguments made some sense to Theo, and yet ... as he beheld her now and saw how she smiled when she noticed him looking ... it was starting to feel like he was drawn to the woman for other reasons.

"What kind of name is Theseus Nil, anyway?" Susanna's question came without warning. "Never known a man to bear either the last or the first."

"You can thank my daddy for that. Rest his soul." After a little while, Theo said more. "The family name is Nilmeier. I just got tired of having to spell it." He turned with a smile that never left his eyes. "As for Theseus ... it's an old name, from an old story."

"Go on then," With a twinkle in her eye, Susanna nodded at the barren expanse ahead. "I got nothing but time."

Theo looked ahead as well. It had been a long while since he'd thought about those times—growing up in Tolerance, Oklahoma. Even longer since he'd talked about them to anyone who wasn't Bram backstabbin' Ramsey. After a few moments of consideration, he took a deep breath and let it out slow.

"My father's name was Samuel. He was a candle-maker by trade. As far back as I can remember, it was just me and him and our little shop. Funny as it sounds, the man knew how to make a damn fine candle. Everyone knew it. You need a candle that'll burn bright and slow without too much smoke ... you go to Sam Nilmeier. Problem was, they also knew what a sucker he was for a sob story."

At this, Susanna looked perplexed. "I don't understand."

"Yeah, well … neither did I." Theo smirked. "All they had to do was mention how their old woman had been sick, or that their corn crop had been damaged by drought or bugs or some such. Didn't really matter because whatever they were selling, my daddy would buy right up. Every time. Trade his own hard work for a promise or a freshly baked peach pie. Other things too. He knew I didn't understand." Theo pursed his lips into a false smile. "*People need light*—he'd always say. After food in the belly and a roof overhead, pushing back the dark is the most important thing. It's what keeps us civilized."

After a long pause, Susanna offered, "Your father sounds like a good man."

"He was also a fool." Theo's expression grew serious as he started to shake his head. "He'd been doing that barter stuff since before I was born. Back when my mother was still …" Theo's voice hitched. "Just before I was born, there was a customer who offered to trade a couple of books for a box of candles. One of them was the account of a man who tried living off the land … out in the woods by a pond. That one was boring. But the other had lots of exciting stories in it. Tall tales from a far-off land called Greece." He turned to Susanna, finding her enraptured. "Daddy said Mama loved that book. That he read it to her most every night when she was heavy with me."

Theo could feel the woman's eyes calling for his own, but he didn't turn. This was the most he'd mentioned of his mother in over two decades. That kind of thing took some easing into.

"Their favorite story happened on an island called Crete. I can't remember it all now but … there was a king who ruled there. A real bad guy by the name of *Minos*. Thing of it was, King Minos had himself a pet monster—kind of a man but, with the head of a bull. Real ugly sumbitch—mean, too. And it liked to *eat* people."

Before going on, Theo checked to see if Suzanna was aghast or offended. As it happened, she was neither.

"So, Minos kept this monster—this *minotaur*—in something called a labyrinth, which, as far as I can tell, is a kind of jail made of twisting hallways and filled with traps. The walls are too tall to climb out and it's all so big, you could wander around till Judgment Day and still never find your way out."

"My goodness, that is certainly of a size." As Susanna shook her head, another smile touched Theo's eyes.

"Anyway," he went on, "whenever somebody did something he didn't like, King Minos would just toss them in that labyrinth. Eventually, the monster would get hungry and find them and, well … that was that." He considered going into more detail, but decided to leave it there. "Theseus and the Minotaur. That was the name of the story."

"So …" Susanna looked unsure. "Theseus was one of the victims of this bull-monster?"

"Oh, no, ma'am. In the end, he kills the damn thing."

"Okay, that makes more sense. So you got named after the hero in your parent's favorite story. A monster-killer." She smiled. "I think I love that."

Theo shrugged. "Yeah, well … tell me how you feel after hearing why he did it about a thousand times. *Greatness* was the thing, you see. Sam Nilmeier wanted more for his only begotten son than a life of wax burns, dipping wicks, and scraping by."

When Theo turned, he met Susanna's eyes easily.

"'One day you'll find your own minotaur, son. Find it and shoot the thing right between the eyes, just like Saint George did with that dragon.'"

As he said this, Theo was wearing a sad smile.

"That's very sweet." Susanna mirrored the man's expression. "Though I'm pretty sure Saint George had a sword."

After a second or two, Theo laughed in his throat.

"So tell me, Theseus Nil … in all your wanderings, did ya ever find it? This *minnow-tour* you're supposed to slay?"

"Might be I have." The man's expression grew suddenly serious. "Very recently, in fact. 'Course, the way I've always understood it … *finding* the thing is only the first part."

As he said this, Theo missed his Spencer repeater more than ever. While he and Susanna had managed to talk a thoroughly unpleasant man called Heathcliff Morrow out of two rusty old hunting rifles and a handful of rounds … the arsenal felt sorely lacking for what was to come.

The strange posse arrived on the outskirts of the area known as the Devil's Claim just before dusk got underway.

It was that most temporary time of day that Joanna Nilmeier used to call the *fire time*. When, for just a few minutes, all the world's colors seemed to blaze. Theo had never heard his mother say this, however. She hadn't lived to see her son's first birthday. But as he saw those colors now, adding yellows to the patches of green and making every brown stone glow like it was hot enough to cook eggs, that was exactly the term that came to mind. They had reached the spot where hell had cracked open … right at the start of the fire time.

"We should stop here." Theo said, staring at the five shallow mounds off to the side.

"Are those graves?" asked Lee very frankly.

"They are indeed." Theo dismounted and began checking the old shotgun for the ninth or tenth time. "My partner and I dug them ourselves. About twenty-four hours ago. Those five were hard men. Good with their iron, from what I saw. Just not good enough." He knelt down and picked up the shovel he'd dropped the previous night. "I told you Dekker and his men weren't going anywhere? Well, that's because one of 'em blew up a whole damn wagon full of dynamite that ended that confrontation right quick. Our men were blown one way and his … well, they went for a swim where there ain't no water."

He tossed the shovel in the wagon, where it landed on a coiled length of rope, a stack of horse blankets and some other supplies.

"Thanks to the rocks we were crouching behind, the explosion missed both myself and my longtime partner, Bram. As far as I know, we were the only two that made it out, not only alive, but completely intact. Add to that, all we had left to do was gather up the remains of our bounties and haul them back to Fort Davis to get paid, and you have yourself a proper damn miracle. Three years of tracking that silver-haired bastard across Texas and Missouri ended with that one BOOM. Handing Bram and me the biggest payday of our lives."

Theo snickered, shook his head. "But the Lord giveth and then he taketh away. Says that in the Bible I think."

"Theo." Susanna had dismounted and was standing with her borrowed long rifle in hand. "How come you walked across the desert last night?"

Content that his shotgun was as good as it was going to get, he checked the revolver. Made sure the only round he had left was in the firing position.

"Because of one simple thing. Just run-of-the-mill, everyday human *greed*."

He looked at the faces of the two sisters and the old man. Though it was the last thing on heaven or earth he wanted to talk about, they were all waiting for more.

"Bram Ramsey was my friend. We've been through a lot together. A lot. But last night, as we were putting these fellers in the ground … I think he had an epiphany. I think he decided that it'd be easier to split the money one way than only two. Even if the guy he was halving it with … was me."

Susanna stepped forward, placed a hand on Theo's arm. Though the man wouldn't turn to look at her, she could tell how hard he was trying to hold back his emotions.

"Anyway …" Theo drew the back of an arm across his nose. Turned toward the Devil's Claim. "The truth is, I don't know what we're gonna find up there. It's possible that in the past day, my old friend Bram has been busy. That he's left us nothing but the stains." He sighed. "It's partly why I wanted to do this alone."

Susanna took another step forward. Now they were so close, Theo could see nothing but her. And that was fine. When a gust blew her hat off, the cord caught on the fine line of her jaw. The woman's skin, her exotic eyes and long black braid—everything blazed in the magic light of the fire time.

"And what happens if some of those men aren't as bad off as you think?" The woman's tone was deadly. "What if a few of 'em were only licking their wounds when your stupid ex-partner came back alone? Might be he's been lying down all day."

"Well, ma'am," Theo's heart was thumping so fast, he could hardly find proper volume for his words. "In that case, I would be much appreciative to have you at my side. All of you."

"Well? Better we leave the horses with the wagon." It was the old man who'd spoken. He was straightening out his bent spine. "From here, we should go on foot."

SEVEN

By the time the group had hiked the rest of the way up and into the Claim, the fire time was spent. Under a full red sky, they continued on—moving as quietly as they could with Theseus Nil in the lead. He crept around familiar rocks and outcroppings until he could see the spot where the gunfight had occurred. There were horses where horses hadn't been. And they were dead.

"What do you see?" hissed Lee, with her Yellowboy at the ready.

"Not sure," Theo whispered back. "I'd like to go on ahead and see. All right?"

The two women exchanged glances with each other and with Blithe. Then they all looked back at Theo.

"Be careful," said Susanna.

Theo gave a look as if to say *When has that helped anything?* Then he gave a nod.

Morrow's shotgun wasn't exactly a showpiece but right then, he was glad to have it. With every step, Theo checked and rechecked the deepening shadows on all sides. But until he reached where the horses were, he was alone. After that, he just wished he was.

The horses weren't just dead, they were hard to look at. Flesh hung off in strips that glistened redly in the dying sun. Neither of the animals was Theo's, but that was a small relief. The tongue of the one on the right was all hanging out and swollen. Its head bent unnaturally far back. A position made possible mostly because the animal's throat was no longer there. As he looked, Theo could feel all that fish he'd eaten, suddenly threatening to rise in his gorge.

Three men of the Dekker gang weren't far. Their bodies were tied up—covered in blood, but in far better shape than the horses. As he beheld the grisly scene, the deputy U.S. marshal began to read it—piecing together the story of what must have happened. The men were bound for transportation, likely by Ramsey himself. He must have hauled them up and started to load them on the horses when … something else entered the story. Something impossible that Theo couldn't possibly have seen stand up on the other side of the ravine.

Gripping the rusty firearm tighter than he needed to, Theo stepped past the bodies, made his way to the edge of the chasm and peered down. The scene below seemed like something out of a nightmare. There were bodies everywhere, some blackened, others no longer whole. They were strewn and splayed over rocks and craggy ledges—in the place where a river once flowed.

Theo thought back to an old song he hadn't heard in years. The words came flowing back, and as they ran through his mine, he could almost hear the tune.

And so it was, in that far-off place, where a river once did flow ...

Theo couldn't recall too many of the words, but the line at the end? That one he tossed into the gaping ravine.

"Turned the Claim, once green and good, into a place where dead men grow."

Stepping away from the edge, he turned to again scan his surroundings. This time he saw the splintered remains of a munitions wagon. The very thing that had so abruptly ended the firefight as well as numerous lives on both sides. Right then, as he stared at that pile of charred boards and metal, Theo couldn't help but wonder. Pete Dekker had a plan for all that dynamite. Something bad and big enough to leave a damn scar in the world.

"Man alive ..."

The voice kicked Theo's heart into a gallop. He spun around, shotgun raised to find Susanna walking up beside. Her hand was on her forehead and her eyes were like saucers.

"No, ma'am." He said trying to hide how startled he was. "I don't believe there is."

Lee and Blithe weren't far behind. Of the four, it was the old man who seemed the most disturbed by the gruesome scene they wandered into. This was evidenced by the way he bent over to retch up all those hits of red-eye he'd pulled from his flask. When the act had played out, Blithe stumbled back and fell on his ass.

"Well," Theo said flatly. "So much for the element of surprise."

It was Lee who stepped in with a comforting hand. "You okay, Ham?"

The man looked disgusted, though mostly with himself. "No. No, I am most assuredly not." He wiped his chin on a shirtsleeve. "I'm sorry, Li-Mei. Sorry for what I've ... you girls deserve better than a useless old drunk." He shook head, tucked his knees up against his chest. "I wish it had been me, that day. If Finn were here, he'd—"

"Hush now. Come on." Lee touched her forehead to Blithe's. "Ain't no point in bringing up the past. What's done is done. What I need from you now is to be present. To stand with me right here, right now. Can you do that?"

Blithe looked miserable, but he started the laborious process of getting to his feet. When he was standing, Lee leaned in to kiss him on the cheek but quickly decided against it. Instead, she produced a handkerchief, spat on it and wiped the man's face as if he were her own child.

"I don't wish it had been you that day," she said with tears in her eyes. "What I wish is that we'd never gone to that blasted town in the first place."

Theo watched in silence.

He had taken in the scene for what it was. A kind of family working through something at the worst possible time and in the worst possible place. Susanna hadn't said anything, but her eyes were far from dry. Right then, he'd wished he'd tried harder to convince these three to let him go alone. Even if that had meant pulling his government-sanctioned title ... or his pistol. The fact was, in the few hours he'd been around them, these citizens of Lazris, Texas had managed to grow on him quite a bit. If something happened to one of them now, he might not be able to forgive himself. Dekker wasn't worth it. Ramsey wasn't either.

"This was a mistake," he whispered, too soft for anyone to hear.

Susanna wiped her cheek, sniffed, then turned with a clear question on her face. But before Theo could repeat himself or think of something better, a sound echoed throughout the Devil's Claim. It was a low, directionless thing that seemed to come from everywhere at once. Like a grinding, guttural moan, it drifted up and through the stomachs of all who heard it.

"What was that?" Susanna's eyes looked like those of a rabbit.

"That's him." Blithe hobbled over, his voice shaky. "The thing that crawled out of hell. Ain't nothing else coulda done that to those horses. The stories were true. But I think you already knew that—didn't you, Mr. Nil?"

Theo's eyes were already shut, but he could feel the women turn to him.

"Theo?" Susanna sounded nervous.

Theseus Nil had done a lot he'd rather forget. Walking all night across a freezing Texas desert after being betrayed by his oldest friend ... burying his daddy behind their cottage—in a plot next to a mother he never knew. And yet ... answering Susanna right then felt like the hardest thing he'd ever done.

"Yeah."

For almost a minute, this was all he said. Then, the sound happened again.

"Last night, when we were trading lead with the Dekkers ... I saw something. It was about this time, about this dark and I saw it rise. Over there, on the other side of the ravine, it stood like a man, but ... it was too big to be one. And, so help me ..." Theo checked the expectant faces of his audience, then turned away again. "I think it had horns."

RRRRUUUUMMMPPHHHH ... The miserable sound came for a third time and all turned in a single direction. The calls were coming from the bed of the ravine, somewhere past the broken bodies of the wicked men.

"Theseus Nil," Susanna sounded terse. "Are you telling me your minotaur turned out to be *an actual, literal minotaur* ... and you didn't think to mention it before this second?"

"Ma'am ... till now I was almost able to convince myself I hadn't seen it at all." Theo looked dejected. "I dunno. Maybe I've been out on the trail too long but I'm not one to put much stock in the fantastic. The only monsters I've ever known didn't have horns. Hell, one of the worst just had silver hair and a paunch."

With that, he walked over and knelt before the bound men who were sprawled beside what was left of the horses. With the end of Morrow's shotgun, he turned their faces so they caught the dying light.

"This one here is called Landsbury, Uncle Joe to his friends, not that he had many. As for those two, the skinny one is the science-man, Doc Blamire, and beside him is a German feller by the name of Edwin Kurtz. Dekker must be at the bottom with the rest."

Lee swallowed audibly.

"Yeah...," she said, as the first touch of fear crept into her voice. "And whatever is making that godawful racket."

Theo nodded. "I reckon those men were tied up for transport to Fort Davis. We've done it like that a dozen times before, Bram and me. Whatever that thing out there is, it must have interrupted him while he was loading up."

"Where are you going?" The voice was Susanna's.

"To find some answers." Theo called back without stopping. "There's got to be a way down, all we gotta do is find it."

EIGHT

By the time the four made it down to the bottom, the moon was up.

"Oh, thank the Lord above." Blithe gasped, finding the closest, most comfortable-looking rock to sit on. "Used to be I could do three shows a day. Now?" The man shook his head. "You all better go on. Don't worry, I'll catch you up once I've rested some."

The girls looked at each other, as if trying to decide if one of them should stay behind too.

RRRRUUUUMMMPPHHHH ... the bestial noise was so close, Theo and the sisters aimed their weapons in the same direction. Lightning coursed through their veins as all three stared hungrily into the ample dark. It was almost a minute before they realized nothing was coming.

"It sounds like it's in pain," Susanna exclaimed, lowering her borrowed long rifle.

Theo's mind was racing around corners. There was a labyrinth of possibilities before him and it was about to drive him crazy. Without a word, he located the nearest of the Dekker boys and strode pointedly over.

Had the man's upper third still been attached, identifying the poor bastard would have been easier. All Theo knew for certain was that the man was too short to be either Dekker or Wraith.

Just as he'd hoped, in the dead man's hand was a pistol. As it took some real doing to pry open that iron grip, no shortage of grunts and swearing did occur. Once the weapon was free, Theo checked the remaining ammunition and stormed back over to where Arthur Blithe was having a sit.

"Take it." Theo pushed the weapon forward. It was an act which produced no discernable reaction.

"Mister? I don't know what your hangup with guns is about and right now, I don't much care. You want to separate from the group, you take this."

The old man just glared at the weapon, then up at the man holding it.

"Stubborn old ..." Theo dropped the weapon on the rock beside Blithe. Then he turned to walk deeper into the ravine. "There's four shots left. You wanna waste 'em, that's your business."

With that, he turned and proceeded to walk toward the maddening sounds with his shotgun gripped and ready.

It didn't take long for the deputy U.S. marshal to realize that he was walking by himself. His first reaction was to swear under his breath. Then he realized that this was secretly what he'd wanted all along.

As he crept along, Theo stayed close to the sheer wall of the ravine, where shadows were the blackest.

Most of the bodies were hard to identify, though that birthmark made one of them a sure thing. Weeping John Wraith lay with his head propped against a rock. The way he was positioned, the man looked almost alert. They said John hadn't been right in a few years. That something had happened that was so traumatic, his brain just broke. Theo didn't know much about that. The way it was splattered on those rocks made it kind of hard to tell.

Including the three men above, Theo had counted eight members of the Dekker gang. All deceased and in various degrees of unsightly. He couldn't definitively recognize every man, but he knew none were the two that mattered most.

With each step, the animal sounds got closer and louder. It got so that he could hear the rattles of the thing's breath. Practically feel the wind of it pressing into his eyes. As he rounded a bit of a bend, he finally saw. There, not twenty feet away, was a hulking thing— a mass of black fur huddled into the same shadows he'd been sticking to. Theo's heart raced as he approached—his finger never leaving the trigger. Sensing a new threat, the mass flinched and uttered a breathy cough which rattled on the intake.

"Well, look who it is."

Theo wheeled around and aimed at the voice.

"You came back."

Bram Ramsey was propped up against a boulder, just sitting on the ground. At first Theo didn't know what to say. Then he noticed how his former partner was cradling his stomach with one arm.

"What the hell happened here, Bram?"

"Oh … you know most of it." He laughed, coughed. "I got stupid, then greedy, then … I got myself killed. That last part is just really taking its sweet time."

Theo walked closer, eyeing a Winchester Yellowboy not far away— just lying in the dirt. When he was close enough, Ramsey met his eyes. And despite looking like absolute hammered shit, the man managed a smile.

"I honestly can't believe you came back."

"Yeah, well …" Theo could see what looked like pale snakes in Ramsey's arm. He was pushing them against his gut, or rather, back into it. "I told you I'd be thinking about nothing else, didn't I? Jesus Christ … what the hell happened?"

"Well," Ramsey's words came very slow, very deliberate. "I found your thing. Your, uh … bull-guy. It's … right over there." He nodded his head up at the undulating hide of the creature. "I know you can't see its face now, but whoo boy, is it ugly." More coughing. "Got them horns though, just like in your daddy's story. Damndest thing, I swear to God."

"Minotaurs ain't real, Bram. It's just … just a stupid story. *It's a … metaphor for making something of myself! That's all it ever was!*"

"Huh," Ramsey took a second to think and a few more to just breathe. The man looked about a week past tired. "Well, that metaphor over there sure gave me a time."

Theo shot a look back at the creature. It was too dark, still too far off to describe much … but it *was* there.

"Yep. That thing and I chased each other around for most of the night and day. Guess there was just something about me it didn't like." He chuckled at this, but the smile died. "In the end, we did each other in, I guess. Now we're having ourselves a race. *Ain't that right, you ugly sumbitch?*"

In response, the creature shifted where it lay, bringing into view part of a smooth, pale face and a horn.

"I reckon I could win if I just pulled these guts out the rest of the way, but ..." Ramsey seized up, tears welling in his eyes. "Funny ... as I've been sitting here these past hours, it ain't the *dying* I'm afraid of ... it's the doing it alone. Is that stupid or what? Me. The asshole who sent his only friend off into the night with barely the boots on his feet, was scared of kicking off by his onesie. Hey, ain't there like ... a fancy word for that or something?"

Theo could feel a tear running down his own face. It felt hot against the cool night air.

"*Ironic*," he said after a spell.

"That's the one." Ramsey chuckled, as the creature gave off another throaty moan. "Lord Almighty, I can't wait to be dead so I don't have to hear that no more. That blasted metaphor of yours has been carrying on like that for hours. I think ... I got it in the lung."

Ramsey glanced over at his discarded Winchester a few feet away when a shudder suddenly coursed through his body. When he could, the man took a deep breath, though it seemed like a real effort.

"Anyway ... I am glad you came back, Theseus. Glad the desert didn't claim ya. But I know it wouldn't."

Theo shook his head. Conflicting emotions were firing all at once. There were so many things he wanted to say. There just wasn't time.

"Answer me one thing," he said at last.

"Shoot."

"How'd you know about that town?"

Ramsey raised an eyebrow as Theo went on. "Lazris was right where you said it'd be but I can't figure out how you knew. Hell, the two of us have been riding for fifteen years and I know we never been out this way. Plus ...you're from *Little Rock*. It makes no goddamn sense."

Ramsey smiled, showing blood-red teeth. "You're gonna kick yourself when I tell ya."

He started coughing again and it was worse than before. When the fit passed there was blood on the gray streak in the man's beard. When he spoke again, it was a faint raspy whisper.

"I had no damn idea what was out that way. I just needed you to think there was something to reach, so you'd get out of my hair. All that business about staying to the right of the mountain or whatever I said … well, that was just flavor. You always said it was those little details that make a story believable. Figured I'd give it a try."

Theo stared in perplexed disbelief. He didn't know what to say—whether he should feel angry or wounded or plain dumb. In the end, he just laughed. They both did. And when the moment had passed, Abraham Ramsey was gone.

NINE

Theseus Nil stood there for quite a while just regarding his friend, to a low chorus of animal sounds.

Eventually, he produced the final gift he'd received from the man and banged out the last round into his hand. Moonlight slid across the tiny thing as he turned it around in his fingers. All day, he had saved it for one purpose. This round was for Bram.

Without a word, Theo kneeled down and dropped the cartridge into the dead man's breast pocket. Unable to do much else, he regarded his former partner, tipping down the man's hat so it covered his eyes.

When Theo stood up, there were three people standing on the other side of the rock. For a while, he simply looked and they looked back. Susanna was the first one to step forward and put eyes on what was left of Bram Ramsey. But before she could ask the question that was brewing, the beast gave a full blast of its rattling misery that demanded everyone's full attention.

Susanna stepped forward slowly, cautiously. Each step, the bravest thing she'd ever done. Despite being three times the woman's size, the furry thing flinched and curled up defensively as she approached. But when it showed that ugly pale face, Susanna stopped. Morrow's long rifle dropped from her hands as she covered her mouth and dropped to her knees.

"Susu?" called Lee, as she ran to join her sister. "What is it—" She gasped. Turned to the old man. "Arthur. Oh, my God … it's *her*."

From his place in the dark, Theo watched as Blithe moved as fast as he could to join the two sisters. As he passed, Theo noticed there was a revolver in the old man's hand.

Perplexed by the collective reaction to the point of scratching his head, Theo joined the other three. The women were crying, holding each other on the ground. And even the old man's face wasn't dry. But this reaction made no sense. Theo looked at the thing again. He still couldn't tell what it was other than black, hairy and of a size. Its face was pale, with great gaping holes for eyes, and … by God, there really were horns.

Susanna pulled away from her sister to touch one of the clawed legs, but it was pulled back.

"It's okay," she said. "No one's gonna hurt you anymore. It's us, girl. Don't you remember?"

This time, when she reached out, the animal didn't protest. Lee put her hands on it next and within moments, the two women were lying prone upon the thing's furry hide. Theo wanted to shout out, to pull them off the beast, to warn them about wounded tigers ... but he didn't. Whatever was happening was beyond his comprehension. And so, he thought it best to let it play out.

"What did they do to you?" The old man's voice shuddered with emotion as he leaned in to inspect that pale smooth face that looked so much like bone up close. "Show's over, darling. You been wearing this long enough." Blithe put his hands on either side of the face, then stopped and got very, very angry.

"Those *bastards. Those motherless sacks of dog shit!*"

The animal gave off another moan and it was just about the saddest thing Theo had ever heard. Whatever the creature was, it was definitely not his stupid minotaur. Needing to understand, he stepped closer. The face wasn't just bone-like ... it was a skull the animal was wearing like a mask or a helmet. Peeking out from the end of the muzzle was a snuffling nose and a set of rubbery lips. This was no demon, no devil escaped from hell ... just an old bear. And somebody, some heartless sumbitch had nailed a goddamned buffalo skull onto its head.

Theo gasped, stepping back in horror. He could see the ends of the nails sticking out of the forehead. Nails that were definitely in the poor thing's brain.

"Lord Almighty," said Theseus Nil, unable to think of anything better.

"We have to get it off!" screamed Susanna, reaching out for the skull.

"No!" Blithe caught her hand and pulled her into an embrace. "No, sweet thing. You'll only hurt her more. There's ... only one way to help now."

The old man pulled out the revolver.

"You can't!" screamed Susanna, her full heart in the words. "We only just found her! We can't—"

Blithe closed his eyes. "Please. Let me protect you from this one thing. I've failed in everything else. I can't have you seein' ..." His voice fractured. "Take her, Li-Mei, please. I'll meet you back at the wagon."

The elder sister nodded and pulled the younger one away. As for Theo, he just watched as would a fly on a wall. The sisters walked arm in arm, each keeping the other upright as they went.

"You too, boy," said Blithe. "I reckon there's a lot of work needs doing in this place ... just not tonight. There's supplies in the wagon for a campsite. Wood and bedrolls and such. Think you can manage?"

"Yes, sir."

"Good." The man sighed. He was stroking black fur as Theo turned away. "Look. I know you've got questions. Just ... hold on to 'em, all right?"

Without another word, Theo did as he was asked. He caught up to the girls, making sure to give them plenty of space. When they reached the top, he thought he could hear soft singing drifting up from where they'd just been.

The gunshot came as they were passing the dead horses. The sound was a force. Like getting mule-kicked in the heart and throat at the same time. After that, for the rest of the evening, no one said a word.

By the time the old man sauntered back into camp, the women were already asleep. Blithe plopped down in front of the fire, just next to Theo. For a few minutes, it seemed like he was gonna say something. Instead, he took out his flask and held it to his lips. Before he could drink, that trembling hand froze in place. Then, without a word or sound on the matter, he hurled the flask into the darkness.

After that, Arthur Blithe got up and said the only word anyone had all evening.

"Night."

EPILOGUE

Sleep was an elusive thing. And for Theseus Nil, it didn't come at all. By his own volition, he had set out at first light on horseback—eventually finding a more roundabout but safer way down to the bottom of the ravine. Theo buried his old friend on a nearby hill, in a spot far enough from the slaughterhouse the Claim had become, yet near enough to share in its legend.

The deputy U.S. marshal returned to camp after seven a.m. with a jackrabbit hanging from his saddle. While the others finished breaking down the site, he dressed and cooked the animal for breakfast. By a quarter past eight, the unlikely four set about their day. The long way down was worth taking for the sake of the horses and, more importantly, the wagon, and by nine o'clock, the real work began.

The dead were collected one by one—each rolled up in an old horse blanket and tied. Most of the Dekker gang were missing bits of this or that, but Theo managed to identify nearly every man. The one with the missing top parts was likely he who'd caused the munitions wagon to blow in the first place—one Standish Poughkenny. But Theo couldn't be sure.

Aside from Mr. Bottom-half, there was John Wraith, "Brushfire" Mason Wood, Old Ollie Hughes and "High Card" McLinty, whose trademark playing cards were strewn about where he lay—some burned, some spattered in blood. There was also Jeff Clevenger, "The Roughneck" Derek Crow, and the youngest of the group, Timmy "The Kid" Kirkland. Counting the three at the top, that only made ten.

"There's three more. Got to be," said Theo, as he handed the body of Kirkland up to Lee and Blithe, who were standing in the wagon. The worry that Pete Dekker had once again escaped somehow was knocking already.

"I found another one!" shouted Susanna from some distance away. "Figuring out who he is might be a problem, though."

When the other three arrived and looked down, Lee made an audible sound of disgust.

"Well. I guess she liked this one even less than the rest. Good for you, girl."

Unlike the other Dekkers, who had seemingly gone unmolested by the brain-damaged bear, this final man looked much as the horses had. His clothes and his flesh were covered in deep gashes, all filled with dried-up blood and rivers of living ants. The flesh of his face and scalp had been forcibly peeled away, revealing some of the bone beneath. Perhaps most disturbing of all though were his hands. They'd been chewed off, by the look."

"Is it *him?*" asked Susanna, hopefully.

Theo shook his head. "'Fraid not. Too short by far." He tried recalling the faces he and Ramsey had seen that first night and compared them with who they'd loaded up in the wagon. As he thought, he continued looking the revolting corpse up and down for any clue. Then his eyes flashed.

"There. You see that?" He pointed at a hammer that was attached to the man's belt. "This here's the Carpenter. Creepy little bastard by the name of Vander Hoeg who had a predilection for torturing folk with a hammer and ... nails." As he said this, Theo's mind raced back to how the moonlight had outlined the nails sticking out of the bear's skull. Both of its skulls. As pieces began fitting into place, he went on in a lower volume. "According to reports, he mostly went by his first name only. *Esau.*"

Blithe was frowning deeply as he stepped up to regard what remained of the man. Then he delivered a swift kick between the legs. The impact was so hard, there was an audible *CRACK*. Offering no explanation, the old man threw down the blanket and began wrapping and tying. Then he carried the savaged corpse off by himself. The bundle was small enough, after all.

For another forty-five minutes, the group wandered, checking and rechecking every cranny and nook for the bodies of the final two men. Besides Dekker, also missing was Mr. Frank Hass, the so-called Rattlesnake. The man was Dekker's oldest known accomplice and surely would have been with him right to the end. And maybe that was the problem. As the minutes went on, it was harder and harder for Theo to ignore the idea that both of those cowardly sons of bitches had run for their horses the second the lead started to fly.

As he looked down at the floor of the ravine, he could feel the sides of his vision start to tremble. Truth was, he didn't give two shits about Hass, but he had tracked Pete Dekker for close to three damn years. He closed his eyes. Tried to recall the things he'd seen in those frantic moments before the munitions wagon went off.

Had Dekker been there then? Had he actually seen him once it all went to hell?

"Shit." Theo kicked a rock. He just didn't know. Maybe if he'd been looking elsewhere instead of across the gap, he'd have seen that shock of silver instead of a monster. No. That wasn't fair. Dekker was the real monster. The other was just a poor old circus bear, Rosie, as she'd been named by her previous trainer. Susanna had filled in some of the gaps when she and Theo had found a quiet moment. The woman didn't go into a lot of detail, but clearly the animal was kin, and what had been done to her was unthinkable. That and some other stuff that the woman left unsaid, had all happened because of one man. The goddamned Silverfish.

Now, as the others continued to look in places they'd checked already, Theo could only stare at the ground. The sun was directly overhead now. The morning had given way to high noon and the sweat was coming down his face in sheets. Removing his hat, the man drew a sleeve across his brow and sighed. Then, Theo saw something new. A shadow on the ground. It looked like a bird with no head.

Inexplicably, he followed it with his eyes—across the ground and up to the sheer rock face of the ravine wall. Once out of the direct line of the sun, he could see it. The bird had landed on a ledge that, from this angle, was almost impossible to see. Approaching with a look of serious concentration, Theo couldn't take his eyes away. It was the biggest damn owl he'd ever seen, and it was pecking at something. Something on that ledge.

Now, standing, gawping just beneath, Theo's heart was racing. His head was already inclined as far as it would go, so he just kept looking. Studying the hunched-over form of that strange owl as it bobbed up and down. It'd found a snake, maybe? Or some small critter it had carried in its claws, that Theo couldn't see because of the sun?

Suddenly, off the side of that hard-to-see ledge, a hand swung out. A big one. Massive fingers were suspended in the air—curled and blackened in death. The owl swiveled its head to look straight down at Theo—fixing the man with its one golden eye. Then, quite abruptly, it flew away.

"Hey!" Theo shouted, pointing. "Hey, look! Right there! There's another one on that ledge!" The others came running, but Theo was the one out of breath.

"Man alive," gasped Susanna. "Is *that...?*"

"Oh that's Dekker all right. Just look at the size of that paw." With hellfire in his eyes, Theo turned to the old man. "Arthur, you stay here to mark the spot. Ladies? You mind helping me figure out how we're getting that heavy sack of manure off that cliff?"

"You bet your ass we don't." Susanna's hand was on Theo's back. He could feel a kind of energy coming off it. Entering him. Giving strength to his limbs. He turned and for a moment that seemed to go on forever, the two locked eyes. His green, hers almost black. For a few seconds, the man forgot to breathe.

Sam Nilmeier had always wanted more for his only begotten son than a life of wax burns, dipping wicks, and scraping by. For him, he hoped for greatness. A life worthy of being put to the page. For a long time, Theo had felt like he had to chase that dream as a way of honoring his daddy. In the back of his mind there had always been that little voice whispering—telling him that old minotaur was just around the bend. Now he realized there was no such thing. No bull-monster. No dragon left to shoot between the eyes.

And as far as Theseus Nil was concerned, that was just fine.

ABOUT THE AUTHOR

Steve Van Samson is the author of the novels *Mark of the Witchwyrm, The Bone Eater King* and *Marrow Dust,* the recent short story collection *Black Honey and Other Unsavory Things,* and numerous published short stories. A fierce proponent of character diversity & of avoiding cliché like the plague, his writing tends to be on the pulpy side—intermingling genres like horror and dystopian with dark fantasy and adventure. When not tapping the keys on his Chromebook, Steve co-hosts the *Retro Ridoctopus* podcast and watches entirely too many black-and-white monster films.

ABOUT THE ARTIST

ENNIE Award-winning illustrator **M. Wayne Miller** continues his quest to synthesize the perfect blend of science fiction, fantasy, and horror with his work. Primarily focusing on science-fiction and horror imagery for limited edition book covers, lavish interiors, and numerous role playing games, Wayne strives for constant improvement as an artist and illustrator through continuous education, training, and pushing the boundaries of his skill set. One of Wayne's goals for 2022 and beyond is to broaden his artistic reach and expand his illustration work to collectable card games, board games, and other media. His list of clients includes Chaosium, HeroMaker Studios, Modiphius Entertainment, Pinnacle Entertainment Group, Thunderstorm Books, and Weird House Press.

www.ingramcontent.com/pod-product-compliance
Lightning Source LLC
Chambersburg PA
CBHW030401020726
47493CB00003B/911